# A DRUG KING AND HIS DIAMOND 2

NICOLE GOOSBY

**Lock Down Publications and Ca$h**
**Presents**
# A Drug King and His Diamond 2
A Novel by *Nicole Goosby*

NICOLE GOOSBY

**Lock Down Publications**
P.O. Box 870494
Mesquite, Tx 75187

**Visit our website @**
www.lockdownpublications.com

**Lock Down Publications**
**Like our page on Facebook: Lock Down Publications @**
www.facebook.com/lockdownpublications.ldp
Cover design and layout by: **Dynasty Cover Me**
Book interior design by: **Shawn Walker**
Edited by: **Kiera Northington**

4

## Stay Connected with Us!

Text **LOCKDOWN** to 22828 to stay up-to-date with new releases, sneak peaks, contests and more…

Thank you.

# Submission Guideline.

Submit the first three chapters of your completed manuscript to ldpsubmissions@gmail.com, subject line: Your book's title. The manuscript must be in a .doc file and sent as an attachment. Document should be in Times New Roman, double spaced and in size 12 font. Also, provide your synopsis and full contact information. If sending multiple submissions, they must each be in a separate email.

Have a story but no way to send it electronically? You can still submit to LDP/Ca$h Presents. Send in the first three chapters, written or typed, of your completed manuscript to:

LDP: Submissions Dept
Po Box 870494
Mesquite, Tx 75187

*DO NOT send original manuscript. Must be a duplicate.*

Provide your synopsis and a cover letter containing your full contact information.

Thanks for considering LDP and Ca$h Presents.

## ACKNOWLEDGEMENTS:

Nickolvien and Cory Walker, this one is for you. Grandma Pepper, thank you for your words of wisdom, which molded me into the woman I have become today. I use this medium to also extend my gratitude to all my readers for their support, encouragement and constructive criticisms. Thanks for following me on my writing journey!

NICOLE GOOSBY

## PROLOGUE

Two weeks had passed since Chanel McClendon moved back into the McClendon Estate. She'd recently been sent to infiltrate the "King's Circle," a group of street players rumored to have something to do with the charges and incarceration of her older brother, Antonio McClendon. Chanel felt it was best she moved into something that showed anything other than the person she was and the things she was capable of. She'd been regarded as the model many claimed she should be. Since it was both feasible and something she'd dipped and dabbled into at one time, she portrayed the image when it came to Kengyon "King" Johnson and his group of associates.

Not only was Chanel to infiltrate his camp in order to discover his part in the charges filed against her brother, but she would also be the demise of him. That was, until she saw him for the person he was and decided to go against the orders of the Circle she was a part of, hoping there could be something else between them.

With millions of dollars at her disposal and a Circle of her own, Chanel made her own rules, played the game with a vision that surpassed the people she started under, and didn't give a care about who thought different of it.

She, along with her right-hand man, Chris, had just conducted a lucrative deal with the guys she supplied in Dallas and were on their way to Fort Worth when she told Chris, "I'm thinking about getting me a truck. I need something different."

Chris looked over at his friend and smiled. "Let me guess, you're thinking about getting you a Lexus truck?"

She shrugged. "I was thinking about looking at a couple of them."

"You want me to be honest with you, Diamond?" Chris felt for his friend. Knowing personally what she was going through, he tried his best to console and encourage her in the process she was undergoing.

Just two weeks ago, she changed horses in the middle of a race many were depending on. Once she decided to confess to King about her involvement, in the race for his fortune and his life, she arrived to find that he was already gone. The home he invited her to and the life he wanted to build with her had all faded away. There was neither sign of him nor the evidence that he ever did live there. Despite her role in the plot against him, Diamond still felt there was something there, which would eventually show him how she really felt, and they'd find a way to get past the events that led to the plot against him in the first place. The times she spent with King painted a much brighter picture than the one she was initially shown when she first agreed to bring about his downfall. It was during those times she knew he was the man she wanted to spend the rest of her life with. And, if going against the Circle was what she had to do, it would be done. If there was a price to pay, she'd cross that bridge when it came.

Chris lowered the volume of the custom stereo he had in his Durango and continued, "Lately, you've been doing all kinds of shit that shouts how you miss that nigga. You might need to be thinking of the possibilities of him coming after you, the way you went after him."

"He never allowed me to explain the shit, Chris. The nigga just upped and left without letting me know. Packed his shit and left without a trace."

"Yeah, that nigga got angles or something, because how else could he have known we were coming for him? Then too, it might have been something else that spooked the nigga."

"There was nothing else, Chris. I knew what he was dealing with and he never spoke of having a problem with anyone in the streets."

"What about the feds?"

"Not even them."

"There has to be something you're overlooking, Diamond, but we can't let that shit cause us to slip. If we ever see this nigga again, we have to include the fact that he just might be on some more shit. You did say this nigga had some killers under him, and you already know I'm not going to let anything happen to you. The way I see it, we find this nigga and take it back to plan-A, Diamond. I mean, take this nigga out, before he has the chance to do it to you."

Diamond smiled, but her thoughts were far from the expression she wore. If only she could speak with King herself. If only she could tell him things had changed between them and she did want the same thing he wanted, when it came to the relationship they spoke about building on. If only she could show him she meant him no harm. If only things were different. "He's not like that, Chris. The nigga owns just one gun."

"Stop underestimating, Diamond."

"I'm not. I'm just saying, Chris. We were wrong about him and I'm more than sure of it."

"Well, that still don't mean we ought to think different about the nigga now. For all we know, he's got someone following us right now and has been for a couple of weeks now." Chris checked his rearview mirror for the third time, fingered the latch to the secret compartment where he stashed his mini-14 with compressor and told her, "You've got to look past that love shit, Diamond, 'cause that shit don't mix. You see how close you got to King using that shit? In the game we in, a nigga worry more about the lies you tell than the love you claim to give, Diamond, and you know this. Fuck that nigga, Diamond. You've got to keep moving, sis. You're a shark now . . . when you stop moving, that's because you're dead. A couple hundred million, remember?" He reminded her of the words she spoke about what she wanted out of the game and the commitment she made seeing it through.

"Oh, now you using my shit against me?" Diamond pushed him playfully and gave a slight nod.

"That's life, Diamond. It's either the shit we do or the shit we say that puts us in money, in graves or in prison."

Diamond thought about some of the words she'd spoke and heard. And, while thinking of the things she'd once said, she could only agree with the very things Chris spoke of. She had her chance with King and she knew what she was getting into. She knew her actions would eventually break him, and now she wished like hell they didn't completely break the bond they shared.

"I'm going to find him, Chris. I'm going to finish what I started."

## CHAPTER ONE

Camille had grown tired of King's sullen and dampened moods and she let him know as much. She'd gone far and beyond to raise his spirits for the past couple of weeks and to see him in such a self-induced funk, she was more than fed up. She'd done things he failed to do and when taking into consideration their livelihoods could have possibly been at stake, she uprooted him and moved him out of the house he wanted to make his home. He'd had one break-up after the other, and it was the most recent one that seemed to break the camel's back.

Seeing her friend attach himself to women he knew little to nothing about, Camille felt it was in his best interest to dig a little deeper for the things she felt he should have known about the women he took a liking to. It was his attachment to a woman he only knew as Diamond that caused Camille to be suspicious, more than he ever would. And, after going behind his back, something she promised not to do again, she discovered Diamond wasn't the woman she claimed to be, and that there had to have been an ulterior motive behind her deceit. A deceit she wasn't willing to see past.

Camille was about to head out the door of her studio home when she noticed King staring out the window, something he'd been doing for the past couple of weeks. She called to him from where she stood. "King!"

"What's up?"

"I'm about to step out for a minute." Camille walked over to where he stood and made him face her. "You straight, or what?"

"Yeah, I'm good, Camille. I'm good."

Camille sighed. If she didn't know anyone else in the world, she knew Kengyon Johnson and she knew when he was lying. "You know what, nigga? I'm tired of you sulking around here as if you're just realizing ya sex change didn't go as planned, and now you regretting drilling another hole in your ass. That bitch wasn't the last fish in the goddamn sea, Kengyon, and if you pulled your head out of your ass long enough to breathe, you'd see that."

"I'm not even thinking about Diamond," he lied.

"Then act like it."

Camille walked off, leaving him alone to deal with the demons that filled his thoughts. She had business to conduct and with him being out of the picture and his right mind, she was doing both his and hers. With over two hundred and fifty thousand dollars to be made, she had her most trusted bodyguard, Buddy, on standby. With him standing six foot five and weighing over three hundred pounds, he was that presence many of the people she associated with feared, when she did come around. They'd been a team since high school and his loyalty was to her and her alone.

"You ready, Buddy?"

"Yes, Boss Lady."

Camille followed him out to the parking garage and climbed into her Audi R58. She was expected in Oklahoma within the next two hours and as always, Buddy would arrive shortly afterwards.

King stepped back, so he could see without being seen. Once Camille pulled out of the parking garage below him, he waited until the huge Dually Buddy drove exited before turning and going about his business. Unlike his break-up with Nava Munez, this time was different. Diamond was nothing like the gold-digger he found Nava to be, nor was she that needy, attention-driven drug addict he tried to rescue. Diamond was everything he wanted in a woman. She was beautiful, street-and-book-smart and the one woman he could see himself settling down with. He'd promised Camille he wouldn't do something as stupid as trying to reach her or even contact her, because once it was found out that Diamond had lied about the woman she portrayed herself as, there was nothing else to know. But, King's heart was already contradicting his words.

He'd been going back and forth between Camille's studio home and his house, ever since she moved him out of his Ravinia home in Dallas. Now that he had a few hours to himself, he began his search. There had to have been something left behind that would tell and explain the story he wanted to know so much about. The one Camille gave little answers to but a million questions for.

***

Silvia had been running the Totally Awesome Hair and Nail Salon ever since she stepped out of the drug game and while being the cousin of kingpin Antonio McClendon, Diamond's older brother, she still had ties and obligations that surpassed her duties at the salon. Along with Datrina Ellis, Chris' girlfriend and Somolia Rhodes, they were responsible for cleaning a good share of the money when her cousin first started out. For the past month or so, Silvia had been doing a little more than she admitted to, when it came to putting Diamond on a level of game even she feared. The money she was entrusted with, along with the secrets she kept, not only interfered with her marriage to her husband KP, but also jeopardized her legitimate business in every way.

Silvia and Datrina took a trip to Miami to conduct a business transaction for Diamond and while they were away, Somolia violated more than the codes the three of them shared and sucked KP's dick, claiming it started as a joke that resulted in an act she couldn't help. It wasn't until Silvia returned, confronted both her husband and Somolia about the incident, that she realized Somolia was still capable of some of the same acts she'd promised never to do again.

"Girl, ain't nobody talking about you, damn," Datrina told her, before rolling her eyes upward and turning back to Silvia, who was now shaking her head.

"Come on in here, Somolia." Silvia waved her in and told her, "And, close the door."

Seeing both her friends wearing questionable expressions, Silvia asked, "What happened now?" Somolia sat on the corner of Silvia's desk and started going through the stack of mail. Something she always did in her attempt to be the nosey woman she was.

"Ain't nothing in there with Somolia Rhodes' name on it," Silvia told her, before leaning back in the recliner she sat.

"I know."

15

"Calling you a nosey motherfucker ain't shit, huh?" Datrina told her, before clapping her hands together as if she was trying to get Somolia's attention.

Somolia finished her perusal and sat the mail facedown on Silvia's desk. "So, what's all the closed door shit about?"

"It's called not wanting everybody in my business, Somolia, so what's said here stays here." Datrina leaned forward, pushed Somolia's leg and told her, "I'm serious, girl."

"Have I ever told some shit we discussed in private?" Somolia smiled. Her words found themselves sprawled on every wall around them.

"You need help, Somolia, that's all I'm going to say," Silvia laughed, straightened the small stack of papers on her desk and raised her brows. "Tell her, Datrina."

"What? Tell me what?" Somolia grew anxious, thinking it was something about her.

"It ain't shit, really. I'm just thinking about buying me a house. Nothing major." Datrina shrugged.

"Yeah, right. Y'all ain't in here whispering about you buying no house." Somolia thought for a second and continued. "Unless you're thinking about leaving Chris."

"Girl, ain't nobody said nothing about leaving Chris," Silvia cut in.

"She don't have to. Why else would she be trying to move? Huh?" Somolia looked from Silvia to Datrina, then back to Silvia.

"See, that's why shit get out the wrong way. Chris' name hadn't even been spoken but all of a sudden, he's the reason. Girl, sit your fat ass down somewhere." Silvia stood, walked around her desk and grabbed the handle of her office door.

"Where you going, Silvia?"

"I do have a business to run, Somolia."

"I'm serious, Somolia. It don't have shit to do with Chris. As a matter of fact, I need you to help me break it to him." Datrina smiled.

"Aw, got to do something, girl. Don't put me in the middle of the shit y'all got going on. You know I don't do that."

"Really, Somolia?" Datrina tsked with closed eyes. "Anyway, I need you to tell him that it would be a good present for me or something like that." Datrina fanned her fingers and said, "Just come up with something, Somolia."

"Oh, so he don't know you want a house?" Somolia looked towards the office door and nodded.

"He has an idea, but I did tell him at one time that I wanted to keep a low profile for a while," Datrina explained, without going into detail.

"What changed? Why you want to move into a house when you have that bad-ass loft?"

"Diamond changed all that shit." Datrina smiled.

"What, you found out they fucking or what?"

"Shut up, Somolia, it don't have shit to do with that. It has to do with me and what I want. Diamond let me stay in her mansion and I can't get past it. I have to step my game up, girl."

"So, now you want a mansion?"

"Not really. If I can get something half as nice as that house she lives in, I'll be fine."

"She does live in a bad motherfucker, huh?" Somolia's thoughts trailed off. If only she'd been able to lockdown either Dell or Raymond. She was more than sure that if things would have worked out with Raymond, she'd be living her dream. And as rich as both of them were rumored to be, it was something she thought of continually. With Datrina and Chris being an item, and Silvia being the cousin of a kingpin, money was nothing to them. Somolia had made a nice income at the salon alone and with her kickback from the Circle, she was able to afford herself a 550 Mercedes Benz, an IS Lexus sedan and a nice apartment in the Mansfield area of Fort Worth. Somolia might not have been as toned as Datrina or as pretty as Silvia, but she felt she had the best head around. With her standing five foot four and weighing close to one hundred and seventy pounds, her compliments came because of her bronze complexion, full lips, wide nose, chubby cheeks with dimples and of course, her slanted gray eyes. Somolia was a big woman with money and she knew what men liked.

\*\*\*

KP had married Silvia, his long-time girlfriend, hoping things would change for them and that she'd become the faithful wife she promised she'd be. But recently, he had every reason to question the validity of her words and the course of her actions. Things hadn't been right between them for a while and after their most recent fight, a verbal fight that turned physical, he was not only kicked out of the home they shared, but he was threatened by both her associates and family alike.

He'd been staying with his best friend, Q, for up to two weeks and was still deciding what measures he'd take to get back into his wife's good graces. His insecurities, along with a past his friend wouldn't allow him to forget, did more than damage his marriage. It pushed him to hit his wife and after realizing his mistake, regardless of hers, he came to regret his actions in every way.

Both he and Q had been waiting on a call from the disaster relief firm he'd contacted, about a possible contract with the state, because of the flooding in Houston and the Gulf Coast. Hurricane Harvey had both destroyed lives and created better ones in the same event. With a team of his own and enough money to rent his own equipment, KP looked forward to the call that would not only get him from under Q's roof for a while, but would also put a nice addition into his savings account. With a wife whose suitors spoiled her with huge amounts of money that dwarfed his best efforts, he was looking forward to amassing a small fortune of his own.

"Nigga, them people ain't going to call you back. Do you know how many organizations are down there right now?"

"Q, I'm tired of your shit." KP walked from the kitchen to the den and plopped down on the love seat.

Q yelled from the kitchen area, "Nigga, don't be diving on my shit like that. That set cost me over two thousand dollars cash."

"Yeah, should have cost your dumb ass two thousand kicks across your ass."

"Yeah, well you up in my shit now, nigga," Q told him matter-of-factly. "And, it's all because of you, so deal with it."

Q walked into the den area, threw his best friend a cold beer and took a seat on the sofa across from him. He popped his beer too and smiled. "You look better."

"What?"

"I said, you looking better. You ain't over there with snot running all out of your nose, crying over no bitch. You looking like potential now."

"Yeah, whatever." KP had been thinking about his situation with his wife, and despite telling Q he was going to move forward with or without her, he was really feeling otherwise. He knew he wasn't about to get over Silvia anytime soon.

"All we got to do now is get you an apartment somewhere," said Q.

"Motherfucker, you got me kicked out of my shit, almost killed, and now you trying to put me out. You got me fucked up."

"You know I love you, but my hoes been coming through here anyway. Ya nasty ass been creeping with Somolia and think I don't know about it."

"Nigga, please. I haven't fucked with Somolia since the last time I got my dick sucked." Q twisted his lips. "You tripping."

"That ain't what she told me yesterday."

"She called you yesterday? What she say, nigga, what the fat bitch say now?"

KP laughed. "Oh, now she's a fat bitch, but when she got her lips wrapped around your dick she ain't 'that fat bitch' then."

"Hell, Somolia always been that fat bitch. When a nigga say shit like, 'that fat bitch,' people know exactly who you talking about."

"Yeah, well she says she's your girl."

"Fat bitch ain't my girl. She sucks a nigga dick and swears we about to get married or something."

"Yep, she's your girl." Feeling the vibrating Samsung in its case, KP held up a finger, signaling Q to be quiet. He took the unknown caller's call. "Pierson Constructions, Kevin speaking."

"Mr. Pierson?"

"Speaking."

"This is Mark Shields from the Ground-Up Foundation Company, and I wanted to know if you'd be interested in getting a contract to do a clean-up in Houston."

"I was just talking to a couple of associates about this possibility and we'll be honored to help out."

KP listened intently to the details of the contract, as well as the possibility of them being on location for months. Hearing him speak of the equipment they'd most likely need and they'd be willing to finance the rental of the equipment, KP's mind started number-flipping. Since he had his own trucks and a crew at the ready, he was more than sure he'd be pocketing a lion's share of whatever they made.

He'd provide rooms for his crew and they'd provide their own food and whatever else they wanted. Once it was understood he'd be responsible for their insurance, he looked over at Q and winked because he knew they would be on their own.

KP concluded his call and looked over at Q, who was looking at him as if he'd turned several shades of color.

"Why? What are they talking about, nigga?"

KP crossed his legs and smiled. "We're going to Houston, Q. We loading our shit up and going down south, baby."

"How long are we going to be down there?"

"Might take as long as a couple of months, maybe more."

"What kind of numbers they talking about?"

KP frowned at his friend and told him, "None-of-your-damn-business kind of numbers."

"Sounds as if you plan on taking some Vaseline with you."

"No need to, you can keep Vaseline up your ass."

Both friends laughed heartily. This was a move they'd been hoping came through, because not only would they be making money with the relief effort, but they'd be gone for a while. KP was hoping this was it what it took for his wife to come a-calling. He wasn't going to call or text her and if she just so happened to, he'd use the "I was busy" excuse to justify it. One way or the other, KP was going to take advantage of the opportunity given him.

*** 

Camille could tell something was off as soon as she turned into the Nichols Hills neighborhood of the north side of Oklahoma. Where there were normally inner city patrol units cruising around, the only car she noticed moving was the same Chevy Cruze that had been trailing her ever since she'd called her connect to announce her arrival. Something she often did, so things would be in order when she did arrive. She'd made several out-of-the-way turns to confirm her suspicions, and while some would at least want to see the occupant or occupants behind the heavily-tinted windows, Camille felt there was no need. One advantage she had was that the product always arrived shortly after she did. All it took was a nod from her to Buddy or a brief text, something she'd already done, that set the big guy off. She made another confirming turn. She hoped they'd realize the plan had been foiled and they'd recalculate and play another vic, but that wasn't the case at all. Camille pumped her brakes, as if she was looking for the address she was given and seeing the obvious reaction from her rearview mirror, she shook her head. "It's a shame how death disguises its face, deceive the deceived and turn predator into prey." She pulled into the driveway of the bi-leveled home and parked. She smiled, seeing the Chevy pass behind her and park at the top of the street, and chuckled when the guy she'd come to see, greeted her with a cheery look himself.

"Camille, it's always lovely to see you," he told her, before descending the front steps of his home.

By the way he subtly glanced at the top of the street, Camille knew this was something he either didn't want to do, or didn't have any confidence in. And, to push him over whichever edge he was standing, she climbed out of her Audi and told him, "It's beautiful out today, isn't it?

He nervously looked towards the top of the street again and nodded. "Yes, it is. It's a good day to get out and put some water under you."

Seeing him swallow, Camille smiled, raised her brows and slightly turned her head. "Shall we?"

After being led to the back of the house and through an out-door archway, the guy turned to Camille, wiped beads of seat from his forehead and told her, "I fucked up, Camille. You know this ain't some shit I do," he pleaded.

"I'll tell you what," Camille pulled out her phone, dialed a number and told him, "I've been having a fucked-up week already, but for that two hundred and fifty thousand dollars, I'm going to make this shit right and you live another day." She looked up at him with a humorless expression and said, "It's up to you."

"Yeah. Make it right. You can have the money. You can—"

Camille cut him off with the wave of her hand and spoke into the phone. "They're low-level looking for a come-up. Be nice." Camille ended her call and smiled. "Where's the wifey?"

Buddy read the short text and smiled. He liked the fact that his Boss Lady was still able to see game from other perspectives. He had not long ago arrived at the same location and after the second call and the instructions to play nice, Buddy pulled past the home where Camille's Audi was parked and the small Chevy sitting at the top of the street. With him, it didn't matter how many people plotted against his Boss, the more the merrier and as long as it was something his Boss Lady needed done, the merrier became the fulfilling.

Buddy arrived, parked his Dually at the corner of the street over and climbed out with his hat low and a clip board in his left hand. He periodically looked towards the numbers sprayed on the curbs as if he was looking for one in particular. Seeing the preoccupied faces of the would-be assailants, he stopped several feet from the car, pulled his MAC-11 from under his left arm and fired a series of silenced shots that shattered the windshield quietly, silencing both talk and movement inside. Buddy walked to the car to make sure his job was done, opened the passenger's side door, fired more silenced shots into both the front and back of the small car and continued up the street as if nothing happened. To confirm no one was in the know of what he'd just done, he walked away, off to where a guy was mowing his yard with his son. Two women continued their daily stroll on the opposite side of the street and none of them noticed the three hundred and fifty pound stranger with the clipboard. Satisfied that things were done up to his standards, he pulled out his phone, dialed a number and said two words, "Nice enough."

*** 

King checked the time on his watch every few minutes. He'd been on social media for over two hours and still hadn't found what he was looking for. This was one way to find out the things people tried to keep under wraps, but his search so far had been for nothing. Kengyon was more than sure Diamond had media ties, but when he remembered she wasn't the woman she claimed she was, he slowly started to understand. He was just about to conclude his search and he thought about the conversation they had just about doing some hosting and not being paid. King was hoping like hell he'd run across a contact related to her, or at least a mention of the booking site, but what he found was so much more.

King looked through Facebook once more, but this time he typed in the name, *Antonio*. More than a few popped up but the one that caught his eye was the one that hadn't been updated in over six months, which had to have belonged to the kingpin, because that was about how long he'd been gone. King pulled up the page and went to the photos. Then, he saw her. Standing beside the exact same Bentley he thought was a loaner car, was his Diamond. He blew up the photo to make sure. She was wearing the same Emmitt Smith jersey he saw on the arm of the sectional in her loft, the one time he did visit. King smiled. He scrolled

23

further, found more pics, saw more captions and froze when he saw the one that read, *Happy Birthday, Sis.* "Son of a bitch," he said to no one in particular. She once told him Antonio McClendon had messed her out of some cash for a party she hosted, but now it was all coming together for him. He now questioned the possibility of her doing something as foul as getting her brother locked up for something so small. Was she some vindictive bitch out to settle some score, or did she conceal who she really was, not wanting to be associated with the kingpin? Several thoughts ran through King's mind as he tried his best to piece together the puzzle before him. The one thing he was certain of was that since Antonio was in the system, he wouldn't be that hard to find.

Knowing Camille would be alerted the minute he used the phone she gave him, King went out, bought a MacBook Pro and hid it in the one place he knew she wouldn't find it—at the top of her closet, under several handbags she hadn't used in a while.

King went to the Federal Inmate site, typed in the McClendon name and once Antonio's info popped up, he sent a short email that read:

*Antonio, I need these words to stay between you and me. My name is Kengyon Johnson and I would like to visit you if this is at all possible. I have more questions than answers and by the looks of it you're the only one that might be able to help me. Please respond at your earliest.*

*KING*

## CHAPTER TWO

Diamond and Chris were leaving their routine stop at the Three Rivers Federal Facility, when she decided to look at a couple of properties in the city. She'd continually told Chris she wanted to at least have a spot closer to where her brother was situated and now that she'd tied a few knots with some of the players there, she was looking forward to doing a little business of her own. Today, she and Chris drove her brother's Rolls Royce and after pulling up an address to a home in the 1604 Chainfield Neighborhood on the north side of the city, they were driving past head-turning properties.

Chris looked over at Diamond and frowned. He said, "I thought you said a little spot, Diamond, not no shit like this." He looked from one home to the next and seeing the teenagers, mostly white, roll past them on skateboards and scooters, and lawn service guys going about their work day, he shook his head.

"These range from two hundred and fifty thousand dollars to four hundred thousand dollars, so I'm told."

"I was under the impression you were talking about an apartment or something, Diamond. These are family homes: kids, jobs, business owners, soccer moms, lawyers and the like." Chris blew the horn at a couple of skateboarders and looked back over at Diamond. "This ain't you, sis."

"Hating-ass, nigga. Who you think my neighbors are now? Ain't shit changing but the city." Diamond pointed, seeing the address she was given. "Pull in that one right there."

Chris turned into the circular driveway and parked in front of a set of steps that led to a winding walkway. As bad as he wanted to tell her he approved of the home, he didn't. He only climbed out and watched her do the same. He noticed they weren't the only people pulling up in the neighborhood and even pointed out the fact that another woman had passed them in a Bentley already.

"Let's walk around to the back and see if we can get in this bitch." Diamond checked the front doors, looked up at the camera above them and continued her search for an entrance.

"You sure we're supposed to be fucking with this house, Diamond?" Chris looked back towards the driveway and across the street to make sure they weren't being watched.

"Nigga, bring your ass on. Money comes in all colors now and I'm more than sure they'll love the color of mine."

"You talked to Dell about this or what?"

"Yep, the nigga told me to look at it and see what I think, so here we are."

"How much one of these go for?" Chris then thought about Datrina. He'd told her they should keep things on the low for a while, but that was slowly becoming a thought not even he agreed with. It was time to get his girl something bigger than the three-bedroom loft they were living in and as quiet as it was kept, he was thinking of a surprise for her himself.

"A little over three hundred thousand, but I'm more than sure I can get it for a little less." Diamond was standing at the rear of the home when she tried the handle. The sliding glass doors on the patio opened. "Found it."

Diamond walked from the huge kitchen with island counters to the first living area she came across. She turned back to Chris and smiled. "I can put a big-ass aquarium right here and fill it with all kinds of exotic fish."

"Get you a bowl filled with sharks, huh?" Chris stood at the entrance and his own ideas filled his thoughts. "Throw rugs and shit. Get some darkened borders going on with the trim and go with a safari theme or something."

"Nigga, I'm not trying to have my shit looking like no jungle." Diamond looked around them at the flooring and told him, "I got to get some marble up in this bitch though."

"You really thinking about moving all the way down here?"

"This will just be somewhere I can come when I'm visiting Antonio, while he's in the hellhole."

"You can get an apartment for that shit, Diamond. You don't have to throw away a bunch of money for a stay-over." Chris walked behind her as they inspected the rest of the home. Forty-five minutes later, they were climbing back into the Rolls Royce.

26

By the way Diamond smiled, Chris knew it was about to be a move he assisted her with, in more ways than one.

Pulling out of the driveway, Diamond thought about King and the conversation they had about living life to the fullest and making something of it. She thought about the ideas he had shared with her and the plans he had to make them a reality. Diamond looked over at Chris, who was now shaking his head at her.

"What?"

"I haven't said anything to you." Chris looked out of the driver's side window, avoiding her stare.

"You don't have to, Chris. What's up?"

"Ain't nothing up, Diamond."

"Girl-ass nigga, why you over there looking like you broke a couple of nails or something?"

"Yeah, whatever, Diamond." Chris' thoughts were of her and the fact that she'd be away from him and he'd no longer to be able to see her on a day-to-day basis, as he had for years now. His little sis was about to leave him.

"Guess what?"

Chris acted as if he didn't hear her but he faced her when she punched his arm, as if surprised. "What? What's up, girl? Damn."

"I should have busted you in your face, nigga. You heard me." Diamond raised up to where her body was facing Chris, and positioned herself where she could swing on him if he chose to ignore her again.

Diamond straightened herself and reclined. She fingered the console between them and found her playlist. She sang Dae Dae's "Spend It" along with the radio, knowing it would agitate the hell out of Chris. If it was one thing Diamond knew, it was when Chris was feeling strange about something, and she was more than sure it would be something they discussed before returning to Fort Worth.

\*\*\*

Dell was seated in the den area of his new home, thinking of another excuse to give, when it came to the money his guys were promised for their role in bringing Kengyon Johnson to his knees. Each of them was promised fifty thousand dollars and now that King was nowhere to be found and the hit had been delayed, they still wanted the money promised to them.

"Just give me a little more time, guys. I'm going to make it worth your while. Things had to be pushed back for a minute, is all."

Dell counted out another forty thousand dollars and handed each of them ten grand for the inconvenience. He knew how it was to be promised something and renege on it at the last minute. The last thing he needed was for them to feel as if they were getting the short end of the stick for whatever reason. "I need you guys to hold off for a minute longer. You know I got you guys."

After leading them out of his home and seeing them leave, Dell walked back into his home and went to stand on his second-story terrace. He rubbed his forehead and neck in frustration. He was out of the loop and didn't know what had gone wrong. He was days away from amassing the small fortune King had built and was more than sure he'd be sitting on a nice supply of product also. Diamond had given him all the intel he needed on King and after hiring a group of guys to handle the bloodwork that was sure to be involved, King just upped and disappeared. He'd contacted Diamond several times to see if she'd had any contact with the famous King, but even she had neither heard from nor about him. At first, Dell thought of the possibility of someone else beating him to the punch, but thought better of it after being assured by Diamond that he had no need to fret.

He'd been paying for the delay himself and if it was one thing Dell hated, it was spending his money on anything. He'd been taught the game by Antonio himself, and after seeing the market for what it was and being given enough money to start their own investment firm, Dell hadn't looked back since. He'd just recently purchased his newest home for a whopping four million dollars and was looking forward to buying more properties in the near future.

Knowing it was about time for Diamond to be returning, he dialed her contact. There had to be something they could do to better the situation he now found himself in. Either way, he had to make money back he just spent.

*** 

Three times, Antonio read over the email he was given. The second was to make sure it was meant for him and the third was to be sure of the second. He'd heard about King and the way things were going with Diamond, but for King to contact him of all people, Antonio couldn't help but laugh. After looking over the sender's info and re-reading the instructions to keep this between them, he decided to make a much-needed call to Silvia. And since he hadn't heard from her in over a week, it was about time they talked.

Silvia had just completed several calls and was looking for a few minutes of down time before she left for the day and seeing her iPhone glow, she rolled her eyes and exhaled. "Silvia speaking."

"Hey, cuz, what's up?"

"Antonio? You got another phone or what?"

"Yeah, you can say that. How're things going with you?"

"Been busy, cousin. This shop, the women and of course, Diamond. Need I say more?"

"Well, whatever happened with you and KP?"

"I haven't heard from him in a couple of weeks, I think. Why?" Silvia reached over and began closing the blinds to her office window.

"Y'all tripping like that now?"

"Call it what you will, Antonio, but I don't have time for more bullshit. My plate is filled as it is."

"Well, guess who got at me today?"

"Bill collectors, 'cause they've been getting at me non-stop."

"Kengyon Johnson."

"Who?" Silvia frowned, hoping she wasn't hearing things.

"Yeah, King got at me today. Wanted to know if he can come see me and some more shit."

"No kidding?"

"No kidding."

"What did you tell him?"

"I haven't told him shit, because I'm yet to get back at him."

Silvia looked towards her office window at the parking lot and asked him, "So, what's up?"

"The hell if I know, I'm going to see what the nigga up to, though. Don't tell no one shit, Silvia."

"Nigga, you act like I'm Somolia or someone."

"I'm serious. I know how you get when you mad. Just chill on this shit, cuz. Let me see across the room on this one, before we do anything else."

"Yeah, I got you." Silvia sighed, nodded and told him, "Keep me posted then and if you need something, don't hesitate."

"I'm good, I'm good. Everything is being taken care of. I'll be back on the street before you know it."

Silvia sat and registered all that was said during their talk. For King to be reaching out to Antonio about anything, told her he was also looking for answers about something that would most likely concern her. The last she heard, King had upped and disappeared and from the looks and sound of things, he'd done that for a reason. Whatever the case though, Silvia was going to let Antonio handle it and if he needed her in any way, she'd be there as she always had.

\*\*\*

King was sitting on the sectional, watching *Sports Center* on Camille's huge one-hundred-forty-inch wall unit when she and Buddy strolled in. He could tell something was wrong off the top and seeing Buddy carrying an extra duffle, so he sat up and watched her. She kicked off her heels and threw her phone on the sectional beside him. He spied her in the kitchen area where she poured a glass of champagne and took a sip by the granite counters she had installed a while back.

"You straight or what?" he asked, knowing she was keeping something from him.

King knew Camille was only trying to look out for him but when she gave him the new phone, he knew it was done in an attempt to keep track of both him and the things he did and now, he was hoping she wasn't onto him in any way.

"Couldn't be better," she told him from where she stood. "And you?"

"I've been chilling, watching Stephen A with his crazy ass and checking out the updates."

"Oh yeah?"

"Yep."

"Um."

King stood, walked over to where Buddy had sat both duffles and asked, "What's this?"

"A gift."

"A gift?"

"Yes, a gift, King. Why are you so inquisitive today?" Camille walked from where she stood and took a seat across from where he one sat and began flipping through the channels. SportsCenter wasn't about to do it for her.

"I'm just trying to see how everything went, is all."

"Yeah, well, if you ask me, you're up to something and trying to throw me for whatever reason, King. I'm not your enemy."

He thumbed through the bills in the first duffle and kicked the other. "You in for the night or what?" he asked her, hoping they could do dinner.

"Plans?"

"Hungry as hell. Feel like having a pizza."

King tried to remember if he'd put the MacBook's setting on ping or vibrate or what. He thought about forwarding it to his phone but decided against it, because he didn't want Camille to discover he'd stepped out to do something as rash as contacting

Diamond or anyone she associated with. Nor did he want her to stumble across his little secret.

"We can order pizza, King."

"I need to stretch my legs, Camille. I'm tired of this hiding shit."

He watched her place the glass she held on the coaster that decorated the glazed table and step into her heels. "Fine, let's go get pizza," she told him.

"I know a nice place in North Dallas we can go."

"You are not about to take me to some eatery you and that woman done sat up in, Kengyon."

"You tripping, Camille. I just know this nice spot. It doesn't matter who I went there with."

"Yeah, well, I'm more than sure we can find something right here in Las Colinas that'll suffice."

King looked over at Buddy, who was now lounged in the huge recliner he frequented when he did come to Camille's apartment. "You riding or what, Buddy?"

"Not this time, King. You two go ahead."

For one of the few times he could remember, King didn't want to be alone with Camille, because he was pretty sure she'd have a few questions for him and he hated lying to his best friend. Not only that, but she'd able to tell and that would start an entirely different conversation itself.

"Las Colinas it is, then," he told her, grabbing the keys to her 911 Porsche.

"We have a few things to discuss anyway," she told him before grabbing her phone and heading out of the door.

## CHAPTER THREE

KP, Q, and the rest of the crew had just exited the 610 High-way when the aftermath of Hurricane Harvey hit them. Debris stretched from one side of the highway to the next and was said to have covered most of the southside of the city. Their instructions were to assist the effort, starting around Clinton Park and would go as far as the Hershal Wood neighborhood. He'd already rented the equipment they'd need and was looking forward to the benefits of it.

Despite Q's perspective of things concerning his marriage, KP still held onto the glimmer of hope he had that things would straighten themselves out. He'd continually checked to see if Silvia had either called or texted and when seeing she'd done neither, he became tight-lipped to say the least. One thing he wasn't about to do was sweat her.

"You hear me, nigga?" Q pointed to one of the sites crewmen were set up at and wanted to make sure KP saw them also.

"We're going to Clinton Park to get things set up, but if you'd like, I could drop you off."

Q replied in a very matter-of-fact way, "Hell, the way things are looking, we could get paid from them also. All we need is some extra hands, equipment and some niggas willing to put in a little work."

"I'm more than sure it's going to take more than that, when you're a legitimate business," KP told him while checking his phone for the umpteenth time.

"Why you keep checking that damn phone like that? That woman ain't worried about you, nigga."

KP looked over at his best friend and shook his head. "Why everything got to be about my wife, nigga? If I didn't know any better, I would have sworn you was trying to push me out of the way so you could pick up the pieces or something."

Q looked at him as if he was crazy. "You stupid as hell if you think I'm going to be chasing a motherfucker that ain't trying to do nothing, but fuck the next nigga with the bigger pockets. Silvia always been about money and I don't have shit to give her." Q looked out of his window in thought and said, "You're stupid."

"Yeah, well, we're about to get this money right now, we'll climb that tree later. Never know, Q, you might even have a little to spend on some woman when we get back."

Before turning into the park's relief effort site, KP checked his phone yet again. Seeing nothing from his wife, he turned it off and threw it in the compartment under the armrest between them.

"She'll get at me," he told no one in particular.

"If you say so," was Q's response.

*** 

Diamond had stopped by Chris and Datrina's apartment early, because they had some business to attend to. When she was pulling into the parking spot next to Chris' Durango, Datrina was hitting the alarm to her convertible.

"Hey, girl, where you headed?" she asked Datrina, before climbing out of her Corvette.

"I've got a couple of stops to make before I head to the salon." Datrina dropped the hood of the car, threw her Prada bag into the passenger's seat and climbed in.

"Well, we'll be through there after a while. We have a few stops to make ourselves."

"Yeah, he already told me."

"Is he up yet or what?"

Datrina laughed. "He said he was up. But, when I walked out of the door, he was still under the covers."

Diamond pulled out her key to their apartment and told her, "Well, let me go get your man."

"Good luck with that." Datrina pulled out of her parking space and waved.

Diamond quietly entered the apartment and headed back to the bedroom. She shook her head at seeing the bulging figure under the designer comforter and looked around for something to use in her attempt to scare Chris. After thinking of something

Antonio had done to her years ago, she ran to the kitchen, grabbed a small plastic bag and walked back into the room where Chris slept.

Chris knew he'd heard something shuffle, but believed it was Datrina going about her business as usual. When she'd awakened him earlier, he told her he was already up but just thinking. He'd closed his eyes for a few minutes longer, his thoughts dwelling on Diamond and the things she had going on. It would be in his best interest to be up and on point.

He exhaled fully and before he could gather his bearings, a plastic bag was thrown over his head and he began to struggle for his life. With him being on his stomach when the assault began, it was difficult for him to reposition himself. He struggled as the grip tightened around the bag and the weight of his assailant held him face down on his bed. For the first time in his life, Chris knew he'd got caught slipping in the worst way. Hoping someone would hear something, he tried to scream, but accidentally sucked the bag in with the effort. Chris reached for the pistol he kept between the nightstand and his bed, but to no avail. Even with nothing to fight with and no oxygen to inhale, Chris wasn't about to give up, it just wasn't in him.

The first thing that came to mind was this was it and the first name to cloud his thoughts was King's. Chris then stabbed at the plastic covering his mouth, and as soon as air flooded his lungs and he was able to breathe, the entire bag was snatched off and laughter filled his hearing. "Diamond!"

Diamond had straddled Chris while he was facedown and to see him at such a disadvantage tickled the hell out of her. She couldn't help but remember the days back when she was sure Antonio was trying to kill her. He'd done the same things to her so often that she didn't even fight it anymore. She'd learned long ago to stab at the plastic covering her mouth and just lay there. The more she would struggle, the harder Antonio would laugh, and it was now she found the same humor in it.

She yanked the plastic from Chris' head and fell over next to him while laughing uncontrollably. She laughed at him with eyes closed and mouth wide open and while being unable to fix her words, she was unable to stop the slobber and snot that came from both her mouth and nose.

"Girl, I don't like that sort of stunt you just pulled on me!" Chris yelled at her.

Diamond laughed harder.

"That shit ain't funny, motherfucker. What if I'd had an asthma attack or something?"

Diamond continued to laugh while clutching the plastic to her stomach.

"I'm serious." Chris yanked the plastic from her and threw it across the room. "Datrina! Datrina!"

Diamond coughed, laughed, and coughed some more. She looked up at Chris, who was now looking as if he wanted to kill her himself and she began laughing again.

"What the hell is wrong with you this morning, Diamond? You don't do shit like that to people." Chris sat on the edge of the bed and shook his head. He looked back at Diamond and started to laugh himself. It was always said that laughter was contagious and after seeing there was no threat, he snatched his comforter from under Diamond. "You got snot and shit all on my Gucci comforter. I ought to make your ass buy me another one."

Diamond straightened herself, wiped her eyes and told him, "Damn, I needed that."

"What you need is a foot in your ass, Diamond. Don't ever do me like that again."

"If your ass would have been up and on point, that shit wouldn't have happened in the first place."

"You crazy, Diamond."

"We got shit to do today, nigga and now that you're up, let's get to it. Go shower and get all that shit from between your ass first."

"I ain't got no shit between my ass."

Diamond began laughing again. "Nigga, you farted like ten times. I thought you found a way to breathe out of your ass for a minute there. You know you got that coming, don't you? I wanted to have your ass saying your last prayer."

Chris made his way to the shower while yelling threats over his shoulder.

"I'm gonna be ready when you lay the payback on me, nigga. Bring it on!"

Chris laughed from behind the door he'd closed.

After walking into their living room, Diamond fingered the remote to his entertainment system and fell onto the sectional. She thought about her brother, Antonio, and the way things used to be. All the fun they had and the promises they made. She then thought about King and the times they spent together. For the first time in over a couple of weeks, Diamond found herself smiling at the memories she held. She found herself smiling at possibilities and just then, the words of Sergio found her. *"We have the ability to choose what's next, Diamond."*

After calling a few contacts of her own, Diamond stood, put on her signature Chanel shades and told Chris, "Let's get to the money, nigga!"

\*\*\*

Somolia had opened the salon herself and after hearing Datrina would be in later and Silvia talking about having a meeting of some sort, she made sure everything ran accordingly. She was logging in entries when her cell phone began to buzz. Somolia looked to find that the caller had blocked the number and instead of playing whatever game they were sure to play, she sent the call straight to voicemail. She thought about her last conversation with Raymond, as well as Q, and being that both of them felt as if she was to respond and react when they wanted her to, she was about to show them she also had things to do.

\*\*\*

Buddy watched King and Camille as they stood below him on the first floor of the bi-level studio Camille owned. The entire group was in attendance because of the shipment they'd just received and the distribution of it. Camille had told him of their need to expand and since this was a bigger purchase than most, it would be a joint effort to get it dispersed.

He'd been thinking about the conversation he last had with the woman he met at the Totally Awesome Salon in Fort Worth, and even thought of contacting her. He dialed the number and after being sent to voicemail, he hung up. Just as he was about to call a second time he thought he heard a ping behind him. He walked towards the kitchen and heard it again. Since he wasn't one to look or snoop into his Boss Lady's belongings, he chalked it up to something she'd handle whenever she got the chance.

*** 

Antonio had decided to get back at King earlier in the day and after knocking out another chapter in his book, he emailed King a response and told him he was to visit as an attorney and he'd have to come during the week. Antonio thought of at least informing him about the protocol, but decided against it, wanting to see just how on point the guy was. After the short email and instructions, Antonio went back to writing in his book he was yet to title.

*** 

Camille and King were standing outside her studio, talking about their next move, when the silver CTS-Coupe entered her parking space. She looked from King to the approaching car, then back to King, who was now smiling as if he'd just found a couple thousand dollars in an old pair of jeans. It was intentional that they kept Terry out of the box they continually dipped into, as well as away from the attention they were sure to gain with their business. Terry was the one that stayed low pro at all times and if anything was to ever keep them from moving themselves, Terry was the legs that would instead.

Seeing him pull up, Camille knew King was up to something and as always, she was going to sit back and observe. Before the day was over, she'd have a pretty good idea of what his role was. She was sure of it.

"What's up, y'all?" Terry greeted them before climbing out of his Coupe that was worth eighty thousand dollars.

"It's always good to see you, Terry." Camille hugged him, stepped back and smoothed the wrinkles she caused.

"Where's the big guy?" Terry looked around them. As far as he recalled, wherever Camille was, the giant was sure to be there.

"He's—"

"What's good, Terry?" Buddy cut in while descending the stairs to Camille's studio.

The four of them stood and talked for a brief minute, before Camille said they all had to do breakfast. And as if her words were law, she walked off, climbed into her Audi, and asked Terry, "Have you lost any money in that thing yet?"

After Terry climbed back into his Coupe and King had jumped into her 911, Buddy brought up the rear in his Dually. He hit redial and after being sent to voicemail for the third time, he pushed his phone deep into his pockets and followed the trio. He'd get at Somolia some other time, he hoped.

*\*\**

By the time Diamond and Chris made it to the salon, Silvia and Datrina were there attending to their prospective clients. Instead of fussing over her hair, Diamond decided to get her feet and nails done. Her little stunt with Chris earlier caused her to rip her wide-legged pinstriped slacks. Therefore, they had to stop by the mansion so she could change out of the barely noticeable torn slacks.

When they entered the building, Datrina was the first to no-tice them, as well as the first to notice she'd changed clothes.

"Diamond, what happened to the pant suit you were wearing?"

"Oh, I ripped the slacks and had to stop by the house for a bit."

"She tripped out, that's what she did," Chris said with a roll of his eyes. He went to hug and kiss Datrina, a move that didn't go unnoticed by Somolia.

"Hey, y'all, where y'all coming from?"

"What did she do now, Chris?" Silvia asked, making sure Somolia's questions went without the answers she was sure to misconstrue.

"Nothing," Diamond answered before Chris could reply to Silvia, looking over at him and trying to not laugh,

"Crazy ass tried to kill a nigga this morning, Silvia, and she thinks the shit funny. That's how she tore her pants."

Silvia smiled when seeing Diamond suppress her laughter. She was sure this story would be topic of many to come. "Keep it to yourself then, because Somolia is just dying to re-edit the script."

"Girl, please, when it comes to them two, nothing surprises me." She looked towards Datrina, perched her lips and continued with her client's hair.

"What she do, Chris?"

Before Chris could respond, Diamond winked at Datrina and told the group, "Me and Chris was in the bed wrestling and he kept pulling at my pants."

The lie was enough to gain Somolia's attention, as well as cause Silvia to walk off.

"I don't know why y'all acting surprised. It ain't like it's the first time." Somolia went in, just as Diamond knew she would and after hearing the rest of the women at the salon engage, she headed to her cousin's office herself. The center of attention was where Diamond kept herself and as long as Somolia Rhodes was co-authoring, it would be a place she stayed.

Silvia fell back into her desk chair. Flipped open her laptop and checked her emails. She even checked her phone to see if there were any text messages from her husband. She might have kicked him out of their home and ignored him until she felt otherwise, but he was still her husband.

"So, what's up, cuz?" Diamond threw herself on the sofa adjacent Silvia's desk.

"I should be the one asking you that. I've been hearing tidbits about this and that as it regards you and Chris." Silvia's intent was to only hint around it and hopefully, Diamond would volunteer the rest.

"If it's Somolia telling the story, then you knew you should have turned the page long ago."

"Somolia? I'm not talking about no damn Somolia." Silvia shifted in her seat and smiled at her youngest cousin.

"What?"

"You tell me?"

"Silvia, you in here tripping, you know I was lying about that shit with Chris."

"Um-hmm."

"I'm serious."

"Yeah, well, what have the two of you been up to lately?"

"We hung out in San Antonio looking at properties, took care of a little business and besides that, we do what we do every day."

"So, what's up with that King situation?" Silvia felt it was time to shoot a little closer to the target she was aiming at.

"The hell if I know. I haven't heard from the nigga, if that's what you're asking me."

"Oh yeah?"

"Yep."

"So, what's the next move?"

Diamond looked out of the window to the left of her and shrugged her shoulders. "The hell if I know. Chris thinks we should get at the nigga, instead of waiting for him to get at me. He thinks he's going to try to cross a few lines in his attempt to cross me."

"And, you think?"

"You know I got to look out for the team." Diamond continued to avoid her cousin's gaze.

"Well, just be careful, Diamond. I understand that things didn't happen the way they were planned, but that's that curve ball life throws at us every once in a while, and at times it's done so we can re-evaluate things."

Diamond looked down at her nails, smiled to herself and said, "Where is all this coming from, Silvia? Where are you going with all of this mother-daughter shit?"

"Call it what you will, Diamond. I'm just trying to get you to see things from a different perspective."

"A perspective other than which?"

Silvia exhaled and began digging into her desk drawer. She told her, "You figure it out, with your smart ass."

Instead of continuing the conversation with Silvia, Diamond told her, "Do my nails for me."

"Get your punk ass out of my office, Diamond. A bitch try to have a real conversation with you and you fuck it up. Get out." Silvia pointed towards her door."

Diamond stood. "Fuck you and that girl-ass shit you got going on. A bitch ain't got to flip all the dominoes over to see what you playing with."

"What?" Silvia frowned, seeing Diamond smile.

"Go figure it out with your smart ass." Diamond laughed, winked at her cousin and walked out, her thoughts taking her to King and the things they promised each other.

She'd just stepped on the floor to the work stations and overheard Somolia say something about Datrina wanting another home. A bigger home.

"It ain't like he ain't got the money to buy it for her," Diamond added.

"As much as he be with you, it's a wonder why you haven't bought them one," Somolia added.

"I thought about it and even tried to. We went to see some properties the other day."

Seeing Datrina smile, Diamond continued. "Quarter-million-dollar houses at that."

"No," Chris said. "*You* went to look at some quarter-million-dollar homes and I only accompanied you." Chris made that statement in a bid to straighten things out, but Somolia was chewing on other thoughts. Thoughts she felt she needed to voice.

"Yeah right, Chris. The last thing Diamond need is another house. It is kind of thoughtful of you, though."

Chris looked from Datrina to Somolia and lastly to Diamond. Their joint effort was sure to cost him a quarter-mil, if not more and he was certain of it.

"Diamond, let's go."

"I'm about to get my nails done, Chris," Diamond pouted.

"We got all day for that."

Seeing Chris make his way to the door, Diamond stood, promised she'd be back later and followed him.

Once they were out the doors of the salon, Somolia looked to Datrina and raised her brows. She asked her," You see what I'm seeing?"

"Yep, about a quarter-million about to be spent." Datrina smiled to herself. It was only a matter of time, before she and Chris were settling in something bigger and better than the three-bedroom loft they'd been staying in. It was about time.

***

During breakfast, Camille had filled King in on the incident that most recently took place and before she had the chance to change the subject, as she'd always done when she felt it was a minute issue, he looked towards Buddy. "So, there was no other way to handle that, Buddy?"

"Boss Lady's orders."

Terry lowered his head and coughed. These were conversations he stayed away from and could tell Camille was sharing it with him as a scare tactic, one which he was feeling personally.

"Some things are inevitable, King and them spilling me at some red light wasn't the option."

"Yeah, I feel that, but damn. In broad daylight?'

"Would you rather someone came by at night to inform you of my demise, King? It is a non-issue. Get over it." Camille took a sip from her glass and sat it down. She looked over at Terry and asked, "So, what brings you out of hiding?"

Before he was given the chance to respond, King spoke up. "I need for him to take some of this cash off of us, just in case."

"Just in case what?" Camille questioned him.

King smiled. "Inevitability, I guess."

"You're real funny, King. Your humor has no bounds." Camille eyed Terry without blinking. She was still awaiting his answer and seeing him swallow without drinking, she understood more than they were willing to admit.

"Um, you know the game, Camille."

"Do I?"

For the next twenty minutes, Camille made it her business to make Terry feel as if he had no place when it came to conspiring against her. She wanted to continually remind him of whom she was, and there was nothing she wouldn't uncover when it came to the secrets he and King had.

## CHAPTER FOUR

It had been two days since the girls put Chris on the spot, regarding the move they felt Datrina deserved and the promise he made to do so. He'd been thinking about the stunt Diamond pulled and couldn't help but relive it in his thoughts daily. With their loft being the only place King visited Diamond, Chris felt it could and would be used to his own advantage.

He'd been well aware of his surroundings for the longest, when it came to the people that came in and out of their complex and knew what he was seeing when he spied the silver CTS Coupe cruise through their spot for the third time. He at first spotted the new car a couple of days ago, but thought nothing of it. Yet, after the second time, he began to pay closer attention. It was just something about the way the driver rolled through with no destination. That became the telltale sign Chris used to gauge the situation, and it was that early morning wake-up Diamond gave him that had him on edge.

"Datrina!" he called after her while spying the same car from their patio window.

"What's up, babe?"

"Um, I'm about to make a run right quick. You need anything from the store?"

"Nah, I'm good."

Chris slid his Glock into his waistband, grabbed the keys to the Corvette Diamond bought him and eased out the front door. With their loft being at the rear of the complex, it was only one way for any driver to go and with that in mind, Chris hurried to the convertible and decided to cut the suspicious driver off at the entrance.

Pulling to the stop where the gates separated their complex from the rest of the world, Chris sat lower in the convertible, slid on a pair of dark shades and waited for every bit of three minutes, before seeing the silver Coupe pull to the same gate awaiting its exit. He tried to get a look at the driver, but the heavily-tinted windows wouldn't allow it. Chris tried his best to remember King and while knowing this would be a move he entrusted to someone else, it was still something he fixed his mind on. If King did send someone to his home, then it would be taken care of sooner than later. And if by chance Chris found himself to be tripping from paranoia, he was about to find out now.

Terry had been through these same cobblestoned streets several times and saw no sign of the Bentley Coupe King described. At first, he thought he spotted the hardtop Corvette King spoke of, but after a closer look, he realized the car was a convertible and although identical to the one he was given a description of, it wasn't the one he was looking for. He pulled up to the entrance to the complex and contemplated his next move. He promised King that he'd find his Diamond and with nothing else to do, this would be done until he did. After checking the area for the hundredth time it seemed, Terry exited the complex and headed to yet another location he was given and when making a mental note to return later, he sighed. For King, he'd continue his search.

\*\*\*

King was pulling into the Three Rivers Federal Facility at nine o'clock on the dot. He'd gotten the response he sought and was more than excited his attempt hadn't been a dead-end. When reading that he'd have to do an attorney visit, King smiled. This meant Antonio really wanted to see him about the matter as well. Today, King dressed in a navy blue suit with tan pinstripes, tan hard-sole shoes with gold buckles and carried a black leather briefcase. The gold-framed specs he wore added sophistication to his person and even before he was able to show any credentials, the prison guards were directing him to the legal visiting area and by the way they spoke the McClendon name, he knew Antonio wasn't just some inmate housed there.

"Thank you," he said, smiling at the female guard. King inhaled deeply and exhaled fully. He'd been waiting for this moment too long.

"He'll be out shortly, sir."

46

Once he was alone in the visiting room, King thought about the day he'd be faced with the same fate. He thought about the game he played and the consequences it promised. King then thought abut Diamond and the reasons he was there. He looked around at the walls that confined many of the players he started with. He didn't wish this on anyone.

*** 

Somolia had just finished setting her client's hair, when her phone started glowing. She wiped her hands before grabbing it. She'd told herself that she was going to ignore both Raymond and Dell and whoever else, but the weekend was nearing and she hadn't gotten her groove on in a minute. Something for the weekend would do her just good. She frowned seeing the number was blocked, but answered it anyway.

"Somolia speaking."

"Good evening, beautiful."

Somolia looked around at various faces, to see if anyone was paying attention while she stayed on the phone. There was only one person she knew whose voice was so deep, it unsettled her. A voice she'd been waiting to hear for weeks now. "Buddy?"

"Yes, ma'am."

Somolia smiled at Datrina while making her way to the back office and with Silvia being out at the moment, she sat behind her desk and continued her call.

"Where are you? I've been waiting for you to call me at least."

"I have been calling, but apparently you've been more than busy."

Buddy's voice caused her to smile, the memory of him caused her to shift and her thoughts towards him brought out the freak she was.

"I haven't been as busy as I'd like to be," she told him with a bit of seduction in her tone.

"Is that right?"

"It's definitely not wet."

When hearing Buddy laugh, she continued, "But, I'm more than sure you have other things to do than meet me at some exclusive location, just to fuck me the way I need to be fucked."

"Um, I'd clear my schedule to accommodate you in that effort."

"I'm serious. I do not have time to play. You've had my pussy throbbing ever since the day we met and—"

Buddy cut her off. "How about tonight around eight o'clock? I'll call with the location and all you have to do is show up."

"Text me instead."

"Yeah, ma'am."

"I'm not going to be disappointed, am I?" Somolia smiled to herself, bit her bottom lip and looked towards the wall clock.

"Only time will tell. You'll just have to meet me and see."

Somolia ended her call and slowly lowered her phone until it was facedown on Silvia's desk. She took a deep breath and shook her head. Not only was Buddy a mountain of a man, but he was one she was more than willing to climb.

\*\*\*

Buddy was lounging on Camille's sofa, thinking of the things he'd planned with and for Somolia later that night. He'd already stepped out and bought her a small token of his appreciation and was hoping she'd like the expensive Prada handbag. He was more than sure he'd be seeing Somolia. As a matter of fact, he was looking forward to it.

Camille walked past Buddy, dropped the medium duffle at his feet and told him, "This shouldn't take long at all." She'd been watching him smile to himself several times, but chalked it up to nothing. That was, until she called his name a second time.

"Something's entertaining you at the moment, so when you're ready, get at me then," she told him before pouring herself a glass of champagne.

"I'm good, Boss Lady. I'm good."

"Plans?"

"You could say that."

"Am I to worry?" Camille walked to where he sat and stood before him.

"No, ma'am. Just thinking of what was said earlier, is all."

Camille never pried in any of Buddy's business and she wasn't about to start. "Well, let's make our rounds, so I won't become the excuse you use to keep you from it."

As soon as she closed the door of her Audi, she thought about King's sudden disappearance. He also spoke of having something to do and since she'd been giving him space, she didn't inquire about his goings or comings.

And, with his location just buttons away, there was no need. Not only could she activate King's phone and camera from where she sat, she could zoom in and look down on the entire area he was at the time.

Despite her talk with Terry and King, she could tell there was more to the explanations they gave her. With Terry being the one kept from all the drama and day-to-day occurrences she and King and Buddy dealt with, she knew he wasn't about to be trafficking any drugs and there was only so much money he could transfer at a time, so there had to have been something else. Something she was sure had to do with the woman named Diamond.

After following the driver of the silver CTS to the freeway, Chris headed to the McClendon estate. He was sure his mind was messing with him because of the little stunt Diamond pulled, but he felt it was time for him to move Datrina into something more secure than the loft they'd been staying. Them cornering him in front of his girl had very little to do with the move he was about to make, because it had to be done sooner or later.

The gates to the estate opened just as he was turning in and after rounding the corner of the mansion, he saw Diamond standing on the stairs, conducting a call of her own and by the way she was cursing, he had a feeling something was about to do down.

"What's up, Diamond?"

"We got hit, Chris."

"What?"

"Yeah, Baby said some niggas hit one of our spots."

"How much he get hit for?"

"A little over sixty thousand."

Chris shrugged it off. "That ain't shit, Diamond. Them crumbs to us."

"It's about the principle, Chris, and I really just played it like that, but I don't believe it at all. I think the nigga wasn't able to get off all that shit and instead of looking like the boss he wants to be, he comes up with some shit like this."

"So, what you want to do?"

"We going to pay this nigga a visit and if for one minute I think he's playing me, I'm going to burn his ass, Chris."

"Fuck that shit, Diamond. Them niggas will need us before we need them."

"I don't need them at all, nigga!"

Chris lowered his head and closed his eyes. He knew this was coming. "Let me stop by the spot so I can get my truck then, just in case."

"When you start buying into all the excuses a nigga comes up with, they'll start selling you anything, and selling me short ain't some shit I'm buying."

\*\*\*

Antonio sat and listened to the events that led to King's sudden confidence in him. He nodded in agreement, hearing that King's experiences in the game didn't allow him to leave loose ends, and he was now doing what he felt he needed to do. To hear King's angle of the game, only confirmed what he already knew, but what confused him was the misdirection he read King. For King to think Diamond was some vindictive bitch out to settle a score by any means saddened him, and hearing King tell him there was a possibility she was behind his incarceration almost broke him. He wanted to tell King how far he was from the truth, but didn't. He instead told him, "I'm going to look into it, King. Thanks for bringing this to my attention."

"I really think someone's putting her up to this, because she's shown me so much more."

"Well, someone's pulling her strings and I plan to find out, but my advice to you would be to stay away from her for a while." Antonio stood. "At least, until I get the chance to feel her out."

\*\*\*

King climbed into Camille's Porsche and sat there. He looked back towards the doors he'd just exited and couldn't help but think of Antonio's situation. He could understand his reluctance to disclose too much information on his sister, because in his mind, who'd be willing to believe someone so close would be the one to do something so deceiving?

Antonio's words captured King's thoughts, but there was also something said long ago that did also. "She'll find me," he told himself before backing out of the parking space and pulling into traffic. Hoping that Terry would have something for him, King pulled out his phone and dialed him.

\*\*\*

Antonio thought about calling Diamond, but decided against it. He smiled, remembering the way King spoke of spending time with his sister, and found himself laughing when hearing about his visiting her in her loft apartment. He was going to sit back and let her do her things and if she just so happened to fall, he'd set provisions in places to pick her up.

\*\*\*

Somolia checked the clock on the wall, more than the text messages in her phone, and it was something that didn't go unnoticed.

"You got some where to be, Somolia?" Datrina asked.

"Aren't we nosey today?" Somolia answered, before making her way to the back for more supplies.

"By the way you're sweating that clock I would have sworn you had someone waiting on you."

Instead of allowing her business to entertain the floor, Somolia lied. "I was trying to see if my six o'clock was going to show, but it seems as if I'm going to have to make a few stops instead."

"What six o'clock?" Datrina asked, knowing both of their schedules like her own.

"The one I scheduled earlier," Somolia said with a slight attitude.

"You ain't made no damn six o'clock appointment. With your lying ass."

Somolia rolled her eyes and laughed. "Y'all some nosey bitches."

"If any of us here is nosey, we all learned it from you." Datrina looked towards the other women, then back to Somolia, who was straightening her station.

"Um, where is Chris and Diamond?" Somolia asked, knowing it would easily shirk the conversation everyone was trying to build around her.

"Buying my house," Datrina smiled. "My quarter-million-dollar house at that."

"Yeah, whatever."

By the time Diamond was climbing out of her Corvette, Chris was pulling in the apartment complex. Since she insisted on driving her car, he followed her as best he could. Seeing her weave in and out of traffic, as she'd always done when she had her mind on something, he slowed and prayed she'd do the same.

Familiar faces stood beside various cars and trucks and seeing a few that he didn't know, he looked towards Diamond, who was now arguing with the guy she'd been dealing with.

"Diamond!" Chris shouted from the truck. He watched several guys assess the same situation he was seeing. "Diamond!"

Seeing Diamond and the guy standing face-to-face, engrossed in the argument they were having, he thumbed the latch on the secret compartment, and pulled out something that held much more than the Glock under his driver's seat, and pulled his truck closer to where Diamond stood. "Let's go, sis. We'll do this some other time."

Before he knew it, Diamond had slapped the guy and before he could react, she'd pulled her pistol and pointed it at him. Chris then pulled up with the M-14 and pointed it at the guys that were hurrying to where she stood. Instead of hoping for a different outcome, Chris let off a series of silent shots as he made his way to where Diamond had drawn down on the other guy. Hearing several shots from that direction and more than a few hitting the hood and passengers' side of his Durango, he grabbed Diamond from the back and pushed her towards her Corvette. "Let's go, Diamond! Let's go!"

## CHAPTER FIVE

Later that night, Somolia stopped by her house, cleaned herself up and slid into a floral summer dress, with a pair of strappy sandals which showed off her fresh pedicure. Underneath the summer dress was a black lace and satin panty and bra set she'd spent over three hundred dollars for earlier that day. Tonight, she was going to blow Buddy's mind and she'd been eating fruit and drinking fruit juice to make sure she enjoyed the experience.

She pulled her Lexus sedan into the parking lot of the Royal Suites Hotel and parked. She closed her eyes and said a silent prayer, needing this to be anything other than her chasing after a ghost. Somolia had been stood up plenty times and it was something she still took a risk at. She glanced at her console and realized that she was twenty minutes early and sighed. This was something she wanted, something she needed. And despite it being something she agreed to just for the night, she was really hoping it turned into something more.

Buddy grew used to the spoils the game rewarded him and while being able to spend thousands upon thousands in and out of the strip clubs he frequented, being escorted by beautiful women began to bore him. He'd bought gifts when he felt the need to and it was just something about the woman Somolia that pulled at him. He could tell that she'd been through her share of ups and downs and kind of understood the woman she felt she had to be. Her aggressiveness towards him, her flirty behavior and the ways she looked at him, stirred his pot of lust and he was now hoping the handbag was enough for a woman of her caliber. In his attempt to be certain it was, he even placed twenty hundred-dollar bills inside.

As soon as he pulled into the Royal Suites Hotel parking lot, he spotted Somolia's Lexus. He pulled alongside her and climbed out of his Dually.

"I thought I was going to have to come and find you," he told her before opening her driver's side door.

"You coming and finding me can be looked at as two separate things." Somolia smiled at him.

"I've been thinking about fucking you for too long and I'm going to make sure you remember this night."

"Oh, really?"

"Really."

Buddy turned her to where she could face him and bent to kiss her. He sucked her full lips and feeling her tongue enter his mouth, he moaned.

"Ummmm."

Somolia broke their kiss and grabbed him by the buckle of his belt. "Let me see what you working with. Your big ass has to have a dick the size of my leg," she told him, before pulling him in the suite and pushing him onto the sectional it provided. She'd been thinking of just that for the longest and tonight, Somolia Rhodes wasn't about to be denied.

***

Diamond made sure they weren't followed and after hitting a few corners and flooring the Calloway Corvette, she found an on-ramp and put miles between them and the area of the shooting. She knew Chris was feeling strange for having to leave his truck, but she was glad they'd stopped to get it. Not only was the truck not registered to Chris or anyone associated with them, but he'd only put so much into it anyway. His Durango could easily be replaced.

"You alright, nigga!"

"Really, Diamond, really?"

"Just make sure."

"I wish you would have made sure before you tripped out back there. You could have gotten us killed, Diamond."

"That's the farthest thing from it, Chris. I read the play as soon as I pulled up. That's why I did what I did."

"And what play was that?"

"He was talking to a couple of guys and when he realized it was me pulling up on him, he tried to act as if I was some bitch he was about to check. I asked about my money and that's when they started making their way for their cars and shit."

"And that meant they were plotting against you?" Chris raised himself and faced her.

"What I did didn't have shit to do with them, Chris. The nigga started telling me a bunch of shit I wasn't trying to hear, and then he tried to kiss me. That's when I slapped his ass."

"He tried to kiss you?"

"That'll be his last time doing some shit like that."

"You shot a nigga, 'cause he tried to kiss you, Diamond?"

"Hell yeah, that and the fact that he was about to pull his shit out on me."

"I didn't see him with a pistol, Diamond."

"And you never will." Diamond took the Illinois exit and drove to Keist and made a right. She knew exactly were she was headed. "Did you leaving anything in the truck or what?"

Chris just watched her. He watched the way she easily detached herself from the incident that happened just minutes ago. He watched her transform into a totally different person. A person he knew better than any. When he looked at Diamond, he was seeing himself. "Where we headed now?"

"I want to show you this house while we're in Dallas."

"Show me a house? Are you serious, Diamond? You just shot a guy. I shot several and you talking about looking at houses?"

"What? You want me to pull over so you can cry, throw-up and clean your ass? We sharks, nigga. We see blood and we eat. Ain't that what you—"

"I ain't said no shit like that, and you know it! You twisting my shit now."

"Well, fuck them niggas. I hope it was worth it to them!"

"What about you, was it really worth it, Diamond?" Chris watched her. "Huh?"

"I would have paid a nigga a hundred grand, but—"

"That's what you need to start doing then, because that's it, Diamond. I'm not going on any runs with you anymore."

"Ya killed eight niggas for my brother and now you ready to thump a Bible and take up an offering. Nigga, please, we in this shit now."

"Are you even listening to yourself, Diamond?"

"This life ain't for everybody, Chris. You have to own this shit and regret nothing. You have to become that bitch, that cold-hearted nigga and if you have a problem deciding which, you need to decide on another game to participate in."

"Your brother wants better for you, Diamond. He doesn't want you out here fucking your life off. Hell, we ain't just throwing stones at prison, we kicking the fucking doors with both feet."

"Well, we knew what it was when we started this shit. The same way we lie in these beds of chance, is the same way we have to lie in beds of consequence."

Chris had been a part of this life for a while and had advanced to a level of game he couldn't climb down from. Despite his reluctance, his hesitance and his failure to do what he knew needed to be done, it didn't bind the opposition from doing the same. The same way he went for guys, was the same way he expected them to come and this was something he owned, this was the person he'd become.

"We always talk about accepting the consequences until they become something we can't. We're quick to become judge and executioner when it profits us, but as soon as we become judged we beg for leniency, sell ourselves short for favors and cry like bitches when it's too late."

"Well, you know I'm not like that, so—"

"That just the thing about it, Diamond, I don't know. You've never been there and truth be told, you can't even say what you'll do."

Diamond faced him. "You really think I'll—"

"Watch the street, Diamond." Chris pointed at the upcoming red light.

"Fuck the street, nigga! You really think that shit describes anything about me? You think I'm one of them finger-popping hoes that scream this shit without knowing the consequences, huh?"

"I'm not saying—"

Diamond cut Chris off. "That's exactly what you saying, nigga. How hard would it be for me to walk down a fucking runaway, and be compared to another bitch with damn near the same shit on? How fucking hard is it for me to suck a motherfuck-er's dick, in exchange for me getting exposure only they claim to be able to give, huh?"

"I'm just saying, Diamond—"

"You ain't saying shit, nigga. If death finds me, then he'd better not be worried about it finding his ass. And if a prison cell one day surrounds me, I'm still going to be me. I'm still going to be Chanel McClendon."

Instead of fueling the fire, Chris nodded. He wasn't one to pacify the tantrum she had and was never one to tell a person what they could and could not do. He'd been her rock from the beginning and as long as she was going to ride, he'd continue to be.

"A couple of hundred-million, huh?"

"Oh now you want to remind me of some shit like that."

"It's me and you, Diamond."

"It was me selling you out a few seconds ago," she told him.

"We'll cross that bridge when we get there."

"How about we burn the motherfucker right now?"

Chris laughed. He knew there was no way for that to be done, but was sure she would come up with something that would change his perception. He watched her pull into a residential area and frowned.

"Just in case someone slipped through the cracks and calls themselves trailing us to whatever location," she told him and pulled past the black wrought-iron fence with a huge lion in its center.

Diamond pulled around to the back of the property, hoping and wishing, and found it as deserted as she once had. She parked. "Get out. I want you to see the inside of this motherfucker."

"This another one of Dell's ideas?"

Instead of lying to him, she said, "Bring your ass on. If you don't buy it, I will."

Diamond gave Chris a full tour of the seven hundred thousand dollar home and pointed out all the possibilities she could think of, thought about the way King presented it to her. Remembered how he wanted to make this her home. Before she knew it, she was standing at the marbled island counter, thinking of the day she came to discover her King was gone.

"Diamond!"

"Yeah, yeah. You like it or what?"

"How you know so much about this house? This was King's spot, wasn't it?"

Diamond nodded.

"You want me to buy the nigga's house?"

"Like I said, if you don't, I will."

Diamond followed Chris out the way they'd come and was about to climb into her car when Chris called out to her, halting her.

"Come here right quick."

Seeing him look off into the wooded distance, she pointed. "Yeah, there's a storage past those trees along that walkway."

"I'm not talking about no storage." He pointed. "Look."

Diamond then noticed multiple dents in the trunk and side of her car and after a closer examination, she cursed. "Son of a bitch!"

Chris laughed.

"Punk-ass niggas shot up my shit, Chris!"

"I see."

"Shit!"

"Don't sweat that shit, Diamond. Throw it in the shop and give it a treatment, another color, slap some nice low profiles under it and you back."

"How about I just give it to you and you do all that shit?"

"Yeah, right." Chris looked at her then began walking towards the passenger door."

"Here," she said, tossing the keys to him. "Silvia is about to be mad as hell at us."

Chris caught the keys mid-air and smiled. It was nothing to call Diamond's bluff and he was more than sure the next time she saw the Calloway Corvette, she'd be wanting it back. He was going to make sure of it.

*** 

Datrina was closing up the salon when she realized that she hadn't heard from either Chris or Somolia in a while. Silvia had checked in to tell her of the dinner she and Raymond were planning and drew the conclusion she'd more than likely be laying low for the rest of the night. But, for Somolia to go missing and Chris not to check in, red flags went off in her mind. She called, then texted Chris and after three minutes of waiting and receiving no answer, she pulled up her GPS app and looked for both him and his truck. Knowing there was only one other person he'd be with, she called Diamond's phone.

"Hey, Datrina, what's up?"

"Why isn't Chris answering his phone?" Datrina asked her.

"Here, ask him."

Datrina could hear the brief exchange before Chris came on the line. "Hey. Babe, what's up?" Chris greeted her.

"You, and you not calling me in over three hours."

"A nigga stole the Durango and my phone was in there."

"Oh, really?" Datrina stopped, looked at her phone and shook her head.

"And which mall would that be, Chris?'

"Um—"

"Or do I need to remind you that finding either is just the press of some buttons away." Datrina could hear Chris' attempt to cover the mic on the phone and instead of going there with him, she said, "Just come home tonight."

"On my way now."

Datrina placed her phone on the counter and thought about the day Chris and Diamond pulled up to the salon in a cab. And, after hearing that Diamond had wrecked the Camaro, but later finding out there had been an incident in the same ordeal, she knew she'd be hearing something along the same lines when they did tell the story.

Hoping that Somolia wasn't about to give a similar story, Datrina called her with a lie of her own.

\*\*\*

Somolia lay spent on the sheets of the queen sized bed while Buddy was stretched out beside her. With him being so big and so strong, he was able to put her in positions she dared to name, as well as put enough weight on her to numb both her legs. He'd hurt her so good, made her so wet and gave her every bit of what she'd been wanting, needing for a while now.

"You fuck everybody like that?"

"No, ma'am. I just wanted to see if the pill worked. Something new."

"And, I was the guinea pig?" Somolia ran her fingers through the hairs on his chest. Made traces down to his stomach and looked over at him.

"I just wanted you to be satisfied."

"Oh really?" She smiled.

"Really."

She looked towards the dresser at her glowing phone and sighed. She was in no mood for the games, but decided to let whoever know she did have things to do, as well as other options.

"Somolia speaking."

"Somolia, I've been calling your fat ass for hours now. Where are you?"

Somolia tsked. "Datrina, damn. Can't a bitch get out every once in a while?"

"Who you with, Somolia?"

Somolia willingly opened her legs for Buddy and once his fat fingers were massaging her pussy, thighs and stomach, she purred. "Um, let me call you back, Datrina. This one can't keep his hands off me."

"You make sure he wore a condom, Somolia!"

Somolia ended the call and laughed. It was always that either Silvia or Datrina said or did something to hate on her and hearing Datrina go in. Feeling Buddy's soft hairs sprinkled across his chest, she said, "Them hoes be hating on a bitch."

While Buddy pleasured her with his hands and fingers, Somolia pulled up her knees, grabbed his wrist and placed his hands on her breasts. "Suck my pussy, Buddy. Lick my ass and give me some more of that fat-ass dick," she told him.

"Yes ma'am, Somolia."

After looking at the clock, realizing they'd been there for over two and half hours and had been fucking for the past two, Somolia closed her eyes, bit her bottom lip and enjoyed the ride. This was one man she wasn't going to let go and when she finished with him, she'd be the one he referred to as "Boss Lady."

*** 

Silvia and Raymond had been together for most of the day and after going over numbers and possible business ventures, it was decided that they'd open other Totally Awesome Hair and Nail Salons, as well as discontinue filtering money through her business. She'd come too far to lose it now and with Diamond doing her own thing and Antonio's lawyers promising this and that, she felt it was time for her to exit the game she knew so well.

She'd be given the three hundred thousand dollars to cover both the cost of the buildings and the first week's booth free for the employees. With Datrina wanting nothing to do with managing, one would be managed by Somolia and the third would be co-managed between the both of them.

"I'm telling you, Raymond, I'm not paying that money back."

"The money is yours, Silvia. We already talked about this. Just look at it as your severance pay."

"Yeah, more like my 'tear your ass' payoff."

Raymond laughed.

"I'm serious."

"You've done more for the lot of us, Silvia and no one's going to protest your exit or the fact that you're leaving with three hundred thousand dollars."

"Well, either way, I'm not paying it back."

"It's about time we all make a clean exit from the game. We've been lucky, Silvia."

Silvia yawned, checked the time on her watch and stood. "I should have been home by now, Raymond."

"You're welcome to crash in the guest room, if you want. I would hate for you to get on the road sleepy anyway."

Silvia thought about the proposal, checked her watch a second time and told him, "The last thing I need is for word to get back that I spent the night here, Raymond."

"Don't sweat that shit, Silvia. We family and if they can't understand that, then fuck 'em."

"Sounds good."

"It is good."

Since there was nothing to go home to, Silvia kicked off her shoes, grabbed them by the straps and made her way upstairs. The guest room was calling her in the worst way.

*** 

KP had been pacing the hospital's waiting area for right about three hours and still hadn't received word on Q's injuries. While demolishing one of the properties, Q violated the safety regulations and proceeded to work without proper protection and as he was trying to secure a support beam of the building, the entire side collapsed, knocked him and another crewman unconscious and severed his right thumb.

He'd cursed Q out several minutes before the paramedics arrived and despite him going in and out of consciousness, KP had very choice words for him. For one, neither of the workers had the insurance he claimed they had and if anyone chose to file suit, it would definitely fall back on KP's construction company.

Seeing the assigned doctor approaching, KP walked towards him and asked, "Is he alright?"

"He should be fine. He's on morphine and stabilizers at the moment, but he should make a speedy recovery."

"Can I?" KP pointed to where the doctor had come from.

"Sure. Go ahead."

KP stepped into the sliding doors, found Q's joint room and walked in.

"You alright?" he asked his best friend.

"Hell naw, ain't alright. Let me yank your thumb off and ask you some shit like that."

KP smiled. "Well, look at the bright side of it."

"Bright side?"

"Yeah, loud-ass, nigga. The bright side."

He watched Q raise his bandaged hand, saw where half his thumb was wrapped and said, "I thought your whole thumb was gone. You had us looking for half a fucking thumb?" KP looked at his friend with contempt.

"Punk-ass nigga, it felt like the whole thing was off."

KP looked back towards the nurses' station, making sure they weren't heard and turned back to Q, who was now sitting up straight.

"Shut your dumb ass up, nigga," KP whispered.

"Fuck that shit!"

KP found Q's shirt and threw it to him, grabbed his work boots and placed them on the gurney beside him.

"What—"

"Nigga, hurry up and put this shit on so we can go." KP looked toward the nurses' station a second time.

"You act like we breaking out or something. What the fuck's wrong with you, clown?"

"Better bring your gay ass on, nigga. You don't have no insurance to pay for this shit."

"What? I thought we—"

"Let's get outta here, man."

"So, I don't get paid by the insurance company?"

"What insurance company? I'll give your ass fifty dollars for a bottle of Advil and something to drink, if that's what you want."

"I thought we had insurance, KP. What if I would have gotten seriously hurt, nigga?"

"Then I would have dumped your ass off somewhere and made up a lie about it. That way, it wouldn't fall back on me, I mean us."

"I wish I could slap the shit out of you, for real. How in the hell am I supposed to work now? How in the hell am I going to pay my bills, nigga? I was counting on that claim, man."

"At least you'll look bigger now." KP smiled at his friend and shrugged his shoulders.

"Look bigger! What the fuck you talking about?"

"Ya dick. You hold your shit in the hand with the short thumb and bitches gonna be like, 'Damn, nigga!' "

Q couldn't do anything else but laugh and go along with the humor of it. "Yeah, stick it right up Silvia's ass too."

"Fuck you, nigga, with your itty bitty, teeny thumb ass. A punk-ass gonna have to wear gloves. One glove."

"You owe me, nigga."

"Yeah, I'll buy your first pair."

## CHAPTER SIX

The following morning, Chris was up earlier than most. He'd made several calls himself and after making arrangements for the Calloway Corvette, he filled Datrina in on the things scheduled to take place within the next couple of days. And since Datrina had a full day scheduled at the salon, it was decided that she follow him at the repair shop to deliver the hardtop and Chris would drop her off at the salon.

"You ready to roll?" he asked Datrina after texting Diamond to let her know where he'd be.

Datrina walked past him on her way to the kitchen area and kissed his lips. "Born ready."

Chris noticed that Datrina wasn't exactly dressed for work, but for something more personal.

"You sure you going to work at the salon?" Chris watched her with a questioning expression.

"Those were my plans. Why, what's up?"

"You're dressed as if you're going to meet up with someone."

Datrina looked over her attire and placed a hand on her hip. "Really? Well then, I guess I am."

Datrina grabbed her handbag, threw her phone inside and scooped her keys. "I wouldn't want to be late for my date then," she told him before heading out.

Chris looked on in bewilderment. It had to be something he was missing.

Outside, he walked her to the convertible and once she was seated inside, he closed her door and began walking towards the hardtop. It was then he saw the same silver CTS parked across the way. He immediately reached for his pistol, then remembered he'd left it in his truck the day before. Chris was slipping in the worst way. He looked back to where Datrina sat waiting and smiled. There was no need in creating panic for her.

Hoping that his mind was playing tricks he could easily best, he looked without looking and once he was seated and felt around in the back for something to arm himself with, astonishment hit him. The Mini-14 he used the previous day was not only disassembled, but scattered between the McClendon estate and the route it took him to get to Echo Heights.

"Bitch!" he cursed the situation and himself for the position he felt he was now in.

Chris pulled past the parked CTS Coupe and watched Datrina do the same. He sighed as she did, but kept a watchful eye on his rearview mirror. Once they were out of the complex and on their way, Chris relaxed. There was still no sign of them being followed, but he knew from past experiences that when a person really knew what they were doing, you wouldn't know anyway. One thing he did know was that as soon as he got rid of Datrina, he was going to visit a pawn shop or two.

***

Datrina looked over herself again. She'd dressed in the same fashion many times before, and for Chris to speak of her doing so now, made her realize that he really hadn't been paying attention to her or the things she wore. She knew his mind had been preoccupied, but never before did she feel as if he'd paid her no attention. She adjusted her mirror, applied a liner to her lips and was about to back out of her parking space, when she noticed the bullet holes in the trunk and rear fender of Diamond's car. She'd heard Chris speak to someone about repairs, but wasn't thinking along these lines. Datrina then thought back to the day before and the fact that Chris spoke of someone stealing his truck from a mall. A mall he couldn't name. She closed her eyes and inhaled. "I knew something wasn't right," she told herself and pulled out behind him. Whatever the case though, she was going to keep it under the hat and what ever he and Diamond had going on, she prayed they be able to solve it.

***

Terry had been parked across the complex ever since spotting both the Corvettes parked under the canopy of the apartments. He started to drive off at first, but before he could do so, a guy and a dark-skinned woman climbed into each of them. He took a pic of them together and sent it to King and seeing his immediate reply—the thumbs-up emoji, he knew he was getting closer. What threw him were the bullet holes in the rear of the car King spoke of as being Diamond's. There had to be something no one was telling him and in his case, it would be something he neither asked nor talked about.

Once they pulled out of the complex and pulled off, Terry did the same. And, before he returned to Dallas, he'd make one more stop by later. After all he'd heard about Diamond, he had to at least see her for himself.

*** 

King made a couple of stops to check on the money he was making and after collecting over one hundred and seventy-five thousand dollars, he headed out to Las Colinas to see what Camille was up to. They both had business lined up for the day and while wanting to surprise her with a dinner and a possible movie, he wanted to get things done as soon as he could. He was pulling into Camille's studio parking when his phone chimed. When he saw Diamond's Corvette, along with a convertible identical to hers, he replied with a thumbs-up. He smiled to himself, knowing he was that much closer to finding his Diamond. Terry had just made a darkened day brighter. Much brighter.

He used his key to enter Camille's studio and was expecting to hear either soft music or the shower and hearing neither, he looked towards her bedroom. He slowly and quietly closed the door behind him, looked for Buddy's hulking figure in his favorite lounge chair and seeing they were alone, he crept across the polished hardwood flooring and suppressed his laughter as best he could. Even though he'd collected over a hundred and seventy thousand dollars, it was nothing compared to the news Terry just delivered.

He eased one of the huge pillows Camille slept with from the bed and raised it. With her being fully under the sheets, he felt this was his advantage and nothing was about to keep him from it.

Just as he was about to send the pillow crashing down on her, she called out to him from behind, her toothbrush in hand.

"Good morning to you too, Kengyon."

King turned to face the voice, looked back towards her bed and then back towards her. "I thought—" he let the pillow fall and pulled at the sheets.

"Thought you were about to make a fool of yourself," she told him before turning and walking back into her bathroom.

"I almost had you, Camille. I almost had your ass."

"I see."

King walked up behind her and wrapped his arms around her waist. He moved her hair and kissed her neck.

"You know I love you, right?"

"What did you do now, King?"

"Nothing. I haven't done anything." He kissed her again.

"So, what you're telling me is that yesterday, you didn't love me, the day before that, you didn't love me and even before then, I haven't been worthy of your love?"

"You're always loved by me and you know it." King kissed her hair, looked at her through the mirror she was watching him from and placed his chin on her head. "Got good news and more good news."

"I'm more than sure you do, King. I'm sure you do." Camille rinsed her mouth, pushed past him and headed for her kitchen,

"I made rounds, picked up over one hundred seventy-five grand and will be free for the night."

"Sounds as if that's the day and life of a King."

"It is, and this King wants to spend the day with you. Let's do dinner and catch us a movie or something."

70

Camille stopped, looked towards her living area then back to King, who was smiling at her as if she'd just shown him the difference in their anatomy.

"Where's Buddy? I haven't heard from him all morning."

"Ain't no telling. He probably went to a strip club or something. The big guy needs love too, Camille." King followed behind her.

"He still would have called." Camille then thought about the way Buddy was acting the day before, as if he either had somewhere to be or was looking forward to it.

"Well, you free or what?"

"Dinner can be prepared here, King, and I'm more than sure the movie you're wanting to watch can be found on Netflix or Hulu."

"I guess I'm just wanting to get out," King spoke the words with less enthusiasm, knowing it would get to her.

"Fine, King. We'll go out, order some popcorn and wipe tears away at the end of it."

"Let's go see Tyler Perry's new movie. *Boo 2*."

Camille searched for the words to say. Told him, "Not Madea, King. I'm in no mood for the humor."

"I wish Diamond..." King cut himself off after hearing his words. He knew how Camille felt about her, what he thought of her and could care less about any of it. He'd crossed the line and he knew it. "I'm sorry, Camille. I—"

"No need, King. It really isn't."

He tried to hug his friend, but she raised her hand, stopping him. "Do not touch me, Kengyon Johnson."

\*\*\*

Somolia strolled into the Totally Awesome Salon hours after opening and went about her day as if it was nothing out of the ordinary. She'd enjoyed her night, and nothing and no one was going to take that from her. She even agreed to see Buddy again. Soon.

"Look at what the whale spit up, y'all." Silvia smiled seeing Somolia put on as if she wasn't about to be topic of the day.

"She looking good," said another woman.

"Want to talk about it, Somolia?"

"Not really, I mean, it wasn't nothing but some hard fucking. And, I do mean hard."

Silvia clapped, as did the other beauticians and clients that knew her personally. And those that didn't only smiled and took it all in.

"Your lips do look fuller, Somolia," said Silvia.

"My legs stayed numb, girl. He did me every which way you can think of."

"Who, Somolia? Who is he?"

"He even bought me this." Somolia held up her new handbag, pulled out a stack of hundred-dollar bills and waved them above her head.

"The power of the pussy!" someone yelled.

"The power of the pussy!" they all said in unison.

Datrina walked into the salon amid the yells and laughter. There were other things on her mind and as soon as she passed her station, she told Silvia, "I need to holler at you in the office, right quick."

Seeing Datrina's demeanor, the women present looked toward each other in search for an explanation and seeing her close the door behind them, they all grew silent. Somolia followed. Silvia sat behind her desk, looked up at Datrina and asked, "What's up?"

"What's up, y'all?" Somolia asked, peeping inside the office door.

"Let me get at her right quick, Somolia," Datrina said, closed the door and stood against it.

Somolia returned to her station with a look that spoke volumes, but still wasn't heard by some.

One woman asked, "What's up, Somolia? What they say?"

"Said get my fat ass out. That's what they said."

Somolia watched how the conversation easily went from being about her to what people thought was being said. Through the blinds, she watched her friends have a hushed conversation without her and for once, she knew it had nothing to do with her.

Raymond sat his glass down and stood. He'd driven out to Dell's home personally to tell him of the things he and Silvia agreed to the day before. And, for Dell to feel as if it was something that should have been discussed with him first, it had him feeling strange.

"So, what are you saying?"

Dell was sitting back on the Italian leather sofa in his pitted den sipping on mimosas when Raymond came over. He'd been thinking about the fact that he was sending out more money than he had coming in and was looking for a way to change that. And here Raymond was telling him they were about to shell out another three hundred thousand dollars to Silvia.

"I'm saying this should have been something we all sat down and discussed. Not some private conversation agreed on by you and Silvia."

"She's just as much a part of this circle as either of us—she has the right to make moves other than the ones we see fit." Raymond walked over and stood next to the Grand piano Dell took pride in. He looked around the room. "All this shit was built on her back, Dell. Don't forget that."

"Money hasn't been coming in the way I projected, Raymond, and for us to give her that amount as a severance or whatever, it's going to put us back a bit."

"Put us back a bit? We've made millions off of the money she and Antonio invested, what you mean, put us back?"

Dell still hadn't told either of them about the loss he took with Camille or the fifty thousand dollars he'd paid his guys for the hit on King. He'd failed to tell them about the monies he used for his own personal reasons, hoping it would be returned because of the things he invested in. Dell had been in charge of the Circle's finances for years now and was never questioned about where money came from or went and for it to be done now, caught him off guard.

"Don't worry about it, Raymond. I'll draw up the check in the morning."

"She agreed to cash and that's why I'm here now. I know for a fact we should at least have half a million on hand, Dell."

Raymond's eyes followed Dell from where he sat to the piano he stood beside.

"I got it. I got the money, so don't even sweat it, man."

Dell stepped around Raymond, unlatched the hook on the grand and raised its top. He then pulled back a thick plastic that looked to have been a covering for the keys underneath. He counted out stacks of five thousand dollars, until they were looking at the full three hundred thousand dollars.

Raymond shook his head. He was more than sure Dell had large sums at other locations, because he was definitely looking at a fraction of the money they'd made together.

"Where's the rest of the money, Dell? And, do not tell me you used our money to purchase this house. Your house?"

"What are you putting this in?" Dell asked, ignoring the question Raymond asked.

Raymond walked over to where he sat and popped the locks on his briefcase, where he kept a folded medium duffle for times such as these. He threw it towards Dell. "Here."

"We have dollar amounts in various locations. This is just where I keep the money at this particular one."

"Me and Silvia went over the numbers last night and after looking at the books, we should be sitting on over seven million dollars in cash and another seven and a half million dollars in assets. Giving her only three hundred thousand dollars is pocket change and she's going to use that to open more salons. In five years, those numbers will be coming back, so it's a win-win for all."

"I also have things in the works—"

"Things no one knows but you, Dell." Raymond grabbed the straps of the duffle with one hand and grabbed the handles of his briefcase with the other. There was nothing more to be said.

"I've always looked out for us, Raymond, always!" Dell yelled after him.

Raymond climbed into his Rolls Royce, threw the duffle and briefcase in the back and looked up at Dell from the driver's window. "Maybe it's time I bought myself a four-million-dollar home." He allowed the suicide door to close itself and pulled off.

\*\*\*

Diamond was smiling, sitting in the first floor study, going over past transactions for both gains and losses. She and Chris made over four and a half million dollars off of the shipment they purchased from Miami and the only loss they took, the sixty thousand dollars they were forced to part with to the guy in North Dallas, was pocket money. She's seen her brother flip these numbers, but she'd done it in less than six months and with half as many people he dealt with. It was then Silvia's words found her and she was thankful for the team she had. She couldn't help but feel her brother and Silvia's influence because once again, if it wasn't for them, she'd be on some cut or in some trap patching up, just to score the crumbs she was now able to throw away.

She thought about how much more she could have been making if only things went as planned with King. Thought about the fact that she really didn't need his outlets and having seen what he was working with herself, there was no way he was the one that stepped on her brother. He'd have been in a more promising position if he had and he wouldn't have been basing his success in the game on a seven-hundred-million-dollar home. Diamond counted out one point seven million for her next drop, and another six hundred thousand. She was going to get at Dell the first chance she got. With King's sudden disappearance, she was certain it would be on the market and she wanted that house. And, thinking about it further, she had to have it. As bad as she wanted to move closer to where her brother was situated, there was a bigger part of her needing to be where King wanted her.

After closing the vault-like door to her safe and loading up her brother's Escalade, she walked the grounds of the estate, remembering the promise she made to herself and him.

## CHAPTER SEVEN

Diamond arrived at Dell's seconds after Chris and by the way both watched her as she climbed out of the Escalade, she was about to be admonished for something.

"What?" Diamond walked around to the rear of the truck.

"Hell, I didn't know who you were pulling up on us in the big ass truck," said Chris.

"Yeah, well, some measures are taken when others can't be," she said, before dragging the cash-filled duffle around.

"Where's your Corvette?" Dell asked.

"I got rid—"

"It's in the shop," Chris yelled, finishing Diamond's sentence.

"I just pictured you jumping out of something a little faster, is all." Dell turned towards his tinted glass doors and told them, "Let's step inside. There is a lot to discuss." He thought about Camille and the fact that he hadn't heard from her in a minute.

Chris grabbed the duffle from Diamond with a questioning expression and followed her into the house. Dell was cool with them, but there was no reason telling what didn't need to be told.

Once inside, Dell led them to where he and Raymond conducted their brief meeting—his den. After offering Chris a drink and Diamond a bottle of water, he took a seat on the piano stool and faced the Circle's newest member.

"What's the money for this time, Diamond?" he asked her, while thinking of a few requests she was sure to have.

"This is six hundred thousand dollars!"

Chris frowned. "You serious, Diamond?"

"Anyway," Diamond turned back to Dell and finished, "I want that house and if Chris don't buy it, I will."

"You sure about this?"

"Does it look like I'm just talking?" Diamond sat back on the sectional, making Chris shift expressions. She knew he wasn't approving of her posture or the fact that she'd pushed his hand.

Dell whistled. "I'll have to make a couple of calls first, Diamond. He could very well have sold the property already."

"Well, get on top of that for me." She looked at Chris and told him, "I also have over half a mil for you."

"I'm not worried about that shit, Diamond. I know where we at." Chris took a swig of the beer he held and shook his head. They'd talked briefly and he still had yet to tell her about the silver CTS Coupe he'd spotted outside of their apartment, or the fact that things were still unresolved with the North Dallas incident.

"Still haven't heard anything from King?" Dell knew it was time to get to the business he needed tending to.

"There seems to be a dead end when it comes to that, Dell." Diamond looked around the room for something other then the thoughts she was having.

"We need to find this guy, Diamond. He knows too much about—"

"I don't think he knows anything other than what we've shown him," Chris cut in, defending her.

"I just hate to let this go, being that we've put so much into it." Dell stood, walked past Chris until he stood behind his fully-stocked bar. He poured himself another drink and offered another to Chris.

"I'm good, Dell."

"The nigga just upped and disappeared, leaving no trace whatsoever," Diamond added.

"If and when he does show his face, me and Diamond already concluded that he has to go."

Dell shook his head. "We first have to locate where he's moved his money and drugs, then we move on him."

"We don't have that edge anymore, Dell. Who's to say he won't be trying to get at either of us while we're waiting to see where he has his shit stashed. We can't risk that."

"Um, well, I'd hate for it to be all for nothing. I mean, we've put a lot into this." Telling them that he'd come out of pocket in the course of the event would have to wait, because now that Diamond had delivered over half a mil, he was sure he could make something happen to compensate his personal loss. He just needed more time. More time than it would take for him to make the calls needed to find out if King's Ravinia home was back on the market.

"Fuck that nigga, Dell. The nigga ain't got no money like that. You had me thinking he'd pushed my brother over for the cash flow, but the nigga isn't even on Antonio's level at all."

"I think he's still filtering both cash and buyers into his equation so it looks as if he's still climbing instead of already there."

"Why would he jeopardize losing out on both money and clientele, just to appease the watching eye?" Chris asked.

"Who knows, maybe the feds have had him in their sights for a minute."

"Well, we'll just have to get whatever we catch him with, 'cause I'm not about to let this nigga move his fortune." Chris looked towards Diamond, held his glass up in a toast and smiled.

Diamond rolled her eyes and immediately noticed the large captions on the seventy-five-inch plasma screen Dell had. "Chris." she pointed.

Chris looked and shrugged as if it was nothing, but when reading the caption detailing "The North Dallas Shooting," he looked towards Dell, then to Diamond. Hearing the reporter speak of three being injured and two deaths, he felt the need to complete what was started. He was never the one to leave things undone.

By the time they left Dell's, Diamond was feeling pretty good about the possibility of owning the house King abandoned. She could tell Chris had something on his mind and was sure he was feeling strange about her insisting on owning the property. As soon as she pulled out of Dell's estate, she stopped and lowered her window, signaling for Chris to pull alongside her.

"What's up?"

Chris leaned over the passenger's seat in order to look up at her. "Head to my spot, we got to talk."

With that being said, Diamond pulled off, fingered the volume of the stereo and drove. No longer was she going to be that selfish bitch that brought King down and if by chance he did catch up with her first, then so be it. All she wanted was a chance and if after that, King couldn't understand, then and only then would she change her perspective also.

***

Datrina filled Silvia in on what she felt was happening and was prepared to hear a totally different story from both Chris and Diamond, but was unprepared for the topic she walked in on after leaving Silvia's office.

"Sure is quiet out here."

"Shh…"

Somolia pointed.

"Reporting live from the Skillman area in far North Dallas where a shooting took place yesterday. Three were injured and two dead. No suspects have been arrested at this time. If you have any information that could possibly help authorities—"

"See, that's what I be talking about right there. Niggas always killing each other and nine times out of ten, it was over drugs," Somolia told them before going back to what she was doing.

"Every once in a while it's even over a woman," another woman added.

"I'm surprised the shooters haven't gotten caught, all the cameras walking around this day and age."

When Datrina turned to face Silvia, she was standing behind her with a shocked expression of her own. Both of them had put the puzzle together and were more than sure Diamond and Chris had something, if not all, to do with it. This would not only be their secret, but it would be the one they both took to the graves with them.

Silvia pulled Datrina back into her office and closed the door. "There you have it." Silvia folded her arms and walked to her office window. "Here I am thinking they're out looking at properties, but come to find out they out there popping pistols."

"Does Diamond even own a gun?" Silvia questioned herself, trying to remember if her young cousin ever did.

"They way the news described it, it was more than one person shooting, Silvia. She's got something."

"We still shouldn't jump to conclusions about this though. We—"

Datrina cut her off, "We know they had something to do with it. Why else would Chris have taken that car to the repair shop the day afterwards? Then, there's the truck he claims to have gotten stolen, while they were at some mall or whatever. Both of their names are all over this, Silvia."

"Well, I—"

"That's why he doesn't have his phone," Datrina added, thinking about some of the lame explanations he gave. "He always keeps his phone either in his pocket or on the console while he's driving and when have you ever known Chris to leave it in the truck while he's at the mall?"

"Have you tried locating it on that app you got?"

"Been there, done that. It's either off or destroyed."

"Everybody knows not to keep the phones of the victim they rob, so—"

"Ain't nobody robbed them. If that would have happened..." Datrina's voice trailed off with the thought. Another piece of their puzzle realized.

Instead of either of them speaking the obvious, they understood the reasons they couldn't, especially on the floor of the Totally Awesome Hair and Nail Salon.

\*\*\*

Raymond parked, saw Somolia's Lexus and knew he wasn't about to hear the end of it. She'd been trying to contact him for the longest and after running out of the excuses he came up with, he just avoided her altogether. The gifts had stopped and the calls were far in between. He entered the salon with a smile.

"Hey, ladies," he greeted the bunch.

He looked towards Somolia's station. "Somolia."

"Hey, Raymond, what brings you by today?" she asked in a dismissive manner.

"Scheduled to meet with Silvia. Is she here?"

"Yeah, she's in her office with Datrina." Somolia nodded in the general direction. "What's in the bag?"

"A little something-something for Silvia and you."

"Me?" Those words caused Somolia to finally look up and meet his gaze. "What about me?" She followed him into the office and this time, she found a seat next to Datrina.

Raymond walked the duffle to Silvia's office closet and told her, "Three hundred thousand. Not a dollar short."

"Three hundred thousand?" Somolia interjected.

"Shut up, Somolia."

"Did you have to fight him for it?" Silvia knew Dell and knew it was probably something she'd hear protest to later.

"Not at all. We all know how valuable you are, so—"

"Hump-umm," Somolia cleared her throat when hearing that statement.

"You also, Somolia and Datrina too. You ladies have sacrificed enough," Raymond continued, stroking Somolia's ego as best as he could.

"And the three hundred is for?" Datrina asked, knowing their method and hoping they weren't trying to get her to operate a salon herself.

Raymond laughed. "Don't even sweat it, Datrina. We know you're not trying to do anything else."

"I have more on my plate than you know, Raymond." Datrina rubbed her temples with both hands and sighed.

"We're opening up more salons and we need you to operate one, Somolia."

Somolia smiled at the three of them. "This money for me?"

"Us, Somolia. Us," Silvia corrected her with closed eyes. Somolia always thought the world revolved around her.

"So…you're running me off?"

"We're actually putting more money in your pocket, Somolia." Raymond explained things from a business aspect while including the numbers they'd discussed the night before and before he was finished, Somolia stopped him.

She raised her hand in pause.

"You and Silvia spent the night together?" She looked as Raymond with slanted eyes.

"Shut up, Somolia. I called you and you were laid up with some man yourself," Datrina added, knowing the words wouldn't come out of Somolia's mouth.

"I'm talking to Raymond." Somolia pointed. "You and Silvia spent the night together?"

"Yes, Somolia. Yes, but we wasn't laying up under each other, if that's what you're asking."

"Really?" Somolia looked from one to the other with a prosaic expression.

"I am still married, Somolia."

"And when has that ever stopped you from fucking off?'

Datrina stood. "Stick ya dick in her mouth, Raymond. She'll forget all about fighting." Hearing both Silvia and Raymond laugh, she pushed past Somolia. "I have some work to do."

"I'm not tripping on them fucking around. I—"

"No one's fucking, Somolia. It had gotten late and I really didn't feel like driving all the way across Fort Worth. That's it, nothing else."

Silvia knew she had to take control of the subject matter, because it would have been something Somolia wouldn't find an end to and to make sure it went no further, she stood also. "I'll just get out of you all's way," she said as she walked past them, leaving them alone. "And, you'd better swallow that shit, Somolia. Don't spit that shit in my trash can."


Somolia faced Raymond. She hadn't heard from him in a minute and was sure they had a thing or two to talk about.

"So, it's like that now?"

Raymond sighed. He knew this was coming. "I've been busy, Somolia. I really haven't had the time to do anything."

"But, you find time to invite Silvia over and—"

"Business, Somolia, business. Nothing more."

"Well, I just wanted you to know that I haven't been sitting up waiting on you to realize how good you had it."

"I'm pretty sure you haven't, Somolia and by the way, Datrina alleged you've been busy yourself." He measured her response with raised brows.

"You know how it is."

"Anyone I know?"

"Nope." Somolia looked up at Raymond, shifted her stance and bit the corner of her bottom lip.

"Is he doing you right?"

"He's learning how to." Somolia stood.

"So, when is the next time I get them lips around my dick?" He stepped toward her until his midsection was pushing against her breasts.

"Um," Somolia looked down at his slight bulge, then back up. "I need to ask you something."

"Ask."

"Can we open up something in Las Colinas?"

"I'll look into it. Is that it?" Raymond pressed harder.

"Yep." Somolia turned, looked over her shoulder and proceeded out the office, leaving him standing there as he'd done her for the last time. For now, she belonged to Buddy and Raymond needed to understand that.

\*\*\*

King had been giving Camille the queenly treatment ever since they left her place and it was beginning to be something she was suspicious of instead of something she was to enjoy.

Camille placed her napkin in her lap and smiled. "With your actions alone, I would have just thought I was deserving, but with Terry's sudden appearance and Buddy's sudden disappearance now, I'm thinking you, for whatever reason, think I'm the fool."

"You tripping. I'm not the enemy, Camille."

"What are you then?"

King looked around them, then back to Camille, who was still smiling at him. "Will you stop it?" King turned his phone so, he could check for a text.

"What am I to stop, King?"

"Faking. Your cheeks ought to be hurting the way you over there smiling."

"You first."

King reached across the table and grabbed her hand, another attempt with his sincerity. "Is me wanting to spend time with my best friend, always a reason to suspect something?" He glanced at his phone a second time in seconds.

"Normally it does and by the way you're monitoring your phone, I can tell you're mind is elsewhere. So, what's up, King?"

"Just thinking."

"About Diamond, I assume?"

"Her too."

Camille pulled her hand from his and took a sip of her water. If it was one thing she knew, it was when he was keeping something from her. Despite it being done in his attempt to worry her less, it was still something she despised. "Am I to worry about these thoughts you're having, King?"

"I just want to see her again, Camille. That's it."

"And, Buddy and Terry are your search engines?" Camille wiped her lips, placed the napkin on the table and looked around for the waiter.

"I have no idea where Buddy is, but Terry has been carrying out some *assignments* for me."

"And what happens when he's found out, King? What happens when he slip at something he had no business doing in the first place?"

"Terry's fine, Camille. He knows what he's doing. He already found Chris and his girl."

"But, he's yet to find the person he was instructed to?" Camille tsked.

"He will. He will." King hoped he was right and since neither of them knew about Terry, he felt it would be the right move and the right time and that time was now.

"That's my brother, King and it something happens to him—"

King leaned forward. "Nothing's going to happen to Terry, Camille. You hear me?" They both looked into each other's eyes. One giving assurance and the other needing it.

They both knew the deadliest games were the ones with no rules, but to not know the rules of the ones played, ran parallel as did the consequences.

"Let's go catch this movie," he told her before rising from his seat and watching her do the same.

"If anything happens to my brother, King, she will die. This bitch you can't seem to see past will become an afterthought, you hear me?"

"Yeah, I hear you."

King followed Camille out of the eatery and said a silent prayer. He remembered the words Chris spoke during their sit-down. Remembered the promise Chris made to him about protecting Diamond at all costs. He even remembered himself acceding to it. It was now he prayed he didn't have to protect her from his best friend.

## CHAPTER EIGHT

That following weekend

A week had passed since the North Dallas shooting and things were somewhat back to normal. Chris had no choice but to come clean with Datrina about the suspicions she had, and after telling Silvia that things couldn't have been avoided, they understood a little better. He made sure he told the story instead of Diamond, because there were some things she was willing to add that would have definitely refuted the story he came up with.

They both agreed to stay cautious, because after hearing that the guy Diamond shot wasn't killed, Chris knew there was a possibility of retaliation. He initially wanted to finish what was started, but after making promises to both Datrina and Silvia, he had no choice but to wait. And, waiting was something Chris wrestled with.

With it being the weekend Diamond was scheduled to visit Antonio, Chris wasn't about to let her make the trip alone. Not only did he have some things they needed to discuss, he had something to give her. As soon as she pulled into their complex, he was standing by the curb nearest the pool, at the entrance. Chris had been on edge all week and took it upon himself to confront the guy or woman driving the CTS Coupe. But, for the past week, he hadn't seen the car or any other suspicious car for that matter.

Chris waved Diamond over.

"What the hell you doing out here, Chris?" she asked, pulling the Escalade alongside him.

"Selling flowers," he told her while climbing inside. "You ready to roll or what?"

"Yeah." Diamond modeled the 'do she wore and asked, "How do I look?"

It was then Chris noticed she'd changed the color of her hair again. The jet-black tussles she wore pulled to one side might have changed her appearance, but Chris still saw the woman she was becoming. "You look good, Diamond, but we know what it's for."

"What's that supposed to mean?"

He looked her over and twisted his lips. "In about three and half hours, you're going to be looking like Young MA."

"What's wrong with that?" Diamond pulled from the curb and drove out of the complex.

"Your front looks so good, but the real you…"

"The real me, what?"

"When you was with King, you stayed this way. You was the bitch every nigga wanted to be with. You was a trophy mother-fucker." Chris smiled at the brief memory.

"Deception was beautiful, huh?"

"Yes, it was."

Diamond watched Chris as she steered the huge truck. She knew what he was implying. She also knew it was the truth.

"Oh yeah, I got something for you." Chris reached under his left arm and came out with a modified Glock. He held it on the seats between them.

"Okay." Diamond looked down at the handgun and shrugged.

"This motherfucker's modified, Diamond. Fully automatic. All you have to do is point and shoot." He then reached in his sock and pulled out an extended clip. "And here's thirty rounds for it. This will not only keep a nigga off you, but it will shred a nigga's ass real nice."

"I thought I told you to get me a HK MP5, or something heavier than this shit. You got sixty-year-old and seventy-year-old women on the news handling assault rifles and you pull out some shit like this?"

"Woman, you stupid. Deadly is deadly and when you can't even hold the bitch up or pull it fast enough, whatever the next motherfucker got becomes just as deadly. While you wrestling with a big-ass rifle, a nigga can use a beer bottle to split your shit and it's shit like that, that creates such an edge." Chris held up the Glock and inserted the thirty-round clip, giving it a totally different appearance and added, "You squeeze on a nigga with this, I promise you he ain't wasting time looking for no beer bottles."

88

Diamond gave an approving nod. "I might work with that."

"Hell, you ain't got no choice." Chris jacked one shell in the chamber and ejected the clip. "Slippers count, Diamond and if you get caught slipping, it's because you want to." He then pushed it in a compartment between their seats. "So, what they say about the car?"

"We'll swing by there when we leave Three Rivers. My boy says he's got a surprise for me."

"What's Datrina talking about now?"

Chris spoke with Diamond about Datrina moving back into the mansion until things died down, but after voicing his concern with his girl, she wasn't trying to hear anything about leaving him. Datrina was going to ride with him against whatever. And, until he bought another home for the both of then, the loft was where she'd stay and if they just so happened to come from there, that's what they'd have to do. This was the reason he bought both of them Glocks and had them modified.

"You know how Datrina is. She's stubborn, just like you."

"Bitch gangster. That's what she is." Diamond smiled.

Chris glanced at his friend and looked away. "She's stupid, that's what she is."

"Niggas hear about bitches like us and call us down bitches. They—"

Chris stopped her midsentence. "That's because they don't know of all the other things they have to offer, but choose to throw life away trying to be the so-called, down-ass bitch."

"If it wasn't for bitches like us, you wouldn't have one. Good girls live the kind of lives niggas continually try to change, because they want something more. Niggas either want a bitch that's going to take it in the ass or want a bitch that's going to bust a nigga in the ass. And, I'm the latter."

She watched Chris for a comeback and when seeing him with nothing to say, she told him. "Bitch-loving-ass nigga."

\*\*\*

Antonio walked into the visitation room with an expression of both anger and concern. He'd received calls all week from Silvia and having been filled in on the things his younger sister was involved in and the fact that he was able to piece together things he'd heard, as well as the things plastered on the news they watched, there were things he needed to say and they all knew it had to be said in person.

He caught Diamond when she jumped into his arms.

"I miss you, nigga. What they talking about?" Diamond began.

After seating Diamond, he walked towards Chris, who then hugged him. "What's up, Gangster?"

"You losing your touch or what?" Antonio asked Chris, knowing full well they were on the same page.

"I got it, Bro. I made a few promises that's binding me at the moment, but I'm still on it, man."

"This is my sister, Chris and—"

Chris nodded and smiled. "I'm not going to let anything happen to her. I promise."

"Nigga, sit down. We ain't come here to talk about that shit. We come to kick it." Diamond pushed a couple of drinks across the table towards where her brother sat and nodded for Chris to take the seat beside her.

"Oh, you the boss now, huh?" Antonio looked at her with raised brows.

"You didn't know, nigga?"

Chris shrugged, opened one of the pastries and slid it over to Antonio.

"You heard her."

"Well, then you need to start taking care of your shit better than you have been. You a boss now, so keep it there. And this little bullshit I'm hearing about all over the news and the streets? You're just growling, you ain't bit nobody yet."

"And what is this you think you've been hearing?" she asked, needing to know just how much he was about to connect.

Instead of entertaining his sister with a play she felt she controlled, he went another direction.

"That you the one set me up with these charges."

"What?" she and Chris asked in unison.

"You know anything about that? What about you, Chris?"

"Hell naw!" Chris then looked towards Diamond, who was still looking on in confusion.

"Where you hear some shit like that from?" Chris wanted to know. He looked from Antonio to Diamond.

Diamond looked over at Chris and asked, "What the fuck you looking at me like that for? I don't know where he got no shit like that from," she told him. Then, she faced Antonio. "Whoever told you some shit like that full of shit, Bro."

Antonio leaned forward. "Exactly, and for both of you to come at me with some bullshit, offends the hell out of me also."

Chris closed his eyes and found himself shaking his head. "I should have known."

"Yeah, you should have, now what's up?"

Antonio sat and listened to the hushed confessions of both Diamond and his most trusted friend. He was now able to see his sister felt disrespected by the guy that withheld sixty thousand dollars from her. He understood. There were other ways to address the situation and he told them as much, but blood had been spilled and he was more than sure retaliation was in order.

Hearing that she gave Dell over a half a million for King's Ravinia home, he laughed, failing to tell them of the visit he had with the man himself and choosing not to. That was another story he was sure to enjoy soon. It wasn't until Chris spoke of going after King that he actually agreed with Diamond. She explained the fact that King wasn't built like that and that if she could only speak with him herself they'd come to terms with each other. The only difference in their theory was that Antonio felt it was best for Diamond to focus on the more pressing issue at hand, instead of some romance that would be the death of both of them.

Antonio was even able to give Chris a couple of assuring nods when talking about King.

By the time the guard informed them their visit was about over, Chris had talked Antonio out of the call he was about to make. The call to some of his guys that would have cleaned up the mess he and Diamond made in North Dallas. Antonio also told her there was no need in moving closer to the facility, because he'd be residing in his own home soon. Those were the words that brought both a smile to Diamond's lips and tears to her eyes. They both knew there was something he wasn't telling them, but Diamond wasn't about to try to extract blood from a turnip.

"Did you ever finish that book you were writing?" Chris asked, remembering it was something they spoke of before.

"What book?" Diamond watched them.

"Not yet, but I'm getting there."

"Oh, now you writing books and shit?"

"I might as well. Never know, this could be big."

"Throw me up in there somewhere." Diamond acted as if she was creating a heading. A title. "Call it, McClendon's Diamond or something."

"How about, 'A King's Diamond?' Or 'A King and His Diamond?' "

Seeing the stare they gave him, Antonio laughed. He couldn't help but laugh.

\*\*\*

The closest Terry came to finding Diamond was locating a car she was said to be the owner of and since then, he hadn't seen any signs of the car or the guy that was driving it. Despite being given the thumbs-up from King, he still felt there was something he could do for his sister's best friend. Since he was in the city, after visiting the Cadillac dealership and having customizations added, he decided to give it one more shot to see what he could come up with. There had to be something he was missing.

Terry pulled into the complex and drove around to the rear of them and seeing the convertible Corvette, he pulled alongside it and parked. He thought about climbing out of the car and waiting for either of the people he saw days before, and seeing the dark-skinned woman round the corner and deactivate the alarm on the car he'd just parked beside, he did so.

"Um, excuse me, Ms. But, do you have a minute?"

Datrina continued to walk towards the man before her. Even with all of the scenarios Chris was about to conjure, Datrina still felt it wasn't something she couldn't handle and seeing the dark-skinned guy climb out of the CTS, she replayed the worst of them in her mind.

"Yeah, what's up?" She pressed a button on the key fob and watched the top fold into the trunk of the Corvette.

"Um, I know this is going to sound crazy and I'm not trying to cause any problems, but do you happen to know a woman named Diamond?"

"Diamond?" Datrina looked at him as if was the first time hearing the name.

"A friend of mine said she drove a hard-top Calloway, and yours and the one I saw days ago parked here are the only ones I've seen, period." Terry pointed to where he last saw the Corvette and smiled at her.

"I'm sorry, but I'm not familiar with that name. Does she have a real name, or is that what you know her by?" She asked, searching him the way he was searching her. Seeing him confused by the thoughts he was having, she smiled also.

"Um, you know what, all I know is that she's beautiful, tall and has hazel-colored eyes."

"I can't say I do and as for the car parked here the other day, my boyfriend did buy it from a woman, but I'm not sure if that's who you looking for." Datrina started the car from where she stood and watched him. The way he deflated when hearing that he'd found a dead-end relaxed her, but she still wasn't about to loosen the grip she held on the Glock tucked away in her handbag.

"Is there any way I can speak to your boyfriend?"

"I'll tell you what, give me your number and I'll have him contact you as soon as he's available."

She watched him light up. Wondering what his angle was, she asked, "Are you from the North Dallas area?"

"Oak Cliff. I was in the area and decided—"

Datrina smiled and nodded. "I got you. I got you. But yeah, give me your info and I'm going to have my boyfriend get at you as soon as he can."

She handed him her phone. Confirming he'd entered the needed information, she smiled discreetly, brought her hand out of her bag and reached for the door handle.

"Thanks. It would mean a lot to me."

"No problem," she told him and climbed behind the wheel of the sports car and pulled off.

\*\*\*

King walked in, just as Camille and Buddy were gearing up to leave. He looked at Buddy and smiled. "He is alive," he told no one in particular.

"Clock ain't stopped yet, King."

"You had Camille worried like hell, Buddy. The way you've been disappearing every weekend and not calling."

"Apologized already. She's good."

Camille pointed at King. She was not in the mood. "Where is Terry, King?"

"He's probably out and about. You know how your brother is."

"Yes, I do and for him not to be returning any of my calls means he's doing something he shouldn't, or he's someplace he shouldn't be. I don't want him getting involved in your shit, King. I'm serious."

"Yes, ma'am." King grabbed Camille as she walked past him. He kissed her neck and squeezed her.

"Don't patronize me, King."

"Where y'all headed anyway?"

"We have business to attend to, unlike some of us." Camille pushed him away and grabbed her phone.

Buddy stood and grabbed his keys.

"Well, I'll leave you guys to it." He looked over at Buddy. "I might need to hit up one of them strip clubs you be sneaking off to for days at a time."

King checked out Buddy's attire. It was evident that Buddy had been shopping, to say the least. He wore a pair of pinstriped linen slacks, a linen shirt that complimented the dark green gator shoes he wore and his facial hair was trimmed to a T. There was definitely something to Buddy's disappearing acts.

"I have a couple of rounds to make myself. I'll be back through here later."

King walked Camille to Buddy's truck and opened the passenger's side door. He told her, "Terry's good, Camille. He's good."

"I really hope so and since you have more influence over my brother than I do, you make sure of it."

Camille closed the door herself, slid on a pair of designer shades and reclined. There was one stop she knew she had to make. "Buddy, let's go."

NICOLE GOOSBY

## CHAPTER NINE

Even before pulling into the lot of the repair shop, Diamond was smiling. She'd seen a couple of cars she liked, but the one that caught her attention was the black Lexus truck parked out front. "That bitch is bad!" she exclaimed.

"Yeah, well, just wait until you see my shit," he told her, knowing they were about to argue over ownership.

Chris pulled around the side of the building and parked next to the owner's Lincoln Continental.

Diamond pointed. "Is that my Vette right there?" she asked, seeing the pearl-colored Calloway with the slightly widened body kit and the twenty-two-inch stance.

"You mean, my shit."

"Nigga, you got me fucked up. You—"

Chris stopped her. "You, my ass. I just put another twenty thousand dollars in this bitch."

Before he could finish his boast, she was already out of the truck and walking towards the car. "Where are my keys at?" she asked the guy wearing the soiled overalls and the Rhino boots.

Chris watched the exchange from the side of the truck and couldn't help but smile. The modifications to the car fit Diamond to a tee. "You owe me twenty grand."

Diamond climbed into her Vette, looked around and nodded. She was definitely feeling herself. "I'll see you at the salon, nigga. You jacked!"

Chris watched her peel out of the parking area and after speaking to the repairman and paying him twenty-thousand dollars, he climbed back into the Escalade and headed to the salon.

Buddy pulled alongside Somolia's Lexus purposely. They'd been secretly seeing each other for most of the week and he was surprised at hearing Camille speak of needing to make a stop to the salon herself. At first, he thought it was done in an attempt to expose the fact that she knew where he'd been and who he'd been seeing. But, after hearing that it was to be done so Terry could be relieved form the duty King bestowed upon him, Buddy felt better. Although Camille hadn't asked him about his doings, he wasn't the one to keep them from her. But, with Somolia being a part of the other team, he knew it would be seen in a very different light.

He followed Camille inside and as always, the talking stopped once he ducked inside.

"Boss Lady?" several of the beauticians inquired when seeing the woman behind him.

Somolia turned, saw Buddy and smiled at the both of them. "Ah, she returns after all." Somolia then looked towards Buddy and said, "I knew you wouldn't call."

"Been busy," he told her with a smile of his own.

"Datrina's not in at the moment, but I'm more than sure she'll be in shortly."

"I was actually hoping I'd see Diamond this time around," Camille said flatly. She walked over to the empty chairs and took a seat. Buddy sat on the sofa across from her.

"As a matter of fact, she called minutes ago and said she was on her way," said another woman.

"Perfect." Camille made use of the selection of magazines before her, while at the same time quietly listening to the shop talk. It was always that one could hear tales of the many things people thought were under wraps while visiting any salon and being that the Totally Awesome Hair and Nail Salon catered to the city's upper echelon of well-to-do women and men, the news therein was considered worthy news.

Somolia glanced in Buddy's direction more than she should have and it was definitely brought to her attention.

"Are you just going to watch the man or are you going to say something?" one of the women asked her.

"Hell, you sound as if you know which questions I need to ask, so you just go ahead." Somolia told her. She tried restraining from the other beauticians, shooting both slugs and subtle hints that they were willing to catch a few themselves, but Somolia went off. "Will y'all leave the man alone, shit!"

"Sounds as if jealousy has arrived," said one woman.

"Is Somolia pissing on trees again?" said another.

"He don't want to hear all that shit and I'm more than sure your husbands wouldn't either." Somolia continued.

Camille smiled. The only time she spoke up in defense for a man was when he belonged to her and he wasn't defending himself. She glanced over at Buddy, who was looking as if the conversation had nothing to do with him, then to Somolia, who was really taking offense to what was being said. Instead of joining in on the fuss, Camille crossed her legs at the ankles and resumed her reading and listening.

"The last time he was here, you was bathing him with your panties and now you acting like he's your man or something."

Somolia knew what was coming next.

"You disappearing throughout the week, coming back with expensive shit and for some reason, you think we don't know what's going on?" said one of the women.

"Whatever." Somolia shrugged. "Believe what you will."

Before any of the other women could dive in on the subject, someone pointed towards the window and said, "Is that Diamond?"

"The woman done went and bought another Corvette."

"Money ain't shit to her. She's a rich bitch and she knows it," Somolia added.

\*\*\*

Diamond knew she was tripping the minute she saw the black Dually, but her thoughts were the farthest things from her mind as she jumped out of the car, thinking King had found his way home. She hurried into the salon, immediately spotted Buddy and began smiling. "King!"

Camille closed the magazine she was holding and greeted Diamond. "I hope you're disappointed."

"Camille?"

"Diamond."

Diamond frowned, looked towards the salon floor then back to Camille, who had now stood herself.

"Where's King?" Diamond asked.

"He, umm, Diamond, I need to explain."

"Hold on a sec, Camille." Diamond looked around at the many faces that watched them and exhaled. This wasn't exactly the way she'd planned its, but this would have to do. "Come with me, Camille." She then called back to Somolia, "Tell Chris I said this is private and I'll be out momentarily."

Camille reluctantly followed Diamond towards the back only after giving Buddy an assuring nod. Once they were out, of the hearing of everyone on the floor, Camille said, "You are definitely not the woman I was introduced to."

"There's a reason for that."

"I'm more than sure there is."

"Listen, Camille. I'm no longer your enemy," Diamond began.

"What's changed, Diamond?"

"The way I feel for Kengyon."

"Don't call him that."

Diamond looked out of the office window, saw Chris turn into the parking lot and turned back to Camille. The words she wanted to speak, now had to be spoken to someone other than who they were intended for.

"I, at first, wanted to see King fall. I wanted him to lose it all, even his life, because I felt he took my brother from me. I wanted King to pay more than anything,"

"And, who might your brother be?" Camille took a seat across from where Diamond stood.

"Antonio McClendon. He was set up a while back and now he's doing a federal bid in San Antonio."

"Really?"

"It was said that King set him up in order to push more product into the flour cities and that the only way to do that was to—"

Camille frowned. "That's not King."

"That's what I found out myself. I had to."

100

"And how was it King entered the equation?"

Diamond thought about the circle she was a part of, them members she'd been knowing for years and told her, "None of that matters now, because King wasn't the wrongdoer."

"And why am I to believe this now, Diamond?"

"Chanel. My name's Chanel McClendon and I'm not expecting you to. I would just like for King to."

"He's not really wanting to see you at the moment, Diamond. I mean, Chanel."

"I can understand that. I also need him to know that if he comes after me in any other way, there have been orders given."

"And, you feel as if it's your call to make?" Camille stood, pulled out her phone and took a couple of pictures of Diamond.

"It's the one I made."

"Well, fortunately, he's not coming after you for any reason. He's moved on and you should also." Camille knew that was the farthest thing from the truth, but knew it was the best for both of them. She'd been given better versions of the stories people told to justify their actions and hearing all Diamond had to say and the way she said them, Camille still had to keep her guards up. If not for herself, it would definitely be done for King.

"I love him, Camille."

Camille stopped, remembered King's confession and told her, "The things we do for the people we love."

"And, I'll do anything for him, Camille."

"Then stop looking for him."

Camille walked out of the Totally Awesome Hair and Nail Salon without acknowledging any of the women that called out to her. There was one thing on her mind. It wasn't until she was out the front door when she noticed both Somolia and Buddy engaged in an obvious conversation. "Really. Buddy? Really?" She climbed into the Dually and tsked. Here she was, trying to save King, and Buddy was about to jump off the same ledge.

\*\*\*

Terry wanted to surprise King with better news, but since he had yet to receive any call from the guy that bought Diamond's Corvette, he wasn't about to tell him of just another possibility.

"Terry, where you at?"

"I'm on my way to the house, King. I had a couple of leads and I'll make another round later in the week."

"Don't sweat it, man. You've done enough as it is."

"I'm close, man. Real close."

"I'm cool, Terry. Just forget about it. I'm cool."

"You sure? I mean, how hard can it be to find this woman?"

King smiled at the words Terry spoke, because he'd been trying to locate his Diamond for a minute now and still hadn't come close. There were some parts of the game only made and understood by some, and telling Terry that he wasn't in that number would only encourage his efforts, and being that he'd already told Camille he'd pulled him off the trail, he lied. "We already found her, Terry."

"What! When?"

King smiled at the naivety displayed and as quiet as it was kept, wished it was true. "I'll get at you later, Terry." He hung up without explaining.

With that being said, Terry floored the CTS Coupe, en route to Oak Cliff, TX.

\*\*\*

Silvia sat and listened to Datrina's account of what had taken place and the more she thought about it, it became obvious that whoever the guy was had to have been working with King's camp. The fact that he neither tried to conceal his identity, his means of transportation or the person he sought after, told her he wasn't a killer. Datrina's being able to capture a photo of the guy, showed how naïve and inexperienced he was as well. She started to tell Datrina about the visit she'd had with Antonio and the reasons for it, but decided against it for not wanting to spill the things Antonio entrusted her with.

102

"Well, it's obvious he's never seen her before, so he can't be one of the guys they ran into during that shooting." Silvia stood, grabbed her keys and told Datrina, "Are you going to tell Chris about it or what?"

"As paranoid as he gets at times, I'm starting to wonder if it would be the wisest thing to do."

Silvia sighed, "I'll be glad when you all this is over with. I mean, everything."

"You seem to be putting it all behind you as we speak." Datrina smiled.

"And you should be also. You need to be getting Chris to want that for the both of you also."

"He does and I know he means well, but he's binding himself to Diamond's well-being."

"Yeah, and for some reason, he feels as if he has to. Not only her, but to us as well."

"He always speaks of being in Antonio's debt."

"Well, he needs to get over that because that's been paid. I assure you that."

Having watched their friendship through the years, Silvia understood more than she claimed to. She understood what it meant to be loyal until the end, and the end only came when that loyalty was sacrificed. Silvia had learned long ago that loyalty would be spoken of by everybody, but only a select few actually lived by it, and as long as Diamond chased her dreams, then Chris would be there by her side.

## CHAPTER TEN

KP read over the citation he was given, a second time. He'd been hit with a hefty fine, due to the safety violations of both Q and the other crewmen, who were injured while performing a clean-up of the Rec Center. He had lied about the insurance coverage of each of the crew he hired and after one of his crew and filed an injury claim, there was only KP's Construction responsible.

Outside of the eight men he employed, KP often went by the labor pools to pick up several more hands when the jobs allowed and this was what he'd done to secure a contract with the cities' Disaster Relief Effort. With enough men and the equipment needed to accommodate such duties, he just knew he was about to be rolling in the money promised. That was, until Q and another guy messed it all up.

"Thirty thousand dollars!" KP yelled, not believing he'd been fined because of another man's mistakes.

"You'd better be lucky it wasn't three hundred thousand," Q told him, hoping he'd see the better side of things.

"Motherfucker, I'm not the one violated the safety regula-tions. I always make sure we have the appropriate safety gear."

"You should have made sure we had safety insurance. With your lying ass."

KP paced the same room. There was no way he'd be able to pay the fine, without coming out of pocket. Then, there was the lawsuit the other crew man was sure to file sooner or later.

"Weak-ass nigga get hit across the head with some sheet rock and act like he died, like I'm the one tried to kill him." KP knew if anyone would be filing a suit, it would be Q and even after losing half his thumb, he was still ready to work.

"The nigga wasn't no regular anyway. You picked the nigga up from outside a labor pool. Hell yeah, he's going to file a suit. Niggas ain't out here working for free and when there's a possibility of a come-up, then it is what it is."

"Shut your punk ass up! You was the one brought the shit up in the first place."

"Nigga, I was just playing when I said I'd sue your ass. I—"

"You coached the nigga into the shit, that's what you did." KP threw the letter across the room, pulled out his phone and began looking through his contacts.

"Who you calling now? Ghost Busters?" Q laughed, he hadn't seen his friend this distraught in a while.

"I'm calling the morgue. I need to see how much it's going to cost to burn a couple of niggas."

"You need to be calling about having your name changed, because when that nigga get at a lawyer, the name Kevin Pierson is going to be last thing you're going to want people calling you."

"I just rented all this damn equipment and these dump trucks." KP slapped the corner of the table, scaring Q in the process.

"Fat-finger-ass nigga, you need to be slapping some money on that motherfucker. All that other shit ain't going to keep them hoes off your ass."

"Where the hell am I going to get the money from?" KP walked back towards the bathroom while thinking. "I got to pay this nigga off, settle out of court or something."

"Call your wife. I'm more than sure she's had time to come up with something. All she has to do is call one of them rich niggas and give 'em some pussy."

"Shut up, Q. Shut the fuck up, nigga!"

"It's as simple as that. You know it's true."

KP thought about the words his best friend filled his thoughts with and knew it to be more than true. They were always falling out because of her suitors and because of the paper trails they left. He'd personally seen her with hundreds of thousands of dollars and now that it was something he was needing, he prayed she had it. "Yeah, I have to call my wife."

"You've been wanting to do that anyway."

\*\*\*

As soon as Diamond's company left the office and the salon, Chris entered. "What was that all about?" Chris watched them depart from the office window.

"That was King's right hand, Camille, and I told her everything."

"You did what?"

Diamond stood and began walking past him. "I said, I told her everything."

"And?" Chris followed her.

"The bitch still don't believe me."

"How'd she even know about the salon or the fact that you'd be here?" Chris stopped her before she could leave the office.

"We talked a while back, Chris, and I guess that bitch remembered."

"I don't know about this shit, Diamond. I mean, come on now. This bitch pulls up on you at your cousin's spot, with some giant-ass nigga in tow and you telling her some shit like that."

"That's Buddy, and wherever she goes, he goes. And, if this was something done so she could get at me, he wouldn't have been standing up in here with her."

"The bitch up to something, Diamond."

"I know exactly what she's up to."

"Really?" Chris watched her with a questioning expression, her calm getting the best of him. There had been too many things done to start slipping now.

"She trying to keep tabs on me in her attempt to keep me and King from each other. Evidently, he's trying to reach out to me and she's doing what she's always done."

"Which is?"

"Protect him."

Chris followed her onto the floor just as Silvia and Datrina walked in. His and Diamond's talk was nowhere near finished and she knew it. "We're not finished, Diamond."

\*\*\*

Silvia acknowledged everyone on the floor and stopped in front of Chris. Seeing his and Diamond's exchange meant she wasn't trying to hear what he was talking about and seeing the recently repaired Corvette, she knew it was time for their talk. "Don't we have a meeting scheduled?"

Chris sighed, smiled and nodded towards her office. "After you."

As soon as Diamond hit the on-ramp, Datrina secured her seatbelt and seeing Diamond floor the sports car while maneuvering through mid-day traffic, she faced her. "What's up, Diamond? It's obvious something is on your mind by the way you driving."

"That bitch, Camille, came by the shop just before you and Silvia got there."

"And?"

"The bitch calling herself keeping me from him." Diamond fingered the sensor on her radar detector and accelerated more.

"You think that's the play?"

"And the bitch had the nerve to take some pictures of me."

"She does have his interest to look after, Diamond. It's not like you went into this with honesty."

"Fuck that bitch."

"Well, check this out." Datrina pulled her phone from her pocket and scrolled through some pics herself. "Have you ever seen this guy before?" She showed her a pic of the guy driving the silver CTS Coupe.

Diamond leaned to get a better look and frowned. "I can't say I have."

"Never? Think, Diamond."

"Naw, I'd remember if I saw him somewhere. He does look familiar though."

"Well, he's the guy that pulled up on me while I was coming out of my apartment, and he was looking for the woman that sold my man the hard-top Corvette."

Diamond swerved through two lanes and looked over at Datrina. "He was looking for me?"

"He described you as a tall, beautiful woman."

Diamond tried to recall all present at the shooting and was sure he wasn't one of them. She then thought about her connects. She'd never seen him before, only someone that looked as if they could have been related. "Let me see that picture again."

*\*\**

Silvia and Chris shared a few laughs, just to break the melting ice they sat on. She could tell he wasn't the happiest camper at the moment, but there were some things she needed to tell him while he was alone.

"I'm through, Chris."

"With what?"

"With all the shit we've been doing for years. I already spoke with Raymond and Dell, and it's been decided that I'm going to open a couple of more salons and go all the way legit."

"You are legit and have been for a while." Chris's smile faded.

Silvia regarded him with incredulity. "Really, Chris? We just got off a charter jet with over a million dollars' worth of drugs."

"You know what I'm talking about, Silvia."

"Well, I'm through with all of it now. They even gave me three hundred thousand dollars to open my salons and to cover expenses, until me and Somolia get on our feet."

"Three hundred thousand, that's all?"

"I'm good, Chris. I've got plenty of money. I haven't been blowing my money on cars, houses and the likes. I've been saving my shit for years." Silvia smiled at him, giving him a visual that she was well off.

"No more Circle either?"

"No more Circle." She shook her head side to side to add emphasis.

"No more kickbacks?"

"I'm out all the way. I'm taking three hundred thousand dollars and that's because Raymond wanted me to."

Chris looked at the parking lot in thought. He knew this day would come for Silvia and even hoped it would come for himself. "I'm happy for you, Silvia and as a matter of fact, I'm going to give you a little something also."

"You keep your money, Chris. I'm good. What I need for you to do is start cutting the strings that bind you to it. It's time for us to do something else, while we have the power to choose."

"I feel you, Silvia, but you know I'm in this shit for as long as it takes."

"How long does it take, Chris?" Silvia shifted in her seat.

"Me and ya brother got ties, Silvia, and now that Diamond is doing her thing, I—"

"You don't owe her anything, Chris. Where you get that from?"

"I know. I just feel as if I have to look out for her." Chris thought about Antonio McClendon and the fact that if it wasn't for his compassion, he'd be dead. Years ago, when Chris first started hustling, he stepped in the game with a grudge in his heart and a pistol in his hand. The way he saw it, there was no need in going after the small fries, just to repeat the process after discovering the chump change they owned. He wanted to hit the big man. He wanted the millions he knew were on hand.

Chris had called himself babysitting Antonio for weeks, only to find that he was nowhere near ready to take on the kingpin and his operations. But, his window of opportunity came suddenly and with nothing to lose but his life, he went for it. It was then he learned that Antonio had his eyes on him also, and it wasn't until the pistols were pointed at a twenty-year-old Chris that he pleaded for his life. And in exchange for it, he'd not only pledged his loyalty to the kingpin, but to his family. After being under Antonio's wing, he then came to realize they weren't that much different at all. The only thing Antonio had that Chris was yet to get, was to have someone else to look after. He had Diamond and therefore, his outlook on his actions took a different case.

"That shit that happened between you and Antonio was just that, Chris, between you and him. It has nothing to do with Diamond."

"I promised her, Silvia and I can't just walk away from that."

"Then get her to walk away from it, Chris."

"You know how Diamond is. When her mind is set on something, that's it. Nothing else matters."

"That's because you're the only one agreeing with her on the things she feel matters, Chris. If you tell her that you're tired of this shit, she's going to have to play a different song."

"I've done that, Silvia, and it seems as if the woman just goes harder in the attempts. That first deal was all her. I was just riding along."

Silvia stood, walked over to her office window and told him, "Then, you're going to have to find something else for her to put her mind to."

Chris shook his head. "A couple hundred million ain't just something you forget about, Silvia. Especially when it's your goal."

"A couple of hundred million! Whose goal is…" Silvia stopped herself and laughed. "That bitch is crazy. I told Antonio he fucked that girl off years ago." Silvia thought about what was just said and looked back at Chris. "And, you crazy as hell for agreeing with her, Chris."

"Loyalty has no bound, Silvia."

"Maybe not, but loyalty can also be the biggest fool there is. That thin line ain't even visible until it's too late."

Chris listened to Silvia's perspective of the game and knew that she'd grown also. He respected her disdain to exit and knew it was best for them all. "The only time Diamond wasn't obsessing over this game shit was when she was with King."

"There you have it." Silvia faced him and pointed. "That's it. King!"

Just as she came to the revelation, her cell phone chimed and seeing that the caller was none other than her husband, she held a finger up.

"I'll just get at you later." Chris walked out, headed for Datrina's work station chair. He grabbed an outdated magazine and took a seat.

Silvia's smile was far from her voice despite her wanting to hear from him. This had been the first time they'd parted ways for over a week and she was missing her husband. "What?" she answered.

"Damn, it's like that? I haven't heard from you in a minute and that's the way you greet your husband?"

"What do you want, KP? I know you're calling for something."

"I'm just calling to tell you that I love you and I'm sorry for everything."

"Really? And why should this apology be looked at any different than all the others, Kevin?"

"Because, I miss you like hell and I love you. I haven't been able to breathe, babe. I'm checking my phone every five minutes praying I haven't missed your call and I'm ready to come home."

Silvia was melting. The defenses she shielded herself with had begun retreating the moment she heard his voice, but there were still things he had to understand. Always was. "Where are you, anyway?"

"I came out to Houston for the disaster relief. Got contracted and everything."

"What—why didn't you stop by the house and tell me?"

"I tried calling, but you wasn't answering so I felt I'd give you more time. Even though it was killing me."

"You should have tried harder, babe."

"I know, huh?"

Silvia placed her phone on the desk and put it on speaker. "You're probably down there fucking around or something."

"The only person I wish I was fucking is my wife. And guess what?"

"What, KP?"

"The rash is gone. Dick smell like perfume now."

"I bet it does, Kevin. You and Q—"

He cut her off. "You know what I'm saying, it don't smell like ointment anymore."

"Yeah, well, what kind of contract did you sign to?"

"Oh yeah, I ran into a little problem with that. You know how they be wanting for us to insure our employees?"

"That's required when doing any sub-contracting, Kevin. You know that."

"Yeah, and I did, but I picked up a couple of workers from the labor pool to make up for the four men I needed."

"So, what happened with that? Did you get the job done?"

"We started, but Q and another guy got hurt."

"Are they alright?"

"Yeah, Q's fine now. He lost half of his thumb though."

Silvia laughed. "He did what?"

"Stupid ass got his finger cut off."

"Hold on," Silvia yelled, "Somolia, come here right quick, Q got hurt!"

"He's good. It's the other guy that's crying now."

"What happened to him?"

Somolia walked into the office wearing a mask of concern. "What's up?"

"Q got hurt in Houston."

"In Houston?" Somolia questioned.

"He's alright though," KP answered hearing her on the other end.

"So, what happened to the other guy?" Silvia asked again.

"Said something about suing me, the company, that is."

"Nigga, you is the company," Somolia cut in, now that she was a part of the conversation. She even took a seat on Silvia's desk.

"I'm going to throw him a little something to shut him up though."

"Did they fine you or anything?" Silvia asked.

"Yeah, thirty-five grand."

"Thirty-five grand?" they asked in unison.

"Yeah. I got that. I'm just needing help with this other nigga."

"How much is he asking for, Kevin?" Silvia looked towards Somolia and rolled her eyes.

"I'm more than sure he'll go away if I give him a hundred and fifty thousand dollars."

"Nigga ain't no smoker, is he?" Somolia asked, knowing a pay-off like that would definitely have whoever he was, on top on the world, if not the moon.

"Naw, he ain't no smoker. He's got a family. Silvia, can you front me the money until I get right? I'll give it back to you."

Silvia frowned, looked at Somolia and twisted her lips. "Where in the hell am I going to get that kind of money, KP?" It was those kind of withdrawals she promised to never do again and here her husband was calling her for just that.

"Come on, Silvia, I know you can get it."

"From where, KP?"

Somolia interjected. "Just give it to him out of the money you just got from Raymond. That's only half—"

Silvia fell back in her seat and pointed towards her office door. "Get out, Somolia."

"Oh, my bad."

"Get your fat ass out of my office."

"Silvia! Please, I really need it. I'm going to have to sell my company if I don't come up with this money."

"You should have insured your workers, KP. Damn!"

"They were, I mean, some of them were."

"Well, now you see the reasons for having the others also."

"Somolia just said you got the money, Silvia, come on now."

"That money is for something else, Kevin. It's already spent, in a way."

"I need that money, Silvia. I really do."

Silvia noticed the change in this tone. She noticed how he went from pleading to subtly demanding. "Nigga, don't call me with no shit like that. Where would you have gotten the money had you not heard Somolia's messy ass, huh? I told you that money was already spent, Kevin."

"Well, get it from one them niggas. They give you everything as it is."

Silvia looked up just as Chris re-entered her office. "Bye, Kevin." She hung up.

"What's Somolia talking about?" Chris asked.

"That fat motherfucker can't hold shit!" Silvia stood, walked around her desk and before walking out herself, she told him, "KP's dumb ass is getting sued and he want me to pay the nigga off."

\*\*\*

KP sat his phone down and sighed. He said a silent prayer that she'd come through for him. Silvia always told him no, only to turn right around and do whatever she protested in the first place.

"What's she talking about?" Q asked, seeing KP end the call.

"She hung up in a nigga's face. That's what she talking about."

"What was Somolia talking about?"

"She said something about Raymond giving her more than enough just recently or something."

"What he giving her money for now? Them ho-ass niggas be paying for some pussy, huh?"

"It wasn't for no pussy, stupid ass."

"What was it for, then? What has it always been for?" Q stood from his seat and walked out of the room. "Stupid ass!"

"Fuck you, punk!" KP yelled after him. "She'll give it to me," he told himself, hoping like hell she would. "If not, I'm just going to have to sell my shit, plain and simple."

\*\*\*

Datrina walked and listened while Diamond vented. This was something she'd gotten used to and as much as she hated seeing

115

her girl stressed out, it was very rewarding. Not only was Diamond spending thousands on shoes and handbags to match, but she was buying Datrina the things she felt looked good on her. "Diamond, you need to slow down and think about this shit."

"Ain't no telling what she's feeding him, girl."

"Look at what you tried to do. I mean, if it was Chris, he'd be doing the same thing."

"The bitch been knowing where I be." Diamond pointed to a tennis bracelet and told the guy, "I want that one."

"That one's two thousand dollars, ma'am."

"Then give me two of them."

"Diamond! You tripping."

"I have two ankles and two wrists. The choice isn't that hard, Datrina."

"You'll have to excuse her, it's her month," Datrina lied with a straight face. She then pulled Diamond out of the jewelry store and continued to hold onto her. "We need to get you some dick, girl, you are strong."

"I'm mad, Datrina. Dick don't suppress my anger. I'll just be a mad bitch getting fucked."

When Datrina laughed, Diamond did also. Reaching in her handbag and pulling out some money, she laughed again.

"You say that now, but as soon as you get some good dick, you can't help but be happy."

"Yeah, whatever, Datrina. Chris ain't got it like that."

"Who said I was talking about Chris?"

They both walked out of the mall in laughter, arm-in-arm and with over eleven thousand dollars' worth of designer items between them. With Diamond, it was always money well spent.

## CHAPTER ELEVEN

Two days had passed since Camille paid a visit to the Totally Awesome Hair and Nail Salon, and she still hadn't told King that she'd been in constant contact with his Diamond. They'd been together for most of the day and he'd been continually treating her like the queen she was. After a light lunch and a lucrative deal she had to come though, Camille knew King was feeling good about the way things were turning out. She could also tell he was still feeling some type of way that she had to lie about something she felt was so small.

"I've been wanting to show you something," Camille told him as they were exiting the pizzeria.

"What you got?" King pulled her to him and kissed her cheek.

Camille pulled out her iPhone 8 and after selecting an app and scrolling through its setting, she handed him the phone.

"What's this?"

"Look."

King stopped at the door of Camille's Audi R8 and fingered the touch screen and noticing the pics of Diamond, he scrolled back and looked at the date.

"This was just two days ago." His excitement was evident.

"I ran into her," Camille told him.

"Where? Where was she?" King faced his best friend with a smile and when he saw that she couldn't look at him, his smile faded. "You've been knowing where she was?"

"I just so happened to stumble across her, King. It was nothing."

"Two days ago, Camille, but you're just now telling me?"

"Why does it matter when, King? I would have preferred to have never seen her again." Camille unlocked her car doors with her keypad and began climbing into her car.

"It's always mattered, Camille. You know Terry was looking for her and you've been knowing her whereabouts all along." King looked off, disbelieving. "Come on, Camille. Really?"

"You're better off without her, King, and I've still yet to complete my investigation."

"Being that you're still looking into her, it means you found nothing." King backed away from her. "I went along with you, Camille, and you've been keeping this from me? What else have you been keeping from me?"

Camille wasn't about to fight King over something she felt needed to be done. She pulled off, leaving him there with the phone he held. He was lucky to have even that.

King continued to scroll through the pics he was seeing. He checked the dates on both, paid close attention to the backgrounds. He searched further, wanting to at least find a contact for her. "Shit!" Thinking of Camille and her efforts, he knew she wouldn't have made the stop alone and there was only one person who would have accompanied her. "Buddy," he told himself before dialing his contact.

\*\*\*

"Tell me something good, Dell." Diamond was hoping Dell would have contacted her by now with matters concerning King's Ravinia home. Now that she knew Camille had been keeping tabs on her, it was time her actions spoke the words she couldn't.

"Well, come to find out, the property has been paid for over a year. But, I have good news also. I was about to get you an alike property for that—"

Diamond cut him off. "I didn't ask you to get me an alike property. I wanted that house, Dell, not a lookalike. That house."

"The property I was able to get was—"

"Fuck that shit, nigga. I needed you to do something and you turn around with some shit like this." Diamond paced the marbled foyer of the McClendon home in frustration. Camille's stunt along with Dell's statement was beginning to rub her the wrong way. She was getting nowhere with either of them. "Have my shit ready, 'cause we'll be through there later," she told him flatly.

"The money's tied up, Diamond, but I—"

Diamond closed her eyes. This was not about to happen. "I don't give a damn about any of that, Dell. Have my money by the time I get there." She ended the call, slid the phone in her pocket and headed to her garage.

\*\*\*

Dell stood on the second-story terrace of his multi-million-dollar home, trying to figure out his next moves. Diamond had never regarded him in such a way and for her to do so, showed him that he was losing his position. Not only was he nearly ten years her senior, but he was the one placed in charge of the Circle. He didn't work for her and by the way she conducted her business with him, that's exactly what she was implying. He'd used the money she gave him as a means of funding his contingency plan and now she was demanding cash he'd spent.

\*\*\*

KP decided to take Silvia's advice and try harder when it came to her. He and Q made it their business to stop by the salon as soon as they hit the city in his attempt to show her that his apologies were sincere, and if a public display of that affection was what he had to show, then he was willing. On top of that was the fact that he really needed money to handle his legal issues.

"I'm serious, nigga, don't go up in here with that soft shoulder shit," Q advised him. "You've been letting her put panties on you for too long. You tell her how it's going to be."

KP sat staring at his friend without blinking. It was because of him and his advice that brought about this whole ordeal in the first place. "Are you finished?"

"I'm telling you, man. Them hoes want a nigga that's stand-up." Q pointed at the cars parked throughout the parking lot of the salon and continued, "When you put your foot down, all these hoes going to respect that shit. Every bitch in there gone be telling that hoe she'd be a fool to lose you."

"Are you finished?" KP demanded.

"Soft-ass nigga! She ought to slap the shit out of you."

KP exhaled, looked over at his friend and smiled. "Let's go see what's up." They climbed out of the truck and headed inside.

Somolia was the first to see the duo enter and when seeing the bandage around Q's hand she said, "Look at what the dogs dropped off, y'all!"

"Hello to you too, Somolia," KP told her before nodding at the other women and looking towards his wife's office.

"Go on back, KP, she's just looking over some paperwork," Datrina told him, then looked towards Q. "You alright, Q?"

"Yeah, I'm straight." He held up his bandaged hand for all to see, knowing sympathy would follow.

"You going to sue KP, too?" Somolia asked. "You've always been for self, Q. We all know that. As soon as you see a lick, you lick it."

Several women around the salon laughed, while others looked on.

"I guess you tripping, 'cause a nigga ain't licking on you?"

"Honey, I don't need you doing anything for me. I have a man and he's more man than you'll ever think about being." Somolia tsked, rolled her eyes and continued doing the hair of the client she had.

"Whatever. A nigga ain't trying to get nothing from you but some head." Q looked back at the women sitting around, exposing the one thing Somolia had going for her.

"And you ain't even getting that any more, with that skinny dick you got."

Somolia knew that would be the blow that folded him over and hearing more than a few women laugh, she continued, "Your dick so skinny, a bitch had to keep her legs closed while you fucked."

"My dick ain't skinny!"

120

"Pull that motherfucker out then." Somolia looked around at the women present and added, "We all grown, up in here. Pull that motherfucker out and prove it."

Q watched the women that were watching him. By the expression they wore, he knew they wanted just that and the last thing he needed was to expose the fact that Somolia had him pegged. "Nigga, I ain't got time to be fucking with your freaky ass, Somolia."

"That's was I thought, nigga. The only thing you had going for you was ya thumbs and now you done went and cut one of them off."

"You feeling yourself right now, huh?"

"Never had to."

"Ya fat ass going to be trying to suck a nigga shit as soon as that nigga cancel your ass, but guess what?" Q patted his pockets. "Bitch going to have to pay like she weigh."

***

Silvia looked over the rim of her glasses when hearing KP enter her office. They spoke briefly on the phone and she was more than sure he got the understanding that it was a non-issue when it came to her money. "What is it, KP? I have tons of things to do."

"Yeah, they already need you, Silvia. It's time we put this petty shit behind us and move forward."

Silvia removed her glasses, placed them on the papers she was reading at the time he entered.

"I've been more than there for you and now that I need for you to do the same, that's what I'm expecting. Like I said, I'm more than sure you can get the money, if you don't already have it and I'm not tripping on what you got to do or who you have to do it with."

Silvia laughed, looked over at her husband and laughed some more. "Are you serious?"

"Hell yeah, I'm serious."

"Well, you're right, we do need to put the petty shit behind us and that's exactly what this is—petty shit. And, what do you figure I'd have to do to get that money?"

"Do what you've been doing."

"Which is?"

"Look, Silvia, I'm not about to go there with you. I need this money. If I don't get this, I might have to sell my shit."

"Well, then that's what you need to be doing, because I don't have nothing for you." Silvia went back to looking over the papers in front of her.

"Really, Silvia?"

"Do you need to use the phone or something?"

KP stood, looked down at his wife and shook his head. "I need this money, I really do."

\*\*\*

Diamond and Chris walked into the salon and caught the end of the conversation Somolia and Q were having. They always fought publically and behind closed doors they'd spend hours making up and figuring out ways to hide the fact.

"Sounds as if someone's going to be meeting up later," Chris told the both of them.

"It won't be with him," said Somolia.

"Silvia and KP in the back or what?"

"Yep," Datrina told her before allowing Chris to kiss her cheek.

"I spoke with Dell earlier and he said something about having a property for us to look at." Diamond knew those words would definitely get a reaction from both Datrina and Chris, as well as become a topic for the floor. And, as soon as the inquiries began, she made her way to the back.

"What's up, KP? What's up, Silvia?" Diamond could tell there was tension of some kind between them and instead of excusing herself, she pushed past KP and took a seat. "Is every-thing alright?"

KP smiled at Diamond, not wanting her to report some tuned-up story to Antonio or Chris for that matter. "Yeah, we good."

"No, he's not," Silvia told her, still not looking up from the papers she was perusing though.

"What's up? Is there anything I can do?"

Those words rang bells in KP's mind. And, instead of allowing the opportunity to pass him by, he told her, "I need a small loan, Diamond."

"How much you talking?"

"About one hundred and fifty thousand dollars."

"What did you do?"

"Yeah, tell her what you didn't do," Silvia chimed in.

KP filled Diamond in on the legalities of what he was sure to undergo and even promised to pay her, with interest, if she'd only come through for him this one time and seeing her look as if she was actually considering the loan, she took a seat next to her cousin.

"So, that's why Q is all wrapped up?" This was something Diamond had been thinking about doing, expanding her fortune, ever since her talk with Sergio in Miami. This could actually be a good step in other directions as far as business was concerned. "I have a much better idea, KP."

"Shoot."

"Instead of the loan, how about I just give you three hundred thousand dollars for the construction company and I hire you to run it? The only thing that changes is the name. Nothing else."

KP closed his eyes. "So, you want me to sell you my company?"

"It's hardly a company, KP, and if I were you, I'd be thanking her for being so generous." Silvia tapped the glass covering her desk with the bottom of her pen.

"I'm not trying to sell my shit. All I need is a little loan."

"Good luck with that," said Silvia.

"Look at it this way, KP. If, and I did say if, you get a loan from the bank and for whatever reason can't pay it back, you lose all the way around. With what I'm proposing, you get a handsome return on the same company you're running. It's a win-win for both of us." Diamond thought about the numbers and was more than sure she could push them in ways he wasn't. For the longest, KP had been doing small jobs here, gaining short-term contracts there, and only scratched the surface of potential he had. Not only was Diamond thinking of the renovations he was known for but she thought about demolishing and building. She'd hire more people and make something of the jewel KP sat on. "We can go by Dell's right now and get the money. The longer you wait, the more time that nigga has to think, KP."

He nodded, not because he agreed to sell his company, but because he was now seeing them working together against him. The company was all he had. It made him the independent contractor he wanted to be, not some employee they made him out to be. And, Silvia of all people knew this.

"And, the next thing you know, I end up getting fired and I'm really on my ass then."

"Business is business," Silvia added with a smirk she couldn't conceal.

"You want to do something or not, nigga! For all I know you could take your regulars and go off and start you something else, leaving me stuck out." Diamond was growing tired of him pouting and thinking everyone was out to get over on him. "But, that's the chance I'm willing to take."

"You'll be able to get me the money today?"

"And, I'll put another three hundred thousand dollars for essentials, equipment, trucks and whatever else we need."

*\*\*\**

What angered King more was that Buddy's story stayed the same and they both knew differently. There was no way Camille hadn't gone over certain details with him pertaining to Diamond and the circle she ran with, but here he was relaying the exact same things she did.

"I'll tell you what, Buddy." King handed him Camille's phone and looked up at him. "You two go ahead and play your little games. I'm good."

"They were going to kill you, King, and if you go after her, they will," Buddy told him, stopping him in his tracks.

"Who told you this?"

"Her circle was under the impression you got her brother knocked."

"That's bullshit, Buddy and we both know that." King walked off, knowing that was just another ploy of Camille's to justify her doings. There was no way it could be true. He'd visited Antonio McClendon himself and that was never topic or even hinted at. "That's bullshit!"

\*\*\*

Camille had been watching the two of them from the bay window of her studio apartment, and for King not to acknowledge the fact that she was looking out for their best interest, was something she couldn't understand. The visit she and Diamond had stayed in her thoughts and as much as she wanted to believe her, there was still something about it all that wasn't sitting well with her. For Diamond to come at her with such a confession not only baffled her, but showed her that she did have feelings for King and they weren't the ones easily dismissed and denied. Unlike Nava, Diamond wasn't going anywhere and she knew it.

"You alright, Boss Lady?"

Camille reached for the phone King had given him. "I'm still trying to figure that one out, Buddy."

"Well, you know I'm here."

"I thought you had a date tonight." Camille waited until King pulled out of the parking area below, and walked away from the window she stood.

"You come first. Always will."

"I wish that was true, big guy. I wish that was still true." Camille scrolled through her phone until she was looking at the woman named Chanel McClendon. She enlarged the picture until the image looked back at her. "I hope I'm not wrong about this one, Buddy. Because if I am, King dies and he's not giving a damn about it."

## CHAPTER TWELVE

With this being his first time visiting Dell's place, KP looked on in awe and envy. This was one of the guys he and his wife had several disputes and fallouts over. This was one of those guys he couldn't compete with and he continually tried to. When Chris turned into the Italian-styled driveway, he leaned forward and asked, "Is this his place or just some property he invites people to look at?"

Chris watched as several cars pulled past them. "Looks as if the nigga did have a little company."

"Yeah, I told him we were on our way and to cancel whatever he was doing, because I didn't need anybody in our business." Diamond checked a few messages on her phone and looked over at the cars that were exiting as they entered.

"You sure he's got the money, Diamond?" Upon seeing the selection of automobiles still parked outside and being told that they were all Dell's, KP said, "Never mind."

Dell was standing at the top of the twelve stairs it took to enter the mirror-tinted doors of the mansion. He smiled when seeing the group. "KP. What are you doing out this way?"

"Just riding with Diamond and Chris."

"Well, come on in." Dell spread his arms. "Welcome to Dell's."

Chris and Diamond looked at one another, before following Dell inside. It was obvious he was a little more than tipsy.

"Would you guys like anything to drink?" he asked the trio.

"I'm good," Diamond told him.

"Yeah, I'm driving at the moment," Chris added.

"Um, I could use a little something, if it's not too much of a problem." KP shrugged when seeing Chris and Diamond turn their lips up at him. He understood they weren't there for some social event, but wasn't about to pass up the chance at getting something from a guy who seemed to have given everything to his wife.

"No problem at all, KP. None whatsoever." Dell led the group to his favorite entertainment room and walked over to his bar. "Dark, clear?"

"Um, dark," KP told him.

"The money's all ready to go." Dell pointed.

"Thanks, because we have other things to do." Diamond nodded at Chris before adding, "I need for you to draw up some papers for us. I'm buying KP's Construction Company and whatever else we need."

Dell watched KP smile from where he stood. "KP, you could have come to me. I would have given you something more favorable."

"Yeah?"

"Sure, your wife's a valuable asset to me, I mean, us."

Chris closed his eyes, knowing personally how Dell rubbed his and Silvia' business ties in KP's face. "From what I'm hearing, even that's over with."

"Well, you know we've always found our way back into each other's lives."

Diamond looked on as KP struggled to find the words to say and when it was clear that he had no come-back, she said, "How long is this process going to take?"

"Give me a few days to transfer everything over and get a bill of sale." With one more slug to shoot at KP, Dell asked, "How much are you selling your company for again?"

"Three hundred thousand."

"That's it? I've recently sold houses for that much. I at least thought you got a million for it." Dell laughed, raised the drink he was nursing and nodded at KP.

By the time KP climbed back into the Escalade, he was seething mad. Not only did he undersell the only thing that made him relevant, but here was his wife's suitor agitating him with both the sale of it and the price he sold it for. With Silvia having her own money, he was able to portray the image that he was doing better than he really was. It was true that she paid the majority of their bills and only obligated him to lesser ones and he knew even Dell knew it.

"You alright back there?" Chris asked.

"Yeah, fuck that nigga. He ain't talking about nothing."

"The first thing I need for you to do is get that nigga out of our hair. Pay him the money, get him to sign the waiver and we'll go from there." Diamond exhaled. She was actually about to do something other than make a drug transaction.

\*\*\*

Q stood around the floor of the salon as long as he could. He and Somolia had been entertaining the entire salon ever since KP took off with Diamond and Chris and he was tired of fighting with her. He'd decided minutes ago that he was going to make Somolia pay for the ridicule and belittlement she placed him under. If he did at one time have a chance to get at any of the women in the salon, that was a done deal. Somolia went as far as telling them of the ways he promised this and that, but continually came up with excuses to keep him from it. She also told the lot of them she was the one that helped him buy several of his cars, that she was the reason he had a bank account in the first place. She detailed the sex sessions they had and how he preferred anal over pussy, because his dick was too skinny. "He got them pretty ass lips for nothing. The nigga just fine, that's it."

Q walked into Silvia's office, fell onto the sofa and placed his hand over his eyes. "Fat bitch."

"I heard y'all out there. Got the whole place laughing."

"Naw, she got them hoes out there laughing. Fat ass be lying her ass off."

"We all know that, Q, but she does know you better than anyone."

"Her fat ass don't be saying all that shit when a nigga's dick in her mouth. Fat motherfucker be moaning and bouncing and all type of shit. Slapping her titties with a nigga's shit and everything.

She's the one that be insisting on a nigga fucking her in the ass! She—"

"Okay, okay. T-M-I. Shit!"

"I'm just saying."

"Yeah, I see."

"Hell, I know how to suck some pussy. I know how to make a motherfucker come hard as hell. I thought her fat ass was having convulsions one time, bitch couldn't even talk for three minutes."

"She couldn't talk? I haven't heard about that one, Q." Silvia sat up.

"I had a vibrator in her ass and I was sucking and licking her pussy so good she couldn't stop coming. Her stomach started cramping up and everything."

"Really?"

"She came so hard, the dick just slid in her ass, she was so wet. I be fucking Somolia's fat ass so hard, she can't even move when I finished. I pop one of them pills and she know she in trouble."

"Umm."

"I'm serious, Silvia. Now, she out there acting like a nigga ain't never put it down. That fat bitch gonna be crawling back for some of this dick. Skinny or not, her fat ass gone pay for it. Again."

"I'll say."

Q's thoughts took him to a place he hadn't been in a while and before he knew it, he told her, "I fuck hard, Silvia. I'll make some pussy cry. For real, for real."

"I bet you will, Q."

"Oh, you think I'm just talking, huh?"

"I didn't say that. I—"

Q cut her off and grabbed himself, showing the erection he now had. "See, you can't take no dick. Not like I be giving it. You'll just run from it."

"Not by Somolia's account."

"See, you have them thick thighs too. A nigga would have to fuck you from the back. Put some pain on you."

130

"Oh, really?"

"Hell yeah, I'll spank the shit out of your ass. Your red ass would be bruised up when I finished."

Silvia shifted in her seat. She could feel how wet she was. She knew what she'd been missing and hearing Q go on and about how he pleased his women in the worst way, she couldn't help but remember that last time she'd been spanked, fucked from the back and bruised in such a good way. Now that the cat was ready to jump from the bag she was in, Silvia tried him. "My pussy wet right now." She eyed him seductively. "Real wet."

"What's up?"

"What you want to be up?"

"And, I know you keep your shit shaved. I wouldn't hesitate sticking my tongue in your ass."

"You know me and KP ain't been doing nothing."

"I know."

"I'm horny."

"I know."

"I'm lonely."

"I'll stop by there later tonight if you want me to."

"You have any of them pills?"

"Yep."

"Take two of them and come by there around one. I need my shit hit good."

"Let me shake KP and I'll be through there. I'll just tell him I'm going to get at Somolia's fat ass."

"That one is getting old. You told him that before."

Q thought about just that and told her, "I'll think of something. You just make sure the patio door is open before you fall asleep."

\*\*\*

"What you think they in there talking about?" Somolia asked Datrina, after realizing Q hadn't left Silvia's office in over twenty minutes.

"Hell, ain't no telling. He probably lying about what they were doing in Houston," said Datrina.

"Or trying to get some pussy."

"Shut up, Somolia."

"Pssst, that nigga been wanting to fuck Silvia." Somolia thought about it a second longer and added, "If he ain't fucked her already."

"You're sick, Somolia. Everyone is not like you, Okay?"

"Yeah, whatever."

Datrina knew Somolia would say some of anything and she only shook her head. She looked back towards Silvia's office and shook her head again. She knew she couldn't put it past either of them, especially when it came to sex and some good dick. "You'll let anything come out of your mouth, Somolia."

"Well, tonight, I know exactly what I'm about to put in it." Somolia snapped her fingers twice, licked her full lips and glanced up at the wall clock. She definitely had somewhere to be later.

***

King was more than sure Camille had Terry tell her everything and as terrified as he was of Buddy, that wouldn't have been hard to manage at all. He started to call and confront her brother at first, but decided to take matters in his own hands. Camille spoke of having to make a drop as she'd done days ago, when she just so happened to run into Diamond and he was certain this was what she was about to do now. With Terry selling him out and Buddy always taking Camille's side, this was something he felt he had to do himself.

He'd told both her and Buddy that he also had things to do and after giving Buddy her phone, he headed straight for the car rental agency. Since they wanted to play the game with such biased rules, he was definitely game.

***

132

Camille checked her appearance a second time. Not only was she going to conduct a little business, but she had plans afterwards.

"You sure about this, Boss Lady?"

"Go enjoy yourself, Buddy. This isn't something I haven't done before."

"Well, hit me up if you need anything."

"Will do." Camille saw Buddy out and sighed. It had been a while since she'd even thought about sex, but today was one of them days. Money had been made and she didn't mind a little entertainment.

She stepped out of her studio apartment in a tan pantsuit and some cream-colored boots, with two-inch heels. She threw on a pair of oversized shades and grabbed a straw floppy hat. The disguise would have to do.

Camille was known for breaking laws but as far as a speed limit went, she was sure to set her own and this was exactly the case, when she blew past the intersection and sped up the ramp en route to the North Parks Mall. She checked her scanner several times, checked her rearview often and kept the speedometer over eighty. She noticed the black Mustang the first time when exiting her parking space, but paid it little attention. But now that the same car had taken the same highway as she and was breaking the same laws she was, she couldn't help but take special notice. Camille switched to the far right lane, dropped her Porsche back and forth and floored it, accelerating past a hundred and forty miles per hour easily. And, with a little adrenaline flowing because of the chase, she decided to play a little game. Instead of losing the factory Mustang totally, she crossed back over four lanes, allowed a Stevens Transport semi to pass and slowed to a speed that allowed her to catch the rear lights of the black Mustang and as it sped past her, she smiled. "Really, King?"

King cursed himself for not selecting something a bit faster than the LX Mustang they gave him at the rental place. The fact that Camille never drove the speed limit didn't cross his mind, until she took advantage of the yellow light at the intersection near her studio. And, even after catching a glimpse of the tail light of the Porsche, he still struggled to keep up with her, "Shit!" He pulled past cars at an alarming speed and still knew it wasn't fast enough. He sped past a couple of people that even cursed him with their horns and when he pulled ahead of the huge semi, he realized he'd lost her. He then realized he'd lost both her and his only means of finding his Diamond.

*\*\**

Later that night, Buddy pulled into the same hotel and parked one spot over from Somolia's Lexus. He couldn't wait for this moment. "How long have you been here?" he asked when opening her car door.

"Just pulled up. I didn't even have time to stop by the house to freshen up. I've been working all day and everything." Somolia climbed out and followed him into the lobby and across to the elevators.

"I'm more than sure we can fix that," he told her as the elevator doors were closing.

"I got something for you." Somolia reached into her handbag and pulled out a small case. She looked up at her man with a welcoming smile." Here, try it on. I got the band extended, just in case."

Buddy looked over the rose-gold watch and smiled. "Thanks, Somolia."

"Just a little something for my man," she added, wanting to gauge his reaction to the admission.

"Those are mighty tall words, Somolia."

"Well, they're true, aren't they?" She grabbed his belt and pulled him to her. His middle pressed against her breasts.

"Come on in this room so I can show you."

Somolia smiled, fumbled with the key card and once the door swung open, she told him, "I'm liking the sound of that already."

134

Once they were inside, Somolia wasted no time stepping out of the dress she wore. She pushed Buddy onto the bed and began undoing his belt. This was her first order of business. "You know I got to suck this dick first, babe."

\*\*\*

KP pulled in front of Q's house, pulled into the driveway and parked. He'd been paid off in such an offending way and blamed Silvia for it. He always blamed his wife for the things that went wrong. "They been plotting on me, Q."

"I told you."

"But, I got the money. Matter of fact, I got more than that and then some."

"Nigga, what the fuck is wrong with you? You sold your shit for crumbs. And, you let your no-good ass wife and her cousin, talk you out of it. I told you not to go in there with that soft-ass shit."

"Nigga, fuck you. I'm going to take this money and make something happen. That's what they not expecting."

"You stupid, KP."

"Motherfucker, you act like you mad because I sold my shit. That was my shit, nigga."

"Well, it's her shit now. I wouldn't be surprised if you found out that your wife really bought the shit, and they just played it like Diamond did."

KP thought about the words Q admonished him with, and thinking of some of the things Silvia used to say about his contracts and the things she'd do to secure more lucrative ones, he looked over at his friend and said, "You think she'll do some shit like that?"

"It's too late now. Fuck it."

KP looked at the time. "So, what's up for the night?"

"I'm going over one of my hoe's house tonight. What you doing to do?"

"I guess I'll chill." KP smiled and shook his head. "You really think I'm stupid, huh? You think I don't know what time it is with you, huh?"

Q's expression changed from anger to questioning. "You tripping now."

"I know you going to fuck with Somolia. All that fronting y'all were doing at the salon. Y'all wasn't fooling nobody."

"Can't lie, nigga, fat bitch got some good-ass head."

They both laughed. It had become something they eventually did every time.

## CHAPTER THIRTEEN

"They did what?" Raymond switched his call from speaker to phone as soon as Dell started going off.

"That bitch is getting besides herself, Raymond, I'm—"

"Whoa, whoa, whoa. Hold on now. Are we talking about the same Diamond?"

"She brought the nigga to my house as if it was nothing. I don't want that broke-ass nigga knowing where I stay, and I sure don't need him pulling up on me, begging and shit."

"You tripping. That man ain't going to be fucking with you."

"That's beside the point, Raymond. I didn't invite this guy to my home and for her to just up and volunteer the shit, didn't sit well with me at all."

Raymond sighed. He sympathized with his partner, but he was more than sure that he was taking things out of hand. "Did you take care of the business or what?"

"Yeah, I got that end."

"I'm glad to hear she's finally doing something with her money though."

"Yeah, well, she's acting as if I'm supposed to drop every-thing I'm doing, just to appease her. She even went as far as telling me to cancel whatever I had going on, just so she, Chris, and KP's punk ass could stop by for twenty minutes."

"So, now she's the owner of a construction company?" Ray-mond laughed. That was something they hadn't thought of and it had been right under their noses for the longest.

"The next thing you know, she's going to be coming after the investment firm. And, the properties we have."

"Yep, you're tripping. She saw a winning situation with KP and she shot her shot. There's nothing wrong with that, is there?"

"Watch what I tell you, Raymond. She's going to be digging into your pockets pretty soon."

"She has her own money, Dell. I don't see that happening anytime soon."

Dell completed his call and refilled the glass he'd been drinking from. He had to come up with something, because Diamond was actually taking over and he was the only one seeing it.

*\*\**

After leaving the shop, Datrina felt this was the best time to tell Chris of the things that transpired between her and the guy driving the silver CTS Coupe. With all that was going in Diamond's world and mind, she felt two heads were better than one and she confided in Chris. Always.

"The other day, I was on my way to the shop and a guy pulled up on me, asking all kinds of questions about Diamond."

"About Diamond?"

"Yeah. I at first thought he was one of the guys present at the shooting, but turns out, he was looking for her for other reasons."

"You sure?"

"Yeah, I'm sure. We talked for at least ten minutes. He was driving a silver Cadillac Coupe. That new one."

Hearing the description of the car he'd been seeing and trailing, he looked over at his girlfriend seriously. "Was this at the house?"

"Yeah, I told you he pulled up on me while I was on my way to work."

"What else did he say?"

"Anyway…" Datrina pulled out her phone and found the picture of him along with the number he'd personally typed into her phone. "Here's everything I could get from him."

"He let you take a picture of him?"

"Might as well have. He wasn't trying to hide the fact."

"And, he was looking for Diamond?"

Datrina looked at him sideways. "Nigga, you tripping."

"I mean, did he—"

"Yeah, he did, Chris. But I told him that you didn't know her like that, and that you only bought the very car he was looking for."

138

"Oh yeah?"

"Shut up and call him. You talk to him, 'cause you're not hearing nothing that I'm telling you."

Chris glanced at the number before pressing dial. "You sure that's his shit?"

***

Terry had just hung up the phone with his sister and promised he would no longer be the one that looked into matters for King. He promised her there was no way for them to get back at him for any reason, but seeing the blocked call come across his phone, his guy began telling him differently. "This is Terry, what's up?"

"Hey, Terry, my name's Chris and my girl was telling me that you were interested in the woman that sold me a Calloway Corvette."

"Oh, um…" Terry looked around his living room. His thoughts not coming together fast enough for him or this timely response. "Um, yeah. There's not too many people driving around in those."

"Well, yeah, you're right. I actually got it for a nice price. I added a few things to it, but it's still a Calloway. Would you like to see it now?"

Terry frowned. This was nothing near the conversation he thought he'd be having and not wanting to create any suspicion about the whole ordeal, he said, "Um, yeah, I'd like that."

"I'll even try to find her contact info in the meantime. Where are you?"

"I'm in Oak Cliff actually."

"Well, let's meet tomorrow and see if we can get down to business."

"Oh, okay. Let's do that."

***

Chris shook his head and told Datrina, "That nigga greener than some fake-ass grass."

"Told you."

"I'm still going to go feel this nigga out to make sure." He scrolled to the top of Datrina's contacts and dialed Diamond.

"Nigga, ain't you tired yet?"

"Guess what?"

"What, Chris, I'm in the tub, nigga."

"You masturbating, ain't you?"

"Yeah, I got the beads in my ass too. What the hell you want?"

"You probably do for real, Diamond. You a freak."

"You go, girl," Datrina yelled over him.

"Where y'all at, anyway?"

"I'm the one asking the questions, Diamond. Guess what?"

"What, nigga? What?"

"I think I found a way for you to get at King, but I have to make sure it ain't no set-up of any kind." He could hear the water she was in, evidence that she'd gotten out of the tub.

"Come get me."

"Tomorrow, Diamond. I hooked it up for tomorrow."

"How'd you do that?"

"Datrina told me about the guy that was stalking us and—"

"Nigga, you act like you was on some double-oh-seven shit. I'm the one told her about the play."

"Yeah, well go on and finish doing what you do and I'll be through there in the morning." Chris handed Datrina her phone.

\*\*\*

"What is it, Camille?"

"How's your evening, King?"

"I'm good. I'm good."

"Where are you?"

"In traffic at the moment. Why?"

140

Camille suppressed her laugh. "You really amaze me at times. You know that, don't you?"

"The feeling's mutual."

"You still mad or what?"

"I have better things to do than trip with you, Camille."

"Is that a fact?"

"It really is."

Camille saw the person she was to meet and told King, "Well, I'm not sure where you're headed, but I made the exit several miles back. And, the next time you choose to follow me, do a better job." Camille pressed *end* and parked. She'd deal with him and his interest later.

***

King closed his eyes and had to smile. This wasn't a part of the game he played, and it was now that she reminded him of just that.

***

Somolia was on her knees between Buddy's legs as he lay back on the huge king-sized bed. She'd given him a gagging blow job while massaging his balls at the same time, and by the way he kept pushing at her shoulders, she knew she was doing him right. "You like that, babe?" Somolia slapped herself with his dick, acted as if she was struggling to find her mouth.

"I love it, Somolia. Shit!"

"Tell me you love it, then." Somolia then pushed his erection as far as she could and was still holding the base of his penis.

"I love it. I love it."

"This my dick now." With a hand still around the base of his dick, Somolia placed both her hands on his chest and rode Buddy slowly. She raised herself until just the tip of him penetrated her and began gyrating her hips. "You like that, huh? You want it like that?"

141

She knew what was next and despite the fight she put up, her strength was no match for his. He grabbed her around her waist and thrust up into her, making her buck violently and in her attempt to run, she tried to stand, only to feel his grip tighten and him thrust upward, harder and deeper. "Aagghhh!"

"This my pussy! This my pussy!"

Somolia's yelps and screams could be heard several doors down she was sure, but this was necessary. She wanted Buddy to feel like the man he was. Wanted him to know that not only was he doing her the way she liked, but that the pussy was his and only his. "It's yours, babe. It's yours, shit! Shit! Aagghhh!"

Just when it became too much for her and she couldn't stop shaking, he flipped over onto her and pushed both of her legs to the left of her with one hand. He poked her as deep and hard as he could, his long strokes hitting the bottom of her continually. The only sounds were those of flesh abusing flesh and wetness escaping her pussy, so he quickened his pace, 'cause orgasm was near. "Fuck me, babe! Fuck it! Fuck it!" she encouraged him, begged him. Before the night was over and they parted ways, this would be done two more times and she was sure of it.

\*\*\*

By midnight, Q walked out his front door, jumped into his sedan and made his way to Silvia's. He'd been waiting for this chance and he was going to make the best of it. He'd already popped two pills and was more than sure he'd satisfy. Once he left his street, he thought about the way Somolia played him at the salon. He thought about how she made a mockery of him. He remembered the promise he made to himself about making her pay. He wasn't about to let Somolia Rhodes make it this time. It was all fun and games and a means for some of the wildest sex at one time, but now that she was seeing some other guy she claimed to be a real man, he was going to see just how manly he was.

"Fat bitch got me fucked up," he told himself before making the exit and heading for her house. It was just something about embarrassing her that appealed to him. "She said that was my pussy and was going to always be my pussy. Little fat mother-fucker."

Q parked several houses away, saw that she was still out for the night and despite them not being public items, jealousy filled him. He popped the trunk, grabbed his crowbar and walked the rest of the way to her house. She prided herself on the fact that she had money and was able to do whatever, and he was about to see just what she really could do.

"Bitch!" Q smashed her windshield, both driver's side windows and flattened all the tires on her 550 Mercedes Benz. When satisfied with the job he'd done on her car, he walked up the same street he came, failing to see the woman that recorded his very acts.

\*\*\*

KP sat and thought about the very things that brought him to this point in his life. He'd been told long ago that the best thing he'd done was gain some form of independence financially. He'd come to realize he was sitting on a gold mine and he owed that to no one but himself. Kevin had worked for all he had and was proud of that. He just couldn't shake the thought that Silvia might have bought his company from under him and made it look as if Diamond was the one. He thought about the things Dell said while they were at his home. KP was more than sure they were said in Dell's attempt to both agitate and fill him with a jealousy that was always present. He then envisioned the ways they always found their way back into each other's life. Dell's words pushed and pulled at him until he stood, grabbed the keys to his truck and headed out the door. If he did find them together tonight, his mind was made up. "I'm killing his punk ass!" He told himself over and over. Either way, he was about to find out what his wife was up tonight.

\*\*\*

Q parked in Silvia's driveway, sprayed himself with Polo Red, grabbed two condoms and jumped out. He looked around the neighborhood to make sure no one was lurking and headed for the front door. "I'm finna fuck the shit out of Silvia's red ass." He wired himself up. The house was dark, no porch light and no visible lights inside. He smiled at the fact that she was waiting on him, just as much as he'd been waiting to get to her.

He rang the doorbell.

\*\*\*

Silvia had been watching television and her clock for the past hour and despite the visuals they gave, she couldn't help but see KP and Somolia together. She'd been wanting to get back at him and her, ever since but decided to put that behind her. She did love KP, but felt the urge to make him feel pain the way she'd been hurt. Diamond buying his company wasn't her plan but she was glad it turned out the way it did. She'd told KP long ago that if he ever messed around on her, she'd take him for everything he had. She knew he thought court was the way she'd go about it, but Antonio taught her years ago that it only had the most effect when they didn't see it coming.

She was deep in thought when the sound of her doorbell startled her. She glanced at the clock, which read 1:12 a.m. Q wasn't her type, but he was there and this was her chance to do the same thing KP had done, fuck his best friend and co-worker.

## CHAPTER FOURTEEN

By the time Somolia opened her eyes, the sun greeted her through the sheer curtain of the hotel's suite. "Shit!" She looked around the room to find Buddy sitting in the living area taking a call. She grimaced when trying to raise herself, her legs still aching from the positions Buddy put her in. She reached over and grabbed her phone, knowing Datrina or Silvia would have texted to inquire of her whereabouts. She then noticed she had six missed calls, as well as a missed video chat.

"Good morning, babe."

"Hey, you." Somolia scooted herself to the end on the bed and allowed Buddy to kiss her.

"You feeling better?"

"Better than I was." Somolia laughed from embarrassment. Earlier, she had a series of convulsions that had Buddy ready to alert a medical staff. Her insides had exploded repeatedly because of the thorough sexing Buddy gave her. "What the fuck!" she screamed when seeing the video sent to her.

"What's wrong, babe?"

"This motherfucker trashed my shit! He—"

Buddy grabbed her phone, started the video from the beginning and frowned. "Is this your car?"

"Hell yeah, that bitch-ass nigga trashed my shit!" Somolia cried. She placed both hands over her eyes and tried gathering her bearings.

"Who is he?"

"A motherfucker that don't know how to let me go. I told him about you and it apparently had him feeling crazy." Somolia didn't feel the need to inform him of the way she exposed him the night before in front of the entire salon.

"Where does he live?" Buddy handed her his phone.

"I'm really not sweating it, Buddy. My insurance will cover it and I'll be back rolling in a month or so," she told him with very little enthusiasm.

"How about I just buy you another Mercedes? Show this guy that you have a real man now."

Somolia looked up at him and smiled. She'd often seen both Datrina and Silvia pull up in cars other men bought for them, and now that Buddy was offering her that same luxury, she wasn't about to pass it up. "I'd love that, babe. I don't want it to be too much of a problem though."

"No worries, babe. You're with me now." Buddy dialed a series of numbers and gave her an assuring smile. He gripped her fat thigh, rubbed it. "I'll have it delivered to the salon today."

"You serious, babe?"

"About you, I'm serious as a heart attack."

Somolia thought about Q and his vindictive attempts. "What if he trashes that one also?"

Buddy looked back at Somolia and stood. "Then, we'll just have to get you another one."

Those words had Somolia thinking she just might have found that one. By the way he was talking and making it seem effortless about making such purchases, it was obvious he had money. Now, she wanted to feel around for the figure range. "My Benz wasn't cheap, Babe."

"I'm sure it wasn't. It was an old model though. I'm going to put you in the latest, with all the bells and whistles." Buddy walked towards the door, turned and asked, "I have two questions. When do we meet here again and what color do you want it?"

"Um, let's meet back here Saturday night, same time and hopefully, I'll be pulling up in my brand new black CLS. I want a camel-colored veneer inside too, babe."

She saw Buddy out and walked back to the bed. She laughed, thinking about the car being delivered to the shop, was really ready to see the faces of everyone present at the time. This would surely be the talk both inside and outside of the salon for a while.

***

Diamond looked up at the clock on the wall of her bedroom. She was expecting Chris's arrival, but that wasn't until another hour. She cursed, thinking of some package needing her signature and cursed even more, thinking of the groundskeepers and the fact that they always sought her approval, before and after doing whatever job they did around the mansion. She heard the chime of the doorbell a third time. "I'm coming, motherfucker!" Diamond grabbed her modified Glock from the drawer, popped in the elongated clip and slowly opened the huge cherry oak doors of the McClendon mansion, hoping this would deter their actions in the future. "Camille?"

"Good morning, Diamond." Camille removed her shades and pushed them into her clutch.

"How," Diamond suddenly remembered the Glock she held and quickly placed it behind her right leg, asking, "did you know where I lived?"

"Really!"

Diamond stepped back, welcoming Camille inside and seeing the dress code of her nemesis, she felt both underdressed and unequal. "Where's Buddy?"

"Only God knows."

"I'm more than sure you're about to afford the same, if not better."

For the first time, Diamond was able to smile without it being done as a façade. It wasn't because they were talking fashion. It was actually because she saw this as her interview, the interview that gave her access to her King.

"Come on, let's take a walk," she told Camille before walking her down yet another marbled hallway, past elegantly furnished living areas, out onto her patio. They both took seats adjacent to the rock formation waterfall. "So, what brings you all the way from Dallas?"

"King's not speaking to me at the moment and he's actually going out of his way, trying to get to you and I'm just making sure there are no planned attempts on his life, and that you're sincere about it."

Diamond took a sip of the bottled water she was drinking and nodded. "I meant what I said, Camille. He's in no danger of that. Not now."

"Convince me, Diamond. Show me that our hearts are in the same place, that we hold King in the same regards. Show me this, Chanel."

"This—" Diamond pointed around her. "None of this is mine. I've worked for nothing, but was given everything. My brother paved a way for me that is beyond the imagination of most and I know this. Against his wishes, I chose to forge a way for myself, create a name for myself. To do this, I felt it was all or nothing, because I couldn't allow anything else to matter—not even family. When Antonio got knocked, I still had it all but with him gone, with that love only he could give me suddenly taken away, nothing was the same. All I wanted from that point on was that. I thought having the world in the palm of my hand would give me that, and to have my brother back out here chasing me up and down these halls, taking out a couple of cars and pushing them to their limits while making outlandish bets, having him assure me that tomorrow would be better than today and that I was loved. That was all I wanted, Camille, and I was willing to do any and everything for it. This life is the loneliest. It really is, especially when you don't have that special someone to share it with. Well, I found that someone in a place I never imagined."

"You found King?"

"I was looking for the man named King, but found Kengyon Johnson."

"Did you know that King just recently broke up with a woman whose agenda might have been identical to yours, and I was the person that didn't give him the chance to find out?"

"He gave a vague depiction of it."

"Yeah, well it really hurt him, but it didn't kill him and I need to make sure this won't either."

Diamond looked out over the landscape in thought. To know that King really did have those same feelings she had for him, creased the corners of her mouth.

"I'll tell you what, Camille. This weekend, I'm going to see my brother and I would like for you to go also."

"For what?"

"To give you more promise than questions or doubt."

"And your brother, Antonio, will be able to do that?"

"He has a way of making me feel as if things will be alright and I'm very sure you'd be easy on the eyes."

"Um, I—"

"I'll handle everything. No one needs to know what we do. Matter of fact, just be here Saturday around eight a.m. It normally takes about four hours, but I've made it there in a little over three."

"Really?"

"Really."

"Um, a woman after my own heart."

"If you are not here, I'll understand. But, that still doesn't mean I'll accept it." Diamond watched her.

"I'm sure it won't, Diamond." Camille looked out over the same landscape as Diamond, her thoughts taking her farther, reminding her of the promises she'd made both herself and King. She'd always pictured herself climbing the stairs of her own multi-million-dollar home, as well as a man of her own to come home to. Camille wasn't about to wait for a knight in shining armor to save her from the pitfalls life was sure to place before her. She was the one that had to make a way for both her and her brother, Terry, and she'd been doing a hell of a job this far. Camille was one of those women that knew what she had to do and she was willing to do any and everything to make it happen, just like the woman sitting across from her.

*** 

KP was sitting on the living room sofa, nursing a cold beer when Q finally emerged from his room. They both said and did some things the night before that neither was proud of and knew sooner or later, it would be something they discussed.

"What's up?" Q asked as he walked past him.

KP remained with the thoughts he was having, the same thoughts he'd been dealing with for most of the morning.

"Hey, you alright?" Q asked again.

"Naw, not really."

"You want to talk about it or what?"

KP looked over at his friend and frowned. "Do you have any idea how it feels when the people you claim to love, the very ones that claim to love you, go behind your back and do something so foul to you. Do you have any idea how that shit feels, nigga?"

Q stepped back wearing a frown of his own.

"I was sitting here thinking late last night and something wasn't sitting well with me." KP wiped his brows, took a swig to the beer he was drinking and finished. "I was just feeling some type of way about my wife, so I get up and went to see what she was up to. I had to see for myself, Q." He watched his friend. Watched for a reaction, was expecting him to do what he'd done so many times before. "Oh, you ain't got shit to say now, huh?"

"Nigga, you said you was through with her. You said that shit."

"Really? That's my fucking wife, nigga!" KP stood and faced his friend. "I drove, nigga. Had a feeling I couldn't describe, a feeling I've been letting guide me for the longest and you know what I found out, nigga? Huh?"

Q lowered his head and thought about his night, his morning. He couldn't believe he'd done something so foul. "I'm sorry, man. I really am."

KP walked towards his friend, bottle in hand.

"I'm sorry, man. I'm—"

KP cut him off as he walked past. She wasn't even with the nigga, Q. I'd been thinking my wife was with that nigga all night and when I pulled up at his spot, she wasn't even there. Never was there. I'd been accusing her of it all the time and she never was. That nigga just made me think she was. He always made me think she was."

Q watched his friend pass him, and he exhaled. He was grateful that KP had checked Dell's home, instead of his own. There would have been no way for him to explain the reason he was parked at his wife's home, or even on his street for that matter. Q remembered the talk he and Silvia had and was looking forward to the promise of it. He never once regretted trashing Somolia's car, but when he pulled up at his friend's home ready to screw his wife, he did feel strange about it but that still didn't stop him from ringing that doorbell. And after minutes of waiting, checking the patio door, Q walked around their home twice before realizing that Silvia wasn't about to answer the door and that she'd most likely told him all those things just to see how far he was willing to go with the effort. As bad as he wanted Silvia, he knew it would violate all codes of conduct when it came to friends, even though he'd been wronged in the same way.

"I've done everything for her. Everything!"

"So, what's the play now?"

"I'm going to bring her shit down, Q. The salon and all. I had to sell my shit because she wouldn't give me the money."

"Regardless of what was done, KP, she didn't have anything to do with that shit with the guy getting hurt."

"Fuck that shit, man. She could have helped me out, but she didn't want to. She don't want to see me with nothing, so why should I want to see her with anything?"

"Divorce her and sue her. Take all she got and make sure she has to split the rest," Q offered.

"I know all about the laundering she did years ago. I know about all the drugs she's held and dealt for and with her family. I know all her shit and she throws me under the bus. She thinks I won't come for her, Q. That's why she thinks, but I'm through trying to love her. I'm through, nigga!"

"Just chill, nigga. We'll come up with something. You've got to hit a bitch where it hurts, KP. You got to flatten they mother-fucking pockets."

\*\*\*

King made several calls himself. He'd been waiting to hear from his Kansas City connect for a couple of days and after promising that he'd sell them fifty kilos for twenty-five thousand dollars each, he was on his way. He ignored the calls from Camille and just as he was climbing into his Lexus truck, both Buddy and Camille pulled into his driveway.

"You're taking the trip alone?" Camille asked with a questioning expression.

"Why not? You do it all the time." He walked past where she stood.

"Buddy, go with him."

"I'm good, Buddy. I got this."

"That wasn't topic for debate, King. You going alone with that much product isn't the way we do things."

"Oh, now it's about the way we do things? You could have fooled me."

"These childish tantrums should be beyond you, King."

"Yeah, they should, shouldn't they?" King climbed into his truck and began backing out.

Camille looked towards Buddy and sighed. She told King, "I went to see her today,"

"I'm sure you did, Camille."

King checked the date of the picture. It was a pic of the both of them standing by a rock formed waterfall and it was dated for the current day. "Photoshop created these very images."

"The picture is real, King. She misses you."

King stopped, looked in Buddy's direction and said, "I've been missing her, Camille."

"I know."

"I need to see her."

"I know, King."

"Well?"

"In due time, King, she has some issues she needs to resolve and she's doing just that."

"Yeah, well, I'm more than sure these issues have something to do with you and what you want."

"And, it does."

"I guess I'll see the two of you when I get back." King checked his timepieces and said, "I'm behind schedule."

"Take—" Before she could finish her sentence, King backed out of his driveway and headed to Kansas. "I'll see you when you get back, Buddy. And, make sure he doesn't do anything stupid."

"Will do, Boss Lady."

Camille looked at the information Buddy left her, along with the specifics he wanted. She was never one to tell him what to do with his money, but seeing him list such basic features for the car he was buying his new girlfriend, she was sure she could make them more interesting. With nothing to do for the next few hours, she climbed into her Porsche and headed for the Mercedes dealership in Fort Worth.

NICOLE GOOSBY

## CHAPTER FIFTEEN

After going over a few numbers and agreeing on a date to purchase their second delivery, Chris tried talking Diamond into letting him take the Corvette to Dallas to meet up with Terry. He'd been putting together his spiel for most of the day and was sure he could break the guy into giving up more information than he was allowed to. And then there was the fact there were still guys in Dallas that wanted both their heads. "I'm telling you, Diamond, let me just feel him out right quick."

"Feel on him for as long as you want, but I'm coming, Chris. Case closed."

Chris sighed, looked around them at the paintings that adorned the walls of the McClendon home and told her, "Well, either put on a disguise or follow me in the truck."

"Now you tripping, a disguise for what?"

"You going to let me do this or what?" Chris checked his watch. "We need to hurry up."

"Let me throw on something right quick."

Chris watched his friend disappear up the spiral staircase and headed for the garage, There was no sense in him leaving, because he knew she'd only follow him. As he waited, he thought about some of the things he and Silvia discussed, the things that bound him. He'd been blessed to make plenty of money under Antonio and now that he was in partnership with Diamond, he'd made both money and enemies, and despite it being something that came with the game he and Diamond played, it was still something he'd been advised to keep at a minimum. One thing Chris learned was that money and murder wasn't something you crossed, and when murder was your means of making money, there were no rules to follow and none to give.

He'd promised Datrina many times that they'd exit the game when the time was right and as always, she agreed to ride it out with her man. This was also something he continually thought about when it came to Diamond and the goals she'd set for herself.

All in all, Chris was a dope man. That was the way he came into the game and was really expected to go out.

"You ready?" Diamond walked up behind him and threw him the keys to the Calloway. She then modeled her outfit. "You like?"

"Who are you supposed to be?"

"You like it or what, nigga? You told me to wear a disguise."

Chris looked her over. The Dak Prescott jersey, the blue hoochie momma shorts and the hoop earrings screamed hood chick and it caused him to smile.

"All you need now is some gum to smack on and you'll definitely be hard to identify."

"I was thinking about applying a coat of matte lipstick and throwing my hair in a high-crowned ponytail."

"Yeah, do all that and please…" Chris walked around to the passenger's side of the car and opened the door. "Please stay in the car. Don't even get out."

"Whatever." Diamond climbed in and slammed her door. "A bad bitch is a bad bitch, no matter what she wears. Remember that."

Chris climbed in and looked over her a second time. "I now see that a bad bitch and a boss bitch present themselves two different ways."

\*\*\*

Silvia, Datrina and the rest of the women at the Totally Awesome Salon were going about their day as usual, and when Somolia finally strolled in all eyes met her with question.

"Long night, huh, Somolia?" Datrina asked.

"Yes, indeed. It was definitely a long night. If you know what I mean."

Somolia walked to her station slowly, fanned herself and acted as if she'd been through more than she could bear.

"Really, Somolia?" Silvia knew she was doing too much, as did all the other women. To them, Somolia was just too dramatic at times.

156

"I've experienced love and hate in the worst way. My man sexed me beyond my wildest imagination and my ex-man destroyed my Benz in the worst way."

"What?"

"I'm telling you, I got fucked both ways, literally." She pulled out her phone and showed them the video clip sent to her.

"Who the hell is that?" one woman asked seeing a guy swing away at Somolia Mercedes.

"Q."

"Who?" Silvia grabbed the phone from her to see for herself.

"Yep, the jealous-ass nigga don't want a bitch to be with no one else. He stood here and talked all that shit and the nigga pulled some girl-ass shit like that."

Datrina couldn't believe Q would stoop to such a level. "Did you call the cops, Somolia?"

"Naw, Bu—I mean, my man told me not to worry about it." Somolia caught herself.

"Don't worry about it, what the hell he mean? How else are you going to have the insurance company replace your shit?" Silvia frowned.

"He told me he was going to get me another one. A better one at that."

"And, you believed him? Come on, Somolia, you can't be putting yourself out there like that. Nigga always want a bitch to think they really got it, but you should have made sure you looked out for you," Silvia went off.

"He hasn't lied to me yet and he's the one that told me to chill. That was the first thing I was about to do, but he stopped me. Didn't want me to sweat it. He said that was small shit to him."

"Small shit? That car cost you over seventy grand, girl and you talking about small shit. You act like the nigga Dell or Raymond."

"Yeah well, it's neither of them. I have a real man and he said he's going to take care of it, so I'm going to let me man do what he do."

"And what about Q's trifling ass?"

"I'm not even going to trip on the hating-ass nigga. He's realizing he lost a bad bitch and now he's feeling it."

The women looked from one to the next. It was now evident that Somolia might have been telling the truth all those times she claimed to have it good.

"Head game vicious, huh?" one woman asked.

"The proof is in the actions and reactions," she told her.

"You need to be trying to get your shit fixed, Somolia. That shit you believing ain't no guarantee."

"From the sounds of it, Somolia, the nigga got you all the way out there, to be believing some shit like that. Nigga got to have some money to back up them words. Some real money at that."

Somolia smiled to herself, 'cause she knew her man was trustworthy. Not only that, but he'd shown her that when it came to her, he'd take care of her. She subtly checked the time and finished setting up her station. They'd all see the results of the game she had shortly. At least, she hoped they would.

\*\*\*

Silvia walked back to her office in total confusion. She was hoping Q's latest stunt wasn't done as his way of acting out, because she'd stood him up and left him hanging the night before. She'd told him things and even promised him more. His arrival not only showed her that he wanted her, but it really showed the level of betrayal he was willing to go. She'd stepped out on her husband plenty of times, but one thing Silvia wasn't about to do was lower herself to that point by sleeping with her husband's best friend.

\*\*\*

Buddy followed King as instructed and being that a guy had come out to meet them halfway, they conducted the transaction in Corpus Christi. It wasn't until Buddy pulled alongside King's truck that King realized he'd been followed.

"You've been following me, Buddy?"

"Boss Lady's orders, King."

King walked around to the passenger's side of Buddy's truck and climbed in.

"Is everything straight on your end?" Buddy asked.

"Yeah, that's a done deal, Buddy. Don't even trip."

"You want me to drive the money back for you or what?"

"Naw, I'm straight, Buddy. What I do want you to do is level with me." King pulled out his phone, thought about sending Camille a short text, but decided against it. He was going to play it by ear. "My baby still looking good or what?" King smiled at him.

"You mean Diamond?"

"Yeah, that's me, you know that right?"

"She was looking good to me."

"Where were you all the first time?" King could tell by the expression Buddy wore that he wasn't about to get anything other than what he already had, but for Diamond, it was definitely worth a try.

Buddy finally laughed. "You know what, King, I'll tell you what. I know how you feeling, but Camille just looking out for you in the ways she knows how."

"Yeah, yeah, I understand that Buddy, but shouldn't that be a call I made for myself?"

Buddy leaned back in the chair and told him, "That's just it, you are not making a call for just yourself. If Diamond and them wanted to bring our ship down because of a call you couldn't or didn't make, then you become the reason we lose." Buddy told King of the things he'd been told and hearing King's initial protest lessen, he really hoped he was getting through to him.

"You're going to have to trust her, King. Camille loves you and you know that."

As soon as King climbed out and was behind the wheel of his truck, Buddy put his in gear. His job there was done. Thoughts of Somolia found him. The way she sexed him was something he couldn't forget and as short as she was, Buddy was able to give her all of him. Where other women cried about the size of him,

Somolia rose to the challenge in every way. He could tell that she enjoyed the sex they had and the ways he made love to her. Buddy had pleased her in many of ways and was looking to do more for her in the near future. All he wanted to do was please his woman and Somolia Rhodes had become just that. He'd told her not to sweat the guy that wronged her and now that he had both his contact and his address, he was going to pay him a little visit. And, after making sure he had a light two hundred rounds in the clips of his sub-machine gun, he was more than sure his visit would be felt. Besides, the rewards from it were sure to have him wrapped in Somolia's arms at the end of the week.

\*\*\*

Camille thought about the last time she'd gone out and bought Buddy a gift of any kind. She hated the fact that it had been that long. It wasn't until he started telling her of the gift he wanted to surprise his woman with that Camille figured this was her chance to impress him also. He'd already given her one hundred thousand dollars to purchase the car and with a few things in mind, she was going to spare no expense. Not only was Camille about to reward Buddy for all he'd done for their team, but she was also about to reward Somolia for her contributions also. If it wasn't for her and her loose lips, Camille wouldn't have known half the things she knew about Chanel McClendon.

Before she was through the doors of the Park Place dealership, she was greeted by the manager.

"Good evening, Ms. Welcome to Park Place South. Is there anything I can help you with?"

Camille placed the medium-sized Fendi duffle on the carpet besides her and told him, "I've a hundred thousand dollars in this bag and I need to spend it all."

"Um." The manager regarded her with a wide-eyed expression, saw she was serious and bent down to retrieve the bag. "Come with me, Ms."

Camille opted for the 2018 CLS and as instructed, selected a beautiful black 550 that sat on the showroom floor. She went over specifics with the guy, to make sure the sedan was fully-loaded and after hearing of the ninety-two thousand dollar price tag, she told him, "I'd like my bag delivered with the car as well." She felt that would be a good enough reason to stop by the salon.

"As soon as the car's serviced, it will be loaded up and delivered."

Camille looked above him at the clock. "How long would that take?"

"Give or take a couple of hours."

Realizing it would be done before Somolia left for the day, she nodded and stood. Now all she had to do was smooth things over with King. And being that neither of them had contacted her yet, she had 'til then to think of the ways.

Q listened to KP vent, plot and even talk about retaliating on his wife for her betrayal. It was something he'd heard many times before and even gave input for, but it was the first time KP started talking about putting the feds in her business.

"I'm serious, Q. I know all about the shit she's been doing for years."

"That means you go to prison too, dumb-ass nigga!"

"So, fuck that shit. I'm not about to let her sit on her high horse, while I'm shoveling the shit they leave behind. I built my shit from the ground up and she knew how hard I've worked at it."

"I'm not saying do no shit like that, KP. Take the hoe for a little money and let the shit fade, man."

"A little money? Motherfucker, them hoes rich as hell. They—"

Q cut him off. "They going to end up doing something to you, KP. I'm telling you, man."

"I'm not scared of that shit. The feds raid her shit, I'm going to be the last person they expect. The first thing they going to think is that Diamond and Chris did something."

"And, when they find out otherwise?"

"They ain't. Hell, they haven't even found out what happened to Antonio yet. How the hell they going to find out." KP stopped mid-sentence and eyed Q suspiciously.

"Motherfucker, don't be looking at me like that. I do all kinds of shit, but I don't do no snitching, nigga."

"If they wave a couple hundred thousand at you, you just might sell a nigga out."

"Nigga, if they wave a couple of hundred grand in my face, your ass is going to come up missing."

"Punk-ass nigga. You would do some shit like that."

"Buy my own trucks and forget all about your dumb ass."

"I ought to run up in the house while she's at work and see if she still has money laying around somewhere."

"Yeah, I'll help you do some shit like that, but all that other shit," Q shook his head as if disgusted.

"They did say something about her receiving three hundred thousand dollars from Raymond a couple of days ago. She might have that laying around."

"If we find it, I get half?"

"Hell naw, you ain't getting half. The shit really belongs to me."

"Well, you'll be running up in there by your damn self. That way, when they find out you broke in your own house, Antonio is going to have you fucked-off, man. You really fucking with the wrong one."

"Motherfucker, I'm the wrong one to fuck with. Say that!" KP went to grab a beer out of the refrigerator and slammed the door.

"You slam my shit again like that and you're going to buy me another one."

"Nigga, I got over half a million in the truck. Fuck that cheap-ass refrigerator. That motherfucker only got one door as it is and the ice machine don't even work right."

"Your ass get found out, you going to be in one and you ain't going to be working."

KP laughed, took a swig of his beer and right before his eyes, the bottle exploded. He looked towards Q and once the glass of Q's aquarium exploded and pieces of the kitchen cabinet flew by them, he yelled, "Drive-by, nigga! Drive-by!"

Q dropped to the floor just as the door and cabinet he stood next to caught an array of silenced bullets. Glass shattered around them. He screamed as loud as he could, hoping like hell it would scare the assailant away. It seemed an hour had passed before the bullets stopped whizzing past them overhead. They both watched each other in confusion and fear and when it was obvious the shooting had stopped, Q stood. He had to see the damage they'd done to his home.

## CHAPTER SIXTEEN

Diamond and Chris pulled into the driveway of a nice three bedroom home and parked behind the silver CTS Coupe. Diamond was the one to point out the fact they'd first run across King at the intersection just up the street and it was also minutes away from King's Ravinia home. "You think he lives here alone?"

"I don't, but then too, you live alone." Chris reached for the door handle. "Do not get out, Diamond."

"Oh, a bitch embarrassing you now?"

Instead of answering, Chris only laughed. And, before he could climb out of the sports car, the front door opened and Terry walked out.

"Hey, Chris."

"What's up, Terry? How's it going?" Chris then looked over the car, gave Diamond subtle glances and continued talking to Terry. "You have a nice home here. I was wondering if you were married."

"Hell, naw. It was just me and my sister for a while, then she moved up and got her own place in Las Colinas."

Chris was sure Diamond was hearing them talk and by the way she'd lowered the passenger's side window, he was certain. The fact that she held her phone and seemed to be indulged in a conversation of her own, he knew better. "Las Colinas? I heard that was a very nice area."

"Yeah, you know how the game is."

"So, what's up? You trying to lose some money or what?" Chris saw the way Terry constantly stole glances of Diamond. He noticed the way he made sure she saw him as well.

"What do you mean?"

"I was under the impression that you was a collector or even raced. My girl told me you was really checking out the car when she met you."

"Oh yeah. I do a little something, but for the most part, I was just doing my sister's best friend a favor."

"You talking about finding the car or the owner of it?"

165

"He was under the impression that some chick named Diamond still owned it, I guess. But, he told me he'd got in touch with her already."

"Really?"

"Yeah, he was really trying to find this chick and I was just trying to help him out."

Chris smiled, seeing Terry walk around to Diamond's side of the car. She was definitely his taste and Chris recognized it. "You know her or something?"

"Huh?" Terry stuttered.

"I was asking did you know her? I saw the way you two were looking and just had to ask." Chris lowered his voice so only Terry could hear him and said, "You know how it go."

"Oh no, I don't know her at all. She's just a bad bitch. I mean no disrespect."

Chris smiled again. "None taken, homie."

"The dark-skinned chick was nice too."

"Well thanks, man."

Terry winked at him. "Where y'all be finding these women, because I be looking in the wrong places it seems?"

"You've got to go out there, homie. Spend a little money, do a little mingling."

"Yeah, that's exactly what King said."

Chris looked towards the house then back to Terry, who'd done the same. The sounds of Rihanna's hit song, "Wild Thoughts" blasted from a stereo system. Chris then looked back at Diamond, who was now bobbing and singing along with the pop star. It was also his cue to wrap things up. She'd heard what she needed and he was certain of it. "Man, let me drop this one off somewhere."

"You never told me what kind of numbers you were talking?"

After entertaining Terry a few minutes more, hearing Diamond switch the songs she was listening to, Chris pulled out of the drive with the confirmation he felt he needed. It was Camille's call when it came to King's sudden disappearance. And, to hear they hung out in Las Colinas, only pointed them in Camille's direction.

Chris knew Diamond had taken several pictures of both Terry and the house they'd parked in front of, and he was more than sure it was done to show Camille just how close to home she'd hit.

***

Q hurried outside in a vain attempt to catch a glimpse of the car or truck used in the drive-by shooting. He ran to the curb in front of his home and saw nothing. No one was standing outside and no one was driving past.

KP slowly followed him, making sure the gunman was no longer in the area.

Q looked around them disbelieving. "Motherfucker, shot up my shit! They shot up my house, KP!"

KP stood on the porch with his mouth agape. Bullet holes were everywhere, shattered glass covered the front porch and as he went to step out onto the grass, he caught himself, empty shell casings causing him to slip and damn near fall. "Whoever did this shit had to have been standing right in the yard, Q. All these shell casings didn't fly from no street."

"Look at my house, nigga. These motherfuckers could have killed us, man! They could have." Q's words faded as did the thought when he saw the paper hanging from his curbside mailbox. He snatched the papers before looking up and down his block.

"Motherfucker did some shit like this in broad daylight, Q. Niggas stood right here in your yard and aired us out!"

Q ready the first four words barely above a whisper, the shock of what had just happened hitting him.

"What it say, nigga?"

Q handed him the paper, unable to find his voice. He walked back towards his bullet-riddled home.

"We move in silence." KP looked back at a stunned Q and continued reading, "The next time, you and your faggot-ass boyfriend bleed!"

"They could have killed us, KP." Q walked over both brick and glass as he found his way up to the porch.

"Whoever did this—" KP stopped, looked at the side of his truck and frowned. He then looked behind it at Q's sedan and noticed the same thing. They were both shot up and covered with bullet holes. "They shot up the truck, too!"

"Nigga, fuck that car, look at my house!"

KP noticed the rear door ajar and ran for his truck. "Hell naw! Hell naw!" He looked into the cab of the truck for the duffle he received from Dell. He found nothing. He ran around to the other side of the truck, hoping he'd put the bag there, but found nothing. KP found himself looking under the seats and even in the bed of the truck. He began looking in places he knew he hadn't placed the duffle. "They took the money, Q. They got my shit!" KP screamed at the top of his lungs and while not knowing what to do or who to call, he leaned against the side of his truck and thought. There was only one person capable of doing something like this. There was only one person they could think of that would send a sick message like this. The name of that person entered their thoughts at the same time and came out of their mouths simultaneously.

"Chris!"

"What the fuck I ever do to him?" Q threw his hands up with question.

"He's the only one that knew we had that money. Silvia must have told him about the argument we had."

"Yeah, she must have told him the way you threatened her," Q said those words while thinking something totally different. He had yet to tell KP of his latest stunt with Somolia and had a pretty good idea this was done in retaliation for his vandalizing her car. Q knew how Chris was when it came to the women at the salon and he now he understood the extent he'd go for them. "He could have killed us, KP."

"And if we go to the cops or even—"

"Fucking with them hoes, man! You see what happens to a nigga when you try to fuck over a bitch?" Q kicked at the hedges that lined the sides of his walkway.

"They took my money, took my business and destroyed my truck." KP closed his eyes. Here he was, thinking about actions to take against his wife, and she'd already put them in motion.

\*\*\*

With a few minutes on her hands, Camille decided to get both Buddy and King together and do dinner. She called a couple of her favorite spots, before remembering the North Dallas eatery King suggested before. She'd just finished making the reservations when her phone began glowing. She read the short text and had to smile. King had been distancing himself and it was getting the best of her. They'd been through too much too many times, for this to be the cut that separated them and if she could help it, it wouldn't.

Since King was being so terse and Buddy's mind elsewhere, she sent both of them short texts also. The five words she used were as direct as she could get them. "Made reservations…Get here. Now!"

\*\*\*

King and Buddy had cut the distance from the trip in half and after sending Buddy on his way, he had a few minutes to himself. He started to drive the money straight to Terry's home at first, but reading the text Camille sent him, he by-passed the Illinois exit and headed for Las Colinas. He figured if he continued with the silent treatment he was giving her, she'd eventually break. With this being her second time interfering with his personal relationships with the women he chose, he needed for her to see that he was capable of making those decisions himself and she needed to respect it.

\*\*\*

Buddy's intentions were to be in the area when the car was delivered, but after reading the text Camille sent, he immediately changed those plans. To him, Camille came before any. He made the wild U-turn, hit the on-ramp and headed for her Los Colinas studio home. His business in Fort Worth was done and he was sure his message was well sent. Always was.

*\*\*\**

Datrina, Silvia, Somolia and the rest of the women in the salon noticed the huge diesel flatbed, the moment it passed the front doors of the salon. It was more than a surprise and seeing the driver walked through the front doors, they all knew who he was about to ask for. They pointed.

"Ms. Rhodes?"

Somolia tried to act as if it was nothing. She was used to receiving gifts at her job and this would only add to the many to come. "Can I help you?"

"I just need for you to sign right here." He handed her a clipboard, which Silvia intercepted.

"Let me see this."

"It's just to show that I delivered the car at this location," the guy told her, before fishing out the three hundred dollar key fob.

"And who owns this car?" she asked him.

The guy flipped a page, fingered a few lines and pointed. "It was purchased earlier today by um," he paused. He looked for the purchaser's name. "It doesn't say."

"Give me this damn board," Somolia told them. She signed her name and followed the guy outside. All the other women followed also.

They each walked around the bow-wrapped Mercedes with approving nods. It was definitely approved of. Somolia basked in the glow they placed upon her and she owed it all to her man. A man she wasn't going to lose.

"Somolia done pulled one in, y'all!" said one of the beauticians.

"And, he's got money too," said another.

Both Silvia and Datrina only looked on. Somolia always talked non-stop about the men she had, the things they did for her, but neither of them knew who this mystery man was. So, she thought.

*** 

Raymond called Dell several times and each time, he was sent straight to voicemail. They had a few things to discuss and after going over a few numbers himself, he realized he was either missing something or money was missing. He pulled into Dell's hedge-lined driveway and parked behind two unmarked cars. He frowned, seeing the heated exchange between Dell and another guy he'd only seen a time or two before. After ascending the stairs towards them, he could tell by Dell's sudden hesitance that they were having an argument he didn't want to have in front of him.

"Is there a problem?" Raymond asked approaching the two.

"Not yet," said the guy.

Raymond stood beside Dell as the guy made his way to his car. There was something about him that was familiar, but Raymond couldn't place it. "You alright?" He followed Dell into his home.

"Yeah, I'm good."

"What was that all about?" Raymond looked back towards the door.

"Don't even worry about that shit. I'll handle it."

"Handle what?"

Dell stopped, turned to Raymond and told him, "Just leave it alone, Raymond. It has nothing to do with you and I'd like to leave it like that."

Raymond looked deep into Dell's bloodshot eyes. It was apparent he'd been doing some heavy drinking, but his aggression reminded Raymond of years prior, when he and Dell dipped and dabbed into some of the best cocaine Antonio had. "You back to using that shit, Dell?"

It was years ago that Antonio introduced them to a circle of investors that prided themselves in the purity of the drugs they brought. The parties they threw and the properties they owned, showed both Dell and Raymond they'd been selling themselves short for the longest and just to be in the presence of that company, the drugs became common denominator and the use of them became the norm. Antonio was the one that showed them the difference between the buyers and the suppliers and it was then he made them promise they'd never become the victims the suppliers used to fund their lifestyles.

"Hell, naw. I've been up all night and half the day." Dell made his way to his pitted den. He poured himself a drink, offered Raymond the same and continued. "I'm tired as hell and I don't feel like no bullshit."

"That guy seemed pretty angry back there. You sure he's not going to be any trouble?"

"I got him. Don't worry about that." Dell walked across the room, took a seat next to his friend and managed a weak smile. "So, what's up? What brings you to Dell's?"

Raymond rolled his eyes. Dell was becoming obsessed with the fact. "I was going over the numbers and—"

Dell waved him off. "I took care of something, don't worry about it."

"So, you already know?"

"Yeah, I mean, I am the one over our finances."

"So, when were you going to inform me that over one million dollars was missing?"

Dell took a sip of the liquor he held and said, "That shit will flip before you know it."

"What's going to flip?"

Dell hadn't been questioned about his ability to manage their funds and for Raymond to do so now, only reminded him of the fact that Diamond had been doing the same. She was also the one that pulled over half a million from under him after he'd acquired several properties that offered promise. He wanted to have things sorted out by the time Camille got back at him, but he hadn't heard from her in a minute. The two point seven million dollar home he was sure to pitch for at least three and a half million dollars, would not only give them a nice return, but would also cover the debt he owed, as well as pay for the new Roll Royce he pre-ordered. "You and Silvia went and made a few decisions without me, so respect the game, nigga."

"Respect the game? What the fuck is that supposed to mean? We owed Silvia that." Raymond leaned closer towards his friend. "We really owed her much more, but she agreed to it and being that it was a win-win for us, I went with it. Nothing was short, nothing was missing and nothing should have been questioned."

"And that's exactly the way it should be now."

Raymond stood, stepped over to where Dell sat and pointed at him, "Don't let this shit go to your head, Dell."

"And, by that, you mean?" Dell crossed his leg over the other, took another sip of his drink and looked up at Raymond.

"Figure it out. Hopefully, it will find your head with something other than the bullshit right now."

Raymond drove away hoping things were better than they were. He'd been warned many times about the power of money, shown what happens to those that hadn't been, and made sure he respected both. That was not going to be the reason he lost it all and before he allowed anyone in the Circle to, he'd happily erase them from that equation. Quiet as kept, he knew the reasons Silvia pulled herself from the same circle she'd been a part of for the longest, the same circle that offered her both money and power.

\*\*\*

Camille sat and watched both Buddy and King conduct their separate business as she ate. She even made conversation for them and after terse answers and suggestions, she placed her napkin on the table and asked, "Is there some other places the two of you would rather be?"

"Why would you say that, Boss? We do what you say do, when you say do it. Why should it be any other way?" King answered, without taking his eyes off the text he was sending.

"I'm here, Boss Lady. Just got word that the delivery happened, is all."

"That's good to hear, Buddy."

"Delivery! What delivery?"

"Buddy made a purchase for the woman he's seeing and I had it delivered to her," Camille confessed.

"Really?" King sat his phone down and faced her. "And, how much about this woman do you know?"

"I'm not about to go there with you, King, so find something else to amuse yourself with."

"So, it's just me, huh? It's my life and everything about it that needs your approval, right?"

Camille met his gaze with the same exuberance he owned. She told him, "Giving a person keys to a car and handing over access to my life, is two different things and as long as I have a say-so about it, it'll be just that. If I say so!" Camille stood before either of them could, grabbed her belongings and told King, "Pay for the dinner you fucked off."

King only watched her. He could see the bend in her. "She thinks she's losing us, Buddy."

"What was that, King?"

"Never mind, Big Guy. Never mind." He never intended or meant to hurt Camille, but this was one time he couldn't let up. His heart was telling him that much.

## CHAPTER SEVENTEEN

Camille pulled to the gates of the McClendon mansion only minutes before the agreed time. She'd thought about this moment for the greater part of the week and still had yet to see the importance of meeting Antonio McClendon. She sighed. The last time she was there, the gates were already opened because of the ground crew, she was sure. But, now that it was just her and Diamond on the grounds, she fought herself when it came to the reasons she was there.

Before she was able to talk herself out of the visit, the black gates opened inwards, inviting her inside.

Diamond was leading against one of the pillars, arguing with Chris on the phone, when the Audi R8 came into view. "I've got to go, Chris. Bye!" She ended her call and stepped forward, just as Camille parked and began climbing out of the supercar. "It looked as if you were having second thoughts?" Diamond smiled her greeting.

"And, third and forth and was about to have a fifth."

"You always told me to never second-guess myself." Diamond led her inside.

"I've been doing a lot of second guessing lately."

"Then maybe you were wrong the first time and knew it, but instead tried to convince yourself otherwise."

Camille took in Diamond's appearance a second time. Just the other day, she sported a ponytail, wore tennis shoes and looked nothing like the woman she followed behind now. The black wide-legged slacks, the heels and the shoulder-less halter, and the coal-black wig she donned now, showed her that the stop they were about to make caused Diamond to be the person she was, or the person they thought she should be. "I take it your brother don't approve of your other appearances?"

Diamond smiled, half-faced Camille and told her, "For the longest, Antonio thought I was actually modeling. He'd set some things up before he left and I didn't tell him any different. I mean, I tried the shit, but—"

Camille nodded. She understood. "That wasn't what you wanted to do, but you didn't want to let him down."

"I've always wanted to follow in his footsteps. Ever since I was a teenager, I wanted to rise in the ranks. Have both money and power."

"You wanted to make your own way, be your own person."

Diamond stopped when they got to the garage. She told her, "Sounds as if you're speaking from experience?"

Camille fell silent. There was no answer to give.

"You ready or what?" Diamond asked as they stepped into the eight-car storage garage.

Camille's brows rose, seeing the selection of luxury automobiles. She walked around the pearl-white Phantom, stepped past the matching Bentley and stopped in front of the diamond-blue '68 Camaro Convertible. "This has to be your brother's?"

"His prized possession."

"It's, it's beautiful."

"Well then, it's settled. We visit him in that."

Camille looked back at Diamond, saw the rebel in her and decided against telling her differently. Instead, she told her, "He's going to kill you."

Diamond shrugged. "Only one way to find out." She grabbed the keys from the key slot and pressed the bottoms to open the garage door. "Let's roll!"

Camille closed her eyes, hearing the sounds the custom exhaust. That deep growl warning them of its potential. "He's put a pretty penny into this project."

"It was restored only after he'd made his first mil. This was the way he rewarded himself." Diamond pulled past cars three and four times the price of the Camaro, but knew the value of it was much more. As soon as she pulled out of the gates and onto the street pavement, she gave it a little gas, which caused the car to fishtail. She blew past the yield sign, flew over two speed bumps and blew the horn at the guy standing in the security booth. "We'll be there before you know it."

"Or in jail."

They both laughed. For the first time ever, they shared a laugh.

***

KP awoke this morning with one thing on his mind. He was going to call his wife and apologize for everything he'd ever done. He was even going to apologize for the thoughts he was having. The idea of him wronging his wife in such a way was sure to get him killed and for the longest, whenever he plotted against her, something happened. He made sure Q was still asleep and walked out in the background. It was early still, but he wanted to get at her before she started her day. Before she had a chance to think of something else to do to him.

***

Silvia had just finished heating the barrel curlers, turned each of the flat screens to a different channel and opened the salon for the day, when her cell phone rang. She immediately noticed it was KP and answered. "You're up early."

"Silvia!"

"Yeah, what's up?"

"You know I love you, right?"

"KP, what the hell you do now?"

"Nothing. I promise I haven't done anything, babe."

She took a seat at Datrina's station, waved at a couple of the other beauticians that just arrived and asked him, "Well, what did I do, KP?"

"You sent Chris to deliver your message, Silvia, and he took the money I got for selling my company."

Silvia looked back at the women that were busying themselves with work and asked him, "What the hell are you talking about? I didn't send Chris to deliver no message. For what?"

"Come on, Silvia. You know how Chris is about you and the rest of them women that work there."

"What does that have to do anything? Where are you?"

"Me and Q cleaned up the house as best we could, but it's still a mess. He even shot up both our automobiles, Silvia. What the hell am I supposed to do now?"

"I have no idea what you're talking about, Kevin, and if this is some stupid joke you got going on, then play it with someone else."

"It's no joke, Silvia, I can send you a pic if you'd like. He could have killed the both of us but he didn't, that's how we know it was him. Besides, he was the only one knew we had that money."

Silvia watched Chris and Datrina walk in. "When did this happen, Kevin?"

"Just days ago."

"Days ago?" She thought about Q's stunt with Somolia.

"Yeah, right after I got the money from Dell."

"I don't know anything about this, KP, and I'm more than sure Chris didn't have anything to do with it."

"He tried to do it last time, Silvia. We know it was him."

Silvia waved Chris over, so he could hear what was being said. "I don't know what you and Q have going on out there, Kevin, but don't bring that shit around me or my salon."

"I really need some help now, Silvia. I have nothing. The few dollars I had in the bank I had to withdraw so I could get me a rental and help Q get this place cleaned up."

"Nigga, you and Q didn't need to pay for a clean-up, that's what you two do. Don't come at me with the bullshit, KP. You sold your company because you saw it was the best thing to do. Now, you're second-guessing yourself and think I'm supposed to feel bad for you. Make use of the money they gave you and—"

"I'm serious, Silvia! Why the hell would I be playing about a nigga trying to kill me, about a nigga shooting up my shit and taking all the money I had? Why would I lie about something like that, huh?"

Silvia handed Chris the phone so he could hear the allegations against him and by the way he was looking at her with questions himself, she knew there was nothing she could do about whatever he had going on. "And, what do you want me to do about it, Kevin? What the hell am I supposed to do? I'm through with all that shit!"

"Please, Silvia. Just tell him to give me my money back. I can do what I got to do then. I'm not going to the cops or nothing, just tell him to give me my shit back."

Chris placed the phone to his ear and told KP, "What the fuck you tripping on, KP?"

"Chris?"

"Yeah, it's me. What you talking about, man?"

"Say, Chris, I was just calling her to say I'm sorry and that I'm not even going to put the cops in her business. I just need that money back, man."

"What money? What the hell you talking about putting cops in her business in the first place?"

"I know you—"

Chris cut KP off and told him, "Listen to me, KP, leave Silvia out of the shit you got going on and keep my name out of your mouth. I haven't taken anything from you and the only reason we haven't come to blows is because Silvia has been protecting your ass. Don't put her in the middle of your shit. I'm telling you, KP."

"I won't, Chris. I promise. I just need that money back. That's it."

"What money?" Chris was growing frustrated.

"What the hell! The money I had in the truck!"

"Hold up, KP. Hold up. I didn't shoot up shit. And, I wasn't the only motherfucker that knew about the money. You might need to be looking at Q's ass. He knew exactly when and where you kept the cash. It might have been him that started the shit you talking about. If a nigga took it that far, why you ain't dead, nigga? And, as far as a message, a nigga ain't going to play with the ink, KP."

"Why would Q do some shit like that?"

"Are you serious, KP? The nigga saw a lick and made it happen. You think a nigga about a punk-ass house getting shot up when he seeing numbers that will buy him bigger and better?"

Completing his call with Chris, he looked back towards the house and thought about the possibility at Q making a move on him. He thought about the way Q cried about not being about to pay his bills, not being able to work, but wanting nothing to do with the lawsuit for some kind of compensation. He thought back to the things he said about selling his business. Q was even the one that rode to the salon to speak with his wife about getting the money in the first place, and that very night he disappeared and came back hours later, acting as if he'd done something only he knew about. KP remembered Q's response when he suggested they call the cops, how adamant Q was about not involving the authorities. And, for a guy who'd just gotten his car and house shot to shit, he was handling it better than he was and it wasn't even his home. KP found himself sitting on the side of Q's house on the air conditioning unit. Chris was able to paint a picture he'd never thought about painting and the more he looked at it, the clearer it became.

***

Diamond and Camille made it to the Three Rivers Federal Facility, only minutes faster than she'd done it in her Bentley, and seconds later than when she drove the Calloway. The conversations about the things they both knew so much about broke more than the ice with them. It had them looking forward to putting a few miles behind them, as well as a few dollars on the line.

While awaiting her brother's entrance, Diamond nervously sat next to Camille and it was more than obvious.

"You alright?"

"I told him I was bringing a friend I wanted him to meet. I never told him who you were."

"And this makes a difference?"

"I hope not." Diamond stood the moment she saw her brother. She ran and jumped in his arms as she always did.

"What's up, sis?" he asked her, while looking past her at the beautiful woman watching both of them. "Where's Chris?"

"He's with Datrina today. I have someone I would like for you to meet." She led him back to the table where Camille began standing. "Bro, this is Camille. Camille, this is my bro, Antonio McClendon."

"It's nice to meet you, Camille."

"Likewise."

Diamond exhaled before finishing, "This is King's right-hand."

Antonio laughed, extended his hand to Camille and as soon as he reached for his, he pulled her to him. "We're beyond handshakes." He hugged her.

Camille was caught off guard completely. She laughed. No man had ever regarded her in such a way. Only Kengyon Johnson. "Wow, I guess we are."

Antonio smiled at his sister, reached across the table and gave her hand an assuring squeeze. He knew exactly what was going on. On both ends at that.

"I'm glad you did. Beauty isn't expected in this place and Camille, you are very welcome."

"Is that flattery?"

"Just an observation."

"Um, would you like something from the machines?" She looked at her brother and winked, knowing she was dealing him in.

"Get me a couple of those carrot cakes," he told her.

"What about you, Camille?"

"I'm good. A beverage maybe." Camille acted as if she was about to pull money from her pocket.

Diamond tsked and walked away, leaving the two of them alone.

Camille looked around them at the walls that confined them, she sighed. "I always wondered how the inside of one of these places looked," she told him, while making small talk.

"It looks a bit different from where I'm sitting and I'm more than sure that once you've dressed out and sat still for a while, you'd wish you never did."

"I'm sure of it."

"I imagined this moment would find me."

"Who's that?"

"Diamond has a way of going out the way to get what she wants. This move is all her."

"Was it a good move?"

"The best."

"Did you know of her intentions beforehand?"

Antonio watched the woman sitting before him. He could tell she was looking for answers, just as King was. He told her, "Me telling her to not do something definitely became the reason she did it and when I heard they were going after King, it was obvious someone had to take the blame."

"But, you knew King had nothing to do with your incarceration?"

"I needed her to find that out for herself, Camille."

"At the expense of King's life?" She watched him with raised brows.

"At the expense of my sister's as well."

Camille watched him. He watched her. They understood.

"The only had one carrot cake, Bro, but I got you a cream cheese pound cake." Diamond placed item after item before him, slid Camilla an iced tea and asked, "What y'all talking about?"

"You," said Camille.

"What about me?"

"Just tripping on the things you do."

"Oh, I've got to tell you something." Diamond looked towards Camille for assurance.

"What did you do now, Chanel?" said Antonio.

Camille found herself smiling. It was something she also did when King did something questionable. Called them by their first name.

"I knocked a little dust off the Camaro."

It was now Antonio's time to look at her with raised brows. "What Camaro?"

"The sixty-eight. I'm surprised it started."

"You drove my car down here, Diamond?"

"Yeah, Camille liked it and wanted to take it for a spin, so—"

Camille opened her mouth in protest, but remained silent. This was nothing to include herself in.

"You drove my car all the way here, Diamond?"

"You act like I tore it up or something, nigga. It ain't all that anyway."

Camille knew Diamond was trying to justify the things she did and acting as if her actions were nothing, was the exact same way King did when it was something he did without thinking.

"If you tear up my shit, Diamond, it's going to cost your ass, I'm serious."

"I got you, Bro. You good."

"I'm telling you, Diamond, and trying to hide the fact is going to get you fucked off."

Camille sat and listened to the brother-and-sister relationship and couldn't help but think about how close she and Terry once were. How they were before she had to become the bitch that did everything for family and the people she claimed to love. She watched Diamond go from being some murderous, scheming bitch to a loveable, beautiful woman, who would do the things she had to. She was looking at Diamond, but seeing herself. It was then she decided to give Diamond a chance. She was going to see what she was really about.

By the time the announcement came for them to wrap up their visit, the three of them had laughed, sorted things out and reassessed things.

"Is this going to be the last time I see you?" Antonio said, looking at Camille.

The things Antonio either did or said continued to catch Camille off-guard. "Um, would you like to see me again?"

"I would love to."

"Well, this is a hell of a place to do it, but I'll see what I can do. I'm not going to make any promise though."

"Sounds good to me."

"We'll be back in a couple of weeks. I'll make sure of it."

Camille and Antonio both looked at one another. They knew Diamond would make sure of it.

"I'm about to get my second drop, Bro."

"You be careful out there when I get home."

"Only death will keep me from it."

"Stop talking like that, Chanel. I hate when you do that."

"Yeah, well, reality is just that, Bro."

Antonio hugged his sister, squeezed her as tight as he could and kissed her forehead. "I love you, Diamond."

"Don't start that shit, nigga."

"Go pull my shit around so I can see it."

After Diamond disappeared through the doors of the visiting room, Antonio stepped closed to Camille. He looked down at her, his six foot two height towering over her five foot six frame. "Guide her, Camille. Show my sister what I can't. I'll give you whatever you want, whatever you need. Just look out for her. I'm seeing her attempts to prove herself to you and I need you to coach her."

"She doesn't like me like that, Antonio."

"She wouldn't have brought you here if she didn't." Antonio pulled her to him and whispered, "She's no threat to King. Love seems that way at times."

Camille laughed. "Whatever I want, huh?"

Antonio kissed her forehead. He knew exactly what she was implying. "Anything besides the sixty-eight."

They both laughed. After following her to where he could see and hear his pride and joy, he waved them off, pointed at Diamond and mouthed the words, "Don't tear up my shit! I'm serious."

***

Q walked through his living area, saw that he was alone and decided to make a brief call himself. He didn't know for sure if Somolia was the one that sent Chris to retaliate on her behalf and without giving anything away, he was going to feel her out. Either way, he owed her an apology.

***

Somolia was just about to step out of her brand new Mercedes when her iPhone chimed. The caller had blocked the call and she was more than sure it was Buddy. "Hey, babe."

"Somolia?"

"Q, what the fuck you calling me for?" Somolia looked towards the front of the salon and decided to finish this call in private.

"What you doing?"

"I'm about to go to work, Q. What the fuck you want?"

"Um, you got something up for the night or what?"

Somolia couldn't believe he was coming at her as if he'd done nothing. She then thought about the fact that he probably didn't even know she knew it was him. "Are you serious, Q? You trash my car and call me talking some shit like this, are you fucking crazy?"

"Trash your car? I didn't—"

"Nigga, my neighbor sent me a video clip of you doing the shit, Q. Your punk ass did some girl-ass shit, nigga."

"Look at what you had Chris do to my house and my car. That nigga could have killed us, Somolia. Me and KP was in the house when he came through, shooting my shit up."

"What? Somolia placed her phone on speaker and sat it on her console. "I didn't have Chris do shit to you. Hell, I didn't even tell Chris."

"Silvia must have told him, because he's the only person that knows where I live and he's the only one known for doing some shit like this, Somolia. I know you had Chris shoot up my shit."

"Bitch-ass nigga, I told you I didn't have shit to do with no shooting. I'm not even sweating that shit. My man…" Somolia remembered Buddy telling her not to sweat it and that he'd take care of it. She remembered putting both Q's contact and address into his phone. She then wondered if he was capable of such actions. Camille's face entered her thoughts and the fact that he'd called her Boss Lady, gave her a better description of the role he played when it came to the woman he referred to as Boss. Somolia was hoping this wasn't the case, but she was about to play it for all it was worth.

"Somolia! Somolia?"

"Yeah, yeah, I'm here."

"I said, I'll pay for the repairs."

"Yeah whatever."

"I'm serious, Somolia, I'm sorry. I'll pay for your shit to get fixed."

"They told me that car was totaled," she lied. After receiving her newer model, she had the older car salvaged.

"I'll do whatever, Somolia. Please."

Somolia thought of a few ways to be compensated. This was her chance to get back some of the money she'd given him through the years. "Just give me fifty thousand dollars and we'll squash it."

"I got you. I'm going to the bank today."

"We'll see." Somolia smiled to herself. Not only did she have a man of her own, but he would do anything for her. Just before she ended the call, Q called out to her.

"Somolia!"

"Yeah."

"Thanks."

\*\*\*

KP walked in on the last part of the conversation Q was having. "Who was that?"

"Aw, that wasn't nobody. A bitch just trying to see what I had up for the night."

"Yeah?" KP walked past his friend, knowing he was lying.

"Yeah."

\*\*\*

King had been thinking of the ways he'd been treating Camille and knew she didn't deserve it. She always called herself looking out for them as a whole and it was something he okayed, for the longest. She was still his best friend and it was about time he showed her as much. The one thing he wanted her to do was trust him when it came to Diamond.

He was just about to climb into his truck when he noticed the familiar face. He stopped, shook off the thought and proceeded about his business.

"Hey, babe!"

King faced the familiar voice. It couldn't be. "Nava?"

"You miss me?"

King sized her up with both confusion and anger. He'd traveled states for this woman, gave his last to this woman and would have even given his life, and here she was standing directly in front of him. His anger gave way to sympathy after seeing how disheveled she looked. Her hair looked as if she hadn't seen a beauty shop in a while, the darkened bags under her eyes were evident and her attire was nowhere near designer. This was the woman he'd gotten engaged to, the woman he was about to marry just months ago. "Nava?"

"I had to come back to find you, King. I haven't been the same without you."

King's heart broke, seeing how frail she now was. Where she was once slightly thicker than Camille and gave some of the most beautiful women a run for their money, she was now rail thin and looked to have been physically and mentally abused. He didn't know whether to hug her or step away from her.

"What happened to you?" He looked past her at the black Town Car parked several feet away." And, who is that?"

"I've been through hell without you, babe. I knew I was making a mistake to leave you, but I didn't have a choice, King. I had to."

King was listening to her, but was more concerned with the occupant in the black car he was sure brought her there. Only a few people knew he resided in this specific location and against Camille's wishes, he made sure Nava knew about it. It was now that he saw Camille's viewpoint. "Who is that?"

"That's a friend of mines that brought me here. He's alright."

"He?"

"He's the only one that's been looking out for me, King. He helped me make it back to you."

King looked back at the woman that once held his heart. "Where are you staying, Nava? What are you doing here?"

"I'm staying wherever I can right now and I came back for you."

King pulled her to him. He squeezed her as tight as he could and seeing her grimace, he let her go. After walking her back into his apartment and seating her on the sofa, he sat next to her, grabbed her hand and kissed it.

"Are you alright?"

"I am now. I went by your other house and noticed you'd moved and was hoping you still had this spot."

"Where have you been, I mean, what happened to you?" King noticed the way she continued to rub her arms as if she was cold. He noticed the way she continued to sniff and rub her nose. It was obvious that she was high. He moved the hair that covered her face, her once beautiful face. King looked into her eyes.

"I worried like hell when you left, Nava."

"I had to leave, King."

"Why?" He watched her take sips of the juice he'd given her.

"Camille threatened to kill me if I didn't and I didn't know what to do, babe."

"You could have come to me, Nava. What about me?" He watched her shake her head.

"I couldn't King. I just couldn't."

His anger returned, his suspicions confirmed. "You took money and left."

"Camille gave me money and made me promise to never come back. She made me promise to forget about you, about us."

King sat and listened to Nava's detailed depiction of all she underwent because of Camille's threats. He listened to her voice crack when reminding him of the life they promised they'd have together, how bad she had it upon returning to Miami and how her dad even disowned her. She reminded him of the promise he made to always be there for her, that he'd take care of her as long as he had breath in his being.

The sudden knock on his door pulled him from the thoughts he was having, as well as the mood he was in. No one was to know of this location for obvious reasons and with Camille having access to entry herself, it was only one person or the other side. He answered it angrily. "What's up?"

"Tell Nava I said, let's go."

King looked the guy up and down. The two gold chains, the gold teeth and the swag the guy had told King that he was a drug dealer and he now understood that Nava could even be broke or in debt.

He watched Nava stand. "You don't have to leave, Nava."

"I can't King. I have to—"

King stepped in front of her, blocking her exit. "Don't go, Nava." Seeing her reluctantly push past him, he grabbed her arm, pulled sixty-five hundred dollars from his pocket and pushed it in her hand. "Here."

He followed both of them to the Town Car and wiped the tears that fell from her eyes, and as soon as King was in the rear view mirror, she pulled the money he'd given her from her pocket. "What I tell you? That nigga will break himself for me." She handed him the thousand she owed.

"What about this Camille chick?"

189

Nava opened the compact she had and cut two lines of the powder it contained. She snorted both lines, held her head back and said, "Fuck that bitch."

"I can't believe you walked away from this nigga, Nava. He's still out there behind your trifling ass," he laughed.

"I knew he wasn't going anywhere. Besides, the bitch was getting in my business."

## CHAPTER EIGHTEEN

Chris was standing at the garage door when Diamond pulled around to the rear of the house. He was dying to hear about how the visit went. He also knew he was going to have to answer to Antonio because of his absence. His mouth fell open, seeing Antonio's '68. "I know he cursed your bitch-ass out when he found out you was driving his shit."

"Hell, naw. He was actually glad to see it.

"Yeah, right."

Diamond closed the door behind her and followed him inside. Chris always knew the codes both inside and outside of the McClendon home. When Diamond wasn't able to make certain stops, Chris could. They trusted him that much. "So, what's up? What I miss?"

"You ain't missed shit. I was at the salon earlier and KP called, talking about Q's shit got shot up and that we took his money and some bullshit."

"What the hell they got going on?" Diamond made her way up the stairs. Now that the visit was over, it was time to slip into something more comfortable.

Chris followed her into her room. "The hell if I know. They up to something, though."

"That nigga had better not fucked off my money." Diamond pulled off the wide-legged slacks she wore and walked past Chris in only her panties and the shoulder-less halter.

"He know better than some shit like that, I hope." Chris busied himself with a few texts before continuing, "Then too, you know money make a person trip out at times."

"Yeah, whatever. A motherfucker gonna feel it fucking with my shit though."

Chris glanced up at her and went back to texting. "What ya brother talking about? Was he tripping on the fact that you drove all the way down there alone or what?"

Diamond checked herself in the full-length mirror. The warm-ups and the retro Jordan's complimented her height. "He was too busy talking about that damn car to notice."

"How's he doing in there?"

"He good."

"So, what are you about to do now?" he asked her, seeing she didn't want to talk about the visit she and her brother had. From past experiences, he knew it was because Antonio had probably told her some things she wasn't trying to hear, and most likely some things she needed to.

"Let's go for a spin in the sixty-eight, see what kind of trouble we can get into."

"I don't know about that shit, Diamond. You know how—"

She cut him off by snatching his phone. "Stop crying, ass-nigga. That nigga can't stop us from driving that old-ass car."

"You wasn't saying that shit when the 'Vette got shopped up."

"That was then, this is now, Chris." She dialed KP's number. There was something she needed to get straight with him.

\*\*\*

King was sitting at the breakfast nook in Camille's studio home when she walked in. He walked over and kissed her cheek. "Where you been?"

"I had to take care of something. Is there a crime in that?" She pushed past him.

He knew he'd been giving her a hard time for the past few weeks and it was expected for her to be with attitude. "You got a minute or what?"

"For what?"

"I just want to talk, see where you at, because we've been tripping with each other lately."

"Have we?"

"You know what I'm saying." He followed Camille to the lounging area and when she sat down, he handed her a glass of strawberry-kiwi juice and sat beside her, an action that made her lean away and eye him suspiciously.

"What did you do now, Kengyon?"

"Oh, I can't love on my bestie?"

"Why is your intention so obvious?"

"Guess what happened to me today?"

"I haven't the slightest, King." Camille gave off an exasperating sigh.

"Just guess."

"You saw Diamond."

"Close, but guess again."

"King!"

"Nava."

Camille faced him and said, "Who?"

"I saw Nava today."

"Yeah, alright, King. Good for you."

"She had some guy bring her by my apartment in Desoto and we had a very interesting conversation."

Camille smiled. "I'm sure you did, King."

"She told me everything, Camille. She told me about the threats you made on her, as well as the money *you* gave her."

Camille sat her glass on the table and shrugged. "I'm sure she did."

"She didn't steal that money, Camille. You just made it look as if she did. You made it look as if she hit her bag and upped and left. But, you never knew about the gift I gave her just days before. The two hundred and fifty thousand dollars I gave her. It always stayed in the back of my mind how she'd leave that amount and only take the sum in the hallway safe."

Camille smiled to herself. She still felt he was fishing and she wasn't about to fold. "Is that it?"

"Not really. Nava never left me, Camille. You're trying to do the same thing with Diamond. Matter of fact, how much did you pay her?" King smiled now. "Oh, she couldn't be paid off? That's what happened?" King could tell she still wasn't believing him about having seen Nava, and she was the last person that would admit to any wrongdoing and that was the reason he pulled out his phone.

"This is how she's looking these days."

Camille eyed the image contemptuously. The date it was taken, confirming King's admissions. "What is she doing here?"

"She came back for me, Camille."

"The bitch must be broke."

"She needs help, Camille."

"That bitch needs a killing, that's what she need." Camille stood.

He grabbed her arm, pulling her back down. "Stop! Just stop!"

"Don't get caught up with that woman, King. I saved her once and I'm not going to allow it again."

"I'm telling you to leave her alone, Camille. I'm not asking you to, hoping you will or trusting you to do so. I'm telling you not to fuck with her. You already fucked her life off."

"What the fuck you mean, I fucked her life off? I wanted nothing more than that, but because of you and the emotions you can't control, I didn't! I'm the reason the bitch still climbing out of holes!"

"I'm going to help her, Camille. She's fucked up because of what you did."

"As strong as you're supposed to be, King, your weakness defines you in ways a person should never be."

"What's that supposed to mean?"

"You'll know when you die, Kengyon. That's what it's going to take for you."

"Promise me, Camille."

"What, that you'd understand it once you're dead?"

"That you won't fuck with her again." King grabbed Camille's chin and made her face him.

"Promise me that you won't have Buddy act on your behalf either."

Camille could only watch him. There was no understanding him. The only things understood were the ones detrimental to him and it was now that she had to accept it. And, thinking about the woman she'd spent the better parts of her morning with, she smiled. "That's a promise, King. I will not fuck with your love interest again."

***

KP looked over his contacts for someone to call. His conversation with Chris didn't go as planned and with Silvia not wanting anything to do with him or the things he had going on, he was on his own. The ringing of his phone startled him. "Chris?"

"Diamond, nigga. What's up?"

"I fucked up, Diamond."

"So I heard."

"So much shit has been going on, that it's hard to put a finger on anything."

"What's up with the money I gave you?"

"After the shooting, I realized that it was missing out of the truck."

"Really?"

"I'm not bull-shitting you, Diamond. I don't play like that and you know it."

"You need to think of all the people that could have pulled it off. I don't do business like this, man."

"I'm sorting it out as best I can, Diamond and if nothing else, I'm going to have to owe you."

"Yeah, that's what it looks like."

"Let me get back at you, Diamond, I have something to take care of."

KP ended the call, just as Q stepped out of his room. It was obvious he had somewhere to be. "Where you headed?"

"I've got to stop by the bank right quick."

"You want me to ride with you?"

"Naw. It'll only take me a minute."

KP followed Q to the door. He would have never suspected his friend and now that he was seeing all the signs he failed to at first, he couldn't believe them.

\*\*\*

Somolia made sure she left the salon in plenty of time to stop by the house and freshen up. She and Buddy had texted and talked about this night for most of the week and now that she was about to see him, she was going to make sure she was right. There were also a few things she wanted to discuss with him.

She parked her new Benz where he'd be able to see it as soon as he pulled up. Now that she'd become a regular at the hotel, she took the elevator to the eighth floor. After removing her clothes and spraying the bed and pillows with her favorite fragrance, she drew the curtains and lit several candles. Satisfied with the way things were, she placed the K-Y Jelly tube into the sink and turned on the hot water faucet. Tonight, she was going to blow Buddy's mind.

\*\*\*

Nava made sure they found a darkened corner at the rear of the North Dallas strip club. She'd performed in this very same club once before and was no stranger to the way things were run. She bobbed her head to the heavy baseline. Hundred-dollar bottles lined their table and it was evident that she was that boss bitch. After tipping the bouncer, she pulled out her compact, cut two lines from the ounce of cocaine she recently bought and meticulously rolled the hundred-dollar bill. This was the life she lived, as well as the life that kept her from living.

\*\*\*

By the time Buddy arrived, Somolia had created both the atmosphere and vibe she wanted to finish her night with. "About time you made it," she called from the back. She opened her arms as Buddy stepped into her embrace.

"Miss me?"

"Like you wouldn't know." Somolia began undoing his belt and at the same time, pulling him towards the bed. He followed her.

"How's your new car turning out?"

"I'm about to show you just that." She pushed him onto the bed and massaged his erection. "Have you been bad, babe?" she asked in her most seductive tone, while looking up at him with her slanted gray eyes.

"You tell me."

Somolia stroked his manhood with both hands. She licked him. "I think you have."

"The good ones finish last and I'm so far from last, babe." Buddy watched her perform. He loved watching her perform.

She took him into her mouth as far as she could. She gagged, laughed and contracted her throat around the head of his dick.

"I took care of that little issue for you."

"Um-hmmm."

"You shouldn't have a problem with him again."

"Ummmm." She slapped herself with his throbbing manhood. "I'm sure of it."

Somolia pleasured Buddy in ways he hadn't been and after hearing that he wasn't the one that took money from either of the vehicles, she believed him. Even if he did, that was Q and KP's problem. She had other things to indulge in. As soon as he came the first time, she swallowed, wiped her mouth and went to retrieve the heated tube she had in the sink. "I've got something for you tonight, babe. And it's only for you."

Buddy watched her climb out onto the bed, smiled when she placed the over-stuffed pillow under her stomach, and raised to his knees when feeling her lubricate his dick with the hot jelly.

"Be gentle, babe. Be gentle," she instructed him. "This is my first time."

## CHAPTER NINETEEN

That following morning, Camille was at King's Desoto Apartment earlier than he expected. She'd given him a full day to himself and now that she was somewhat sure of the plan she'd devised, it was time for her to make her first move. She used her key to enter, prepared to see the woman she despised for reasons of her own.

Camille threw her handbag on the sofa and made her way to the bedrooms. "Why am I not surprised?" King called out from the kitchen.

"Why should you be?" Camille continued her search and when seeing that King was without a guest, she told him, "I need for you to make a stop with me this morning."

"Where's Buddy?"

"Unable to be reached, evidently." She walked past him, opened his refrigerator door and sighed. "Is pizza the only thing you eat, King?"

"It's both a convenience and a luxury." King walked into the living area and fell onto the sofa. "Where is this stop you're needing to make?"

"Fort Worth."

"Fort Worth? What's in Fort Worth?" he asked with a mocked expression.

"Get dressed. My appointment is within the next hour."

"Appointment?"

"Yup. Get dressed now!"

King walked over to his bay window and checked the parking lot. This was something he'd done all yesterday and ever since he awoke this morning. He was expecting Nava to return and was hoping she wasn't in any trouble or even hurt. Despite the signs shown that she was back on drugs, King still believed if only she continued to surround herself with people that cared about her well-being, then she'd eventually climb out of the rut she continually found herself. If only Camille wouldn't have ran her off. "I need to be here just incase she shows up, Camille."

"I need you to make a stop with me, so get dressed. I'm more than sure she'll crawl her way back here as soon as she runs out of the money you gave her."

"And, how did you know I gave her any money?"

Camille only shook her head. "When have you done anything other than that, King? She knows you and knows that's the first thing you're going to offer. First, your money, then your life." She found a seat on the same sofa he arose from, crossed her legs and reached for the novel he had on the smoked glass end table. "Looks as if you've been entertaining yourself for a while here,"

"That might be something you need to try sometime." King walked towards the back of the apartment. There was no need in dragging the inevitable.

"You're entertaining enough, Kengyon!" Camille walked over to the same window King did just seconds ago and looked over two parking lots as well. With her, there was never reason to trust Nava then and now that she'd reneged on the deal that allowed her to live a while longer, there was no need to now. "You know you have to move, don't you?

King, now appropriately dressed, walked up from behind her and said, "We already talked about this, Camille."

"Did we?" Camille snatched up her handbag and headed for the door.

King followed. "It isn't like Buddy to be unreachable."

"Buddy has a girlfriend now, King."

"Oh, really?"

"And, she sees the benefits of him being alive, unlike the women you attract."

Camille sent the short text, looked over at King and rolled her eyes. As promised, she wasn't going to interfere with his love interest and neither was she going to have Buddy do so, but having his love interest followed was another story.

***

After hearing they'd pick up the anticipated drop from the DFW Airport, Chris tried to get Diamond to see things from his point of view. The first time the transaction happened, they had to fly to Miami, but now the drop had landed close to home.

"I'm just saying, Diamond, there has to be another reason he was willing to bring all that work himself."

"He had some business here and felt it was best to travel with only money."

Chris followed Diamond from the theater room through the hallway to the safe room. "How you know this isn't a set-up, Diamond? You have to look out for your better interest in this."

"Well, you stay here. I'm going to get my shit, nigga."

"There are too many variables with this shit, Diamond, and getting caught up when you don't know the plays of the opposing team is always likely."

Diamond stopped, turned to face him and said, "You tripping, but I'm going to let you call this shot. What are you proposing?"

"Just have someone else pick it up."

"And, who the hell is going to go pick up two hundred kilos and not want half my shit, Chris?"

"Someone who doesn't know shit about it. Someone who owes more than they have to pay." Chris smiled.

"You've got to be kidding me?" Diamond soon realized he wasn't and told him, "Silvia will kill us if she found out some shit like that."

Diamond phoned her contact to confirm the things she already knew. She also wanted to make sure one of his guys stayed until the money had been dropped and the product received. And, for a gift, they even told her she could keep the Cadillac Escalade the drugs were in. "Let me call this nigga, KP, right quick."

\*\*\*

KP was awakened by the sound of his ringing phone. He groggily reached for it, hoping to see his wife's face but instead was looking at the image of his new employer on the phone screen. He answered, "What's up, Diamond?"

"Rise and shine. I need you to do something for me."

"When and where?" KP climbed out of the bed and stretched.

"Right now and at the airport."

"The airport?"

"Yeah, I had Antonio's truck looked at and I need for you to pick it up for me."

KP looked around him. "Um, let me get myself together. Where is it parked, Diamond?"

"I'll text you the info."

Before he could question her further, she ended the call. He dressed and made his way into the living room, where Q was already preparing for his day. KP was looking forward to having a few words with his friend to better understand the lie he told about having to go to the bank on a Saturday. He also wanted a few answers, pertaining to the events that led to the shooting and the taking of his money.

"Hey, I need for you to drop me off at the airport."

"For what?"

"None of your motherfucking business, nigga!"

Q frowned. "Damn, nigga, what's wrong with you?"

"Guess?"

"You woke up like you just realized the bitch in your dream was a man."

KP walked towards the door. "I don't have time for that shit, nigga. Diamond needs me to get her truck."

"You think she's just trying to get you out there so she can kill you?"

"Not right now, Q. I have shit to do, man." KP walked outside, handed Q the keys to the rental he'd been driving and climbed into the passenger's side. He looked over the directions Diamond sent him and closed his eyes. "Something has got to give. Shit!"

"Them baggage people going to find your ass coming down a conveyer belt or something." Q pulled out and made way for the location KP gave. "Early as it is and she wants you to pick up a damn truck from the airport."

"Shut the hell up, bitch-ass nigga! I know you had something to do with the shit already!"

"Better lower your damn voice, crazy-ass nigga, before I kill your ass first. Saying some shit already!"

They stared at each other. Each man with thoughts of his own. Each man needing to see the actions of the next.

KP broke the silence. "I've never killed a nigga in my life, but if I find out you had something to do with my shit getting stolen, you're going to be the first."

"Ain't nobody had nothing to do with that shit, nigga. You think I'm going to tell a nigga to shoot up my shit, just to get some money from you? Come on, super dumb-ass nigga. That's just dumb."

"Like I said, let me find out."

For the rest of the ride, they both sat in silence. A silence that began the division of friends.

***

King was sitting in the lobby, looking through several outdated *GQ Magazine* when the chocolate-skinned woman strolled in. He'd greeted a couple of women already, but she was the one that made him take more than notice. He stood as she passed. He definitely knew her from somewhere. "Trina?" he asked, really questioning himself.

Datrina walked past the waiting clients. She had minutes before her first appointment showed and she wanted to be ready. Hearing the guy call out to her she half-turned, finger waved at him and when actually seeing who he was, she stopped and faced him. "King?"

"Yeah, I knew you from somewhere, but it's not coming to me." He took a step towards her, extended his hand and smiled. "Where do I know you from?"

By this time, a couple of the beauticians took notice and one even spoke.

"Her name is Datrina."

"Datrina. That's right."

"Miami," she told him.

"Weren't you with a woman called Dimond?"

"Really, King? It hasn't been that long." Datrina walked to her station. He followed. "What are you doing here?"

"I'm here with my girl." King pointed over at Camille, whose head was in a sink, getting a rinse.

"Your girl?" Datrina glanced at him with raised brows.

"Not girlfriend. I mean my girl as in best friend."

"Oh, okay."

"Um, when was the last time you saw Diamond?"

"Why don't I just call her for you, King? I'm more than sure she wants to speak with you also."

King walked over to her station without hesitation. It was now clear as to what Camille was up to. This was where she ran into Diamond.

"Please tell her where I am."

Datrina pulled out her phone and dialed the woman he'd been looking for the longest.

***

Diamond and Chris watched as the money was picked up and driven off. Chris pointed at several possibilities when it came to the set-up but he could see they weren't convincing her in the least bit. There were no suspicious vehicles parked around, no construction crew or clean-up workers playing the part and no evidence of a jack. The fact that Sergio's men were still alongside the Escalade, only added to Diamond's observation of Chris's paranoia.

"You got me paying this nigga for nothing."

"Better safe than sorry, Diamond. You shouldn't be the one handling this shit anyway. You're supposed to be sitting up awaiting word, not sitting here in the midst of the shit."

"Yeah, you right and one day, that'll be exactly what we do." Diamond reached for her phone and when seeing Datrina's contact she answered, "Hey, Datrina, what's up?"

"King is standing right in front of me, Diamond, and he wants to talk to you."

"Bye, bitch." Diamond hung up, looked over at Chris and smiled. "Ya black ass girlfriend got jokes."

"What's she talking about?"

"Nothing."

Her phone chimed a second time. Chris answered, "Hey, babe. What's up?"

"Where's that girl at, Chris?"

"Sitting right here, looking crazy."

"King's here and he wants to talk to her."

"King?"

"Yeah, King."

Chris knew Datrina played a lot, but he had more than a feeling she was sincere. "Put him on the phone right quick."

***

KP waited for the text to come and once it did, he made his way to the rear of the parking garage. He spotted the black Escalade parked several feet away. This was the same truck he'd seen enter the garage under an hour ago. Diamond's text told him that the keys would be in the glove compartment, and that he was to take the truck to yet another location he wasn't familiar with. It was as simple as that, but when he saw three guys exiting the trucks parked alongside Diamond's, his mind began flipping a thousand miles an hour. Q's words bounced off the walls of his mind. "This bitch done killed me," he told himself once they began watching him. KP's first mind was to keep walking and act as if he was in the wrong section of the airport but it was too late. He nodded at the guy standing closest to him and before he could scream and run, they began climbing back into the trucks around him.

As soon as he climbed into the Escalade, he reached over and opened the glove compartment, grabbed the keys and pulled off. "I'm not ever doing this shit again," he promised himself.

Diamond watched as KP pulled out of the garage and head for his next stop. She and Chris would follow her shipment until Chris was content and she'd let them switch. "Told you." She watched Chris act as if he was talking to someone other than Datrina and seeing him look towards her and smile, she knew they didn't have anything else to do besides mess with her. Either way, it would have to wait, because she'd just spent one point seven million dollars and she was about to oversee its distribution.

Chris laughed when seeing Diamond refuse the phone. "She's preoccupied at the moment, King, and you know how she gets when her mind is on something."

"Yeah, I do. That's what I love about her."

"I'll tell you what. Give Datrina your contact and I'm going to make sure Diamond gets back at you, once we're in pocket." Chris looked over at Diamond and shook his head. He drove her crazy at times and he knew it, but once she found out that King was really on the other end of the line, he wasn't going to hear the end of it.

*** 

King handed Datrina her phone, looked to where Camille was getting finishing touches on her hair and asked Datrina, "Is this her first time here?" He nodded in Camille's direction.

"Who, Boss Lady?" another woman asked him.

"Boss Lady?"

"Yeah, that's what the big guy called her."

King laughed. That was all he needed to hear. "Make sure she gets at me, Datrina."

"Oh, she's definitely going to call you, King. I promise you that."

\*\*\*

Q had called Somolia and even stopped by her house, hoping he'd be able to get at her in private. He knew of only one more place she'd be and that was the reason he pulled in front of the Totally Awesome Hair and Nail Salon, grabbed the package containing the fifty thousand dollars he just withdrew from the bank and rushed inside. "Somolia!"

Both beauticians and clients turned to face him. "What the hell you running up in here screaming for?" asked one of the beauticians.

"Where's Somolia?"

"She's not here yet and after what you did to her car, you shouldn't be here at all."

Camille listened as best she could. She'd put the pieces of the puzzle together days ago that Somolia was the woman Buddy called himself dating and was wanting to hear all she could about her.

"I need to talk to her." Q walked past King and looked towards the back of the salon.

"There ain't nothing back there for you to tear up, Q, so sit your ass down."

Datrina always liked Q, but his latest stunt had her questioning the reasons she did in the first place.

"I have something for her." He handed her the package.

"What's this? A bomb or something?" Datrina weighed the package by bouncing it.

"It's the money I owe her. Ya boyfriend came through and shot up my shit and I'm just trying to make it right."

"There you go with that shit, Q. Chris ain't fucking with you like that."

"Well, somebody did and I think Somolia was behind it."

Datrina walked over, got behind Q and literally pushed him out of the salon. They all knew he said some of anything and they weren't about to entertain it at all. "Bye, Q. We'll have her call you when she get here. 'Til then, don't ever come back."

The majority of the women present laughed. Q always weaved unbelievable tales in his attempts to gain sympathy for the things he did and didn't do.

"That man is crazy, girl. I'm telling you," said another of the women present.

"Yeah, he does have problems, don't he?"

"Hell, if my shit got shot up in broad daylight, I'd most likely have some problems too," another woman laughed.

Datrina's curiosity got the best of her. She had to see what the package contained. "Well, evidently his problems are very real. Look." She then held up the stacks of bills it contained.

*****

Nava rang the doorbell until she was sure King was elsewhere. She tried the door's handle to no avail. "Shit!" she cursed. She'd run through the money he'd given her days ago and was looking forward to him giving her more. The spiel she had for him was one not even he could refuse and if all went right, she'd be moving back in with him tonight.

She walked back towards the Town Car and climbed in.

"So, what's up?" the guy asked her.

"His truck is parked in the back, but he must be out somewhere." She pulled the compact from her purse, cut a couple of lines and filled her nose.

*****

King leaned over and kissed Camille every few minutes it seemed. He was more than grateful for what she'd done, despite it being done as soon as she heard of Nava's presence. "You know I love you, right?"

"Keep your lips off me, King." Camille drove past two car lots and several stores. She made the turn on Wintergreen and was about to pull up in King's apartments, when he suggested they stop and grab a bite to eat. "Keep going, Camille, I'm hungry as hell," he told her when spotting the black Town Car posted out front.

Camille sighed. "Are you serious, King? We just passed a hundred eateries."

"I know, I know. Just keep driving. I'm not ready to go home."

King subtly glanced in the direction of the Town Car, but the heavily tinted windows kept him from seeing who was inside. He knew Nava would return and he knew he'd most likely be the only one that could help her. It was now that he had that decision to make and he wasn't about to lose his Diamond again.

*** 

Buddy sent a short, but sweet text to Somolia and as soon as the Town Car pulled past him at the top of the street, he placed his phone on the seat beside him and gave the occupants his undivided attention. He half-smiled when seeing Nava climb out of the car and hurry across the street to King's apartment. His smile widened when thinking of the plan his Boss Lady devised and as ordered, he was going to sit back and trail Nava Munez and he was going to make sure she paid the debt she owed.

NICOLE GOOSBY

## CHAPTER TWENTY

"Look at what the dog dropped off, y'all," said one of the beauticians as soon as Somolia walked into the salon.

"Thought you fell off the face on the earth," said another woman.

"Rest, babe. Rest. A bitch has to get a little more rest," Somolia told them while heading to her station.

"Well, you've been missing out on all the good stuff, girl."

"I doubt that very seriously." Somolia walked past Datrina towards the rear of the salon. "Been breaking in the new whip."

"You look crazy as hell, jumping out of the big-ass car. Your little fat ass had to get the biggest they had, huh?"

"You know what they say, you give up the ass, they give up the cash." Somolia slapped her ass, faced Datrina and smiled.

"Speaking of giving up the cash, Q stopped by earlier and left you some."

Somolia frowned. "Really?"

Datrina held out the package he gave her. "He said you need to get at him."

She thumbed through the stack of bills and laughed. "That nigga was serious when he said he was going to pay me for my shit."

"Someone's been giving up more than some ass."

"I thought the two of you were at each other's throats?" Datrina shook her head.

"Or in each other's throats," said another woman, who'd been sitting there.

"Let's just say the nigga's realizing that I've moved on and is feeling it."

Somolia held the stack of the bills in the air and continued, "This is how they're supposed to pay. My head ain't cheap, the pussy ain't average and the ass—"

"Shut up, Somolia, we don't need to hear all that." Datrina stopped her, knowing she was about to go there with the topic.

Silvia walked in amid the laughter and with Somolia on the floor, it wasn't hard to figure out who was behind it. "Sounds like a slumber party up in here."

"Oh, we're just a group of hoes, doing what hoes do," Somolia told her.

"Naw, you're the one whoring, Somolia," said Datrina.

"That ain't nothing new." Silvia headed for her office.

"Q brought Somolia a shitload of money this morning," one of the women said.

"Looks like it's about fifty grand in there," Datrina added.

"Damn, bitch. Your nose got a calculator in it and everything," Somolia went off.

"Oh really?"

"Make 'em pay. That's the way I play this game. Make their ass pay."

Silvia thought of a few things to say, but decided against it for not wanting to expose certain things she really didn't know the half of. If nothing else, she was going to look into it.

"I should have gotten more than this, shit." Somolia fanned herself with the bills. She had a thing or two in mind for her man and with the money Q had given her, either could be easily done.

"How long is it going to take?" KP was looking at Chris, but his question was directed at Diamond. He was still leery when it came to their intentions for him.

"Stay here, KP. Just chill. By the time you're through eating, we'll be back."

KP watched as they drove off, leaving him at the IHOP restaurant alone. It was just something about the way Diamond's attitude towards him changed and the way Chris continued to look, that created a panic in him. He wasn't sure what their plans were for him, but he had a pretty good idea who would. After placing his order, he pulled out his phone and called his wife.

\*\*\*

Silvia sighed when seeing KP's contact. She had things to do and hearing him talk about the things he had going on wasn't something she was up for at the moment. "What is it now, Kevin?"

"I think they're going to kill me, Silvia."

"What the hell are you talking about now? I have a lot of shit to do today and I—"

"They dropped me off at a fucking IHOP, Silvia. Diamond said they'd be right back and I'm thinking they're going to—"

Silvia closed her eyes, rubbed her temple with one hand and said, "Hold up, hold up. What's Diamond got to do with this?"

"She called me earlier this morning, because she wanted me to pick up Antonio's truck from the airport, then she and Chris brought me here and she told me she'd be right back."

"Pick up Antonio's truck from the airport?"

"Yeah. I thought she was going to have some guys kill me, but they just left when I got there."

"What guys, KP?"

"Some Cuban-looking guys or something. They were waiting for me at the airport parking garage."

Silvia couldn't believe how stupid KP had gotten. He'd been thinking everyone was out to get him, and looked right over the fact that Diamond just did.

"Um, let me handle my business. I'll call you later, and stop thinking that woman is trying to kill you. You're making even that harder than it is."

"What you mean—"

She ended her call and immediately called Diamond. For her to include KP in something as crucial as the delivering of some drugs wasn't sitting well with her. That was the least she needed right now.

*** 

Diamond helped Chris unload the shipment into the storage unit. For the next couple of days, nothing would be touched and that was because Chris was about to show Diamond the way she was to do things differently. The past eight months, they'd been delivering drugs across four states and that was something he didn't want her doing anymore. From now on, he was going to be in charge of things and she'd oversee the operation. "Let me find out you're trying to push me off the cut, nigga."

"It's time for me to boss you up, Diamond. Niggas want their work, they coming to get it. I'll have control over the transactions, I'll be able to look over the cash before the drugs are picked up and once everything checks out, they go get their work from the location I choose. Ain't no setting us up shit like they tried to pull in North Dallas."

"Yeah, alright, but..." Diamond answered her phone before finishing her response. "What's up, Silvia?"

"You tell me."

"Just chilling with Chris."

"Oh yeah?"

"What the hell do you want? Asking me all these damn questions."

"Where y'all at? Where y'all chilling at?"

Diamond looked over at Chris and smiled. KP's contacting his wife now became evident to Diamond.

"What that nigga say, cuz?"

"Who?"

"Ya husband. I know he called you and said something. You wouldn't be playing crazy if he hadn't."

"Well, as a matter of fact, he did just call me. He thinks you're trying to have him killed."

"He what?"

"Yeah, he doesn't understand the reason you had him pick up Antonio's truck from the airport, when you had Chris with you the whole time. He thinks the Cuban guys you had waiting for him froze up at the last minute and decided to just leave."

Diamond laughed. "Okay, okay. Stop it. Please."

"Well you started it."

"I had the nigga put in some work, Silvia, it wasn't shit."

"So, you think?"

"Yeah, I was just trying something new."

"And, what exactly did you think would happen had things gone wrong and KP got jammed up with that shit, Diamond?"

She knew where this conversation was headed and even though it was Chris's idea, she wasn't going to throw him under the bus. "Ya husband just paying off the debt he owes, Silvia."

"At the expense of you losing all you have. He's not built for that shit, Diamond, and you know it. He actually thinks you're trying to kill him. Him working off some debt is the last thing he's thinking of."

"You know how that nigga is. He's always thinking a mother-fucker out to get him. I'm putting his ass to work. That's all."

"Well, do it in some other fashion, Diamond. Scary people make very rash decisions, act impulsively and you don't need that, I'm sure."

"I got it, cuz. He's good."

"And how much are you paying him, Diamond?"

"Quit calling my damn name like that, make a bitch think you the laws or something."

"Then start allowing your actions to cause you to think the same. So, how much are you paying him?"

"I told you, he's working off a debt."

"Respect the game."

"I am."

"Give him reason to also."

"I will."

"Pay the man, Diamond. He's on his ass as it is."

"I'm giving him the truck they gave me."

"And that makes it right?"

Diamond was fighting a losing battle and she knew it. "I'll give him ten grand."

"Fifty thousand dollars."

"I'll give him twenty-five grand."

"Fifty thousand dollars, Diamond. That ain't shit to you. You a boss now."

"Fifty-grand. Bye." Diamond hung up and told Chris, "Snitching-ass nigga called Silvia, talking about we trying to kill him."

"He what?"

"Now, I got to pay his ass fifty thousand dollars."

"I thought you were going to give him the truck?"

"And that. I'm going to put his ass to work for real now. He'll really be crying about a bitch trying to kill him then."

"Well, don't even let him know you talked to Silvia. Allow him to think these are your own actions."

"Yeah, I got him." Once things were locked away, she told him, "Let's go get this nigga."

\*\*\*

KP sat and mulled over a couple of ideas and the one that refused to allow him to focus on anything was the fact that Q was actually becoming more of a suspect than a friend. Where Q was always the one wanting to know what he had going on, he was now distancing himself, while claiming to be getting himself together. Something had to give and soon.

He watched through the huge windows of the restaurant as Chris and Diamond entered the lot and waved back when Chris waved for him to come out. He reluctantly stood and made his way outside.

"Y'all ready or what?"

"There's been a change of plans," Diamond yelled from the inside of the Corvette she was driving.

"What's up?" He caught the keys Chris threw him.

"You go ahead. The Escalade is yours, and here," she said as she handed him five stacks of hundred-dollar bills.

"You giving me the truck?"

"Nigga, get your ass in the truck and go on about your business. And, stop telling every damn thing."

KP smiled. If there were strings attached, he'd deal with that later. He now had a brand-new Escalade truck and fifty thousand dollars in his pocket. He couldn't wait to tell his friend, Q.

\*\*\*

Nava looked over her selections of outfits, thought about visiting King with a more presentable look, but decided on the Walmart bought jeans and t-shirt. She'd been snorting on the same ounce she'd gotten days ago and was getting low. She promised herself that once she'd made it back to Dallas, it would only be a matter of time before she was back on. This time, she was going to do something with the money she got from King.

"You sure this nigga still on, Nava? The guy moved out of the house you told us about and moved back into an apartment."

Nava cut herself another line and filled her nose. "A couple of hundred thousand ain't nothing to this guy. Him and that bitch he roll with swimming in money," she told him.

NICOLE GOOSBY

## CHAPTER TWENTY-ONE

"Somolia, you got a minute?" Silvia asked, beckoning for her to come back to her office.

"Yeah, what's up?"

After the door was closed and Silvia was seated behind her desk, she looked across the room at Somolia and smiled. "Seems like a pretty nice payoff, huh?"

"Girl, please, that wasn't shit, compared to all the money I've put into Q and the ideas he had."

"It's just coming at a bad time, Somolia, and now that you've made it known that it came from Q, don't you think it's going to paint a picture we're really not trying to see?"

"I have nothing to do with what they have going on, Silvia, and you know that. The nigga told me he was going to pay for my shit and he did. How he got the money, what he had to do to get it and who he got it from, has nothing to do with me." Somolia tsked.

"Well, I'm just trying to get you too see what's going on around here and what's sure to be said about it."

"Yeah, well, as long as they keep me out of it, I—"

Silvia cut her off, "You've got to prepare yourself for the day you're running your own shop, Somolia. You already know that the shit done here is going to follow you, regardless of your role in it. I'm trying to get away from all this shit and I'm going to need you all to help me with it."

"What do you need for us to do?"

"What do you know about the shooting, Somolia? And, don't tell me nothing."

Somolia sighed, looked back towards the door and told her, "He thinks I had Chris to do the shooting, because of what he's been doing and the nigga thinks that if he reimburses me for the damage he did to my car, I'll tell Chris to let him make it. I just went with it, because he promised to get me some of my money back. That's all I know." Somolia didn't see the need in telling her about Buddy and his assurance that Q wouldn't bother her again.

She wasn't about to tell of his role in the shooting for not wanting things pointed in her or her man's direction. As for now, that would be something she kept to herself and as long as she was getting some of what she'd given for years, it would remain that way.

"You've been coming in late lately. What's up with that?"

"I'm starting a new chapter, Silvia, and it's been keeping me busy is all."

"New salon on the way, new man apparently and what else?" Silvia smiled at her friend. It had been a long time coming and she was glad for her.

"We'll see. As of right now, it does look promising but you know how that is."

Silvia stood, signaling the end of their little talk. "Well, just be careful, Somolia. We've come too far to turn back now and the people we associate ourselves with can easily be determining factors."

"Yeah, tell me about it."

"So, when are you going to bring your new man around?" Silvia gave her a knowing smile.

"In due time, Silvia. In due time."

***

Camille forked through her salad for the chunks of chicken it contained. She could tell that King had things on his mind, because of the way he was picking over the things he ordered and she let him know as much. "What is there to think about, King?"

"She needs me, Camille."

"Does she?"

"You should have seen her. The drug use was evident."

"Maybe that's something you'll never be able to change, King. This woman has shown you this before and now that she's returned in the same state, doesn't it cause you to question the way things happened the first time? For all we know, she's had her sights set on you and you fell right in the mine she's been digging out of for the longest."

"She's not like that, Camille."

"Let me tell you something, King. For her own father to disown her, there has to be something that caused it. Something you're not trying to see for reasons of your own."

"This was the woman I wanted to marry, Camille. I just can't—"

"No, what you can't do is mess this off with Diamond. I thought you loved her?"

King nodded. "I do."

"Then, what is there to think about?"

King fell silent, looked over the food he toyed with and thought about Nava. He thought about the promise he made to her. The promise of him doing all he could for her as long as she made an attempt to stay off the drugs, leave all the partying alone and make something happen for herself. The quarter-million dollars he gave her just days before her disappearance was for just that. She told him how bad she wanted to open her very own boutique and how she'd been studying the trade for the longest. How all she needed was for someone to believe in her, help her and give her that very much-needed way out. King had become just that for her. He'd brought her all the way up and now that she was back, he was still seeing the need to do something.

"Seeing that you have no answer for that one, think about this one, why is she here now? I mean, she took enough with her to have done what she needed to do. And, let's say I did make her promise to never return, don't you think she would have made the most out of what she had? The way you tell it, she'd stopped doing drugs long before she left and for her return so easily to that which kept her bound in the first place, I find that hard to believe, King."

"She never wanted to leave, Camille. You did that."

"Really? I wanted Diamond to do the same, but you see how that turned out."

"Diamond's a different story."

"I'd rather you became characterized in hers, instead of Nava's."

"Why now, Camille? I mean, you've known where Diamond was all this time and you kept me from her and now that Nava has returned, you're throwing me at the same woman you insisted on keeping me from. Why now?"

"Diamond's shown me more than Nava can. Diamond's shown me that she's not some gold-digging tramp that's out to get whatever she can, from whoever talks about giving it."

"Is this the same woman I'm talking about?"

"Diamond took me to see her brother, King."

It was now King's time to look on incredulously. "She did what?"

"I told her to convince me that she had your best interest at heart. I made her prove it."

"And?"

"She really does love you, Kengyon, and I don't want to lose you to anyone that doesn't care for you the way I do. I'm more than sure you can understand that."

Those were the words that caused him to reach across the table and grab her hand. He told her, "And, I want the same for you, Camille. I want nothing more than that."

"Then, there's nothing more to think about. You have Diamond. Let that be enough for you, King."

"Now that that's settled, I want to move you back in my home." He was referring to his Ravinia home, the same one Camille moved him out of against his wishes.

"Not just yet, King. If Nava had no knowledge of it, I would approve, but with this bitch still breathing, we can't risk it."

"Nava's not like that, Camille. You tripping."

"What you think she's going to become?" I said. "What? When a woman realizes her man's cheating and has been cheating, she becomes some bitch, but when a bitch like Nava realizes her gold mine belongs to another, that's a different story to tell, King. Believe me."

"Just let me handle Nava."

"While you're doing that, let me get in touch with Dell and see what he has on the market. I'm more than sure I can get something nicer."

And, to show King the urgency of it, she pulled out her phone and dialed Dell. "Hey, Dell, we need to talk."

***

Chris ran a list of things down to Diamond. The things he was about to change as well as implement. He told her about the way money was about to be spent as well. He thought he'd find protest at first, but she only continued to nod, as if agreeing to all he said. "It's time to follow the blueprint, Diamond, and why change what's been working for the longest?"

"Let me find out, Chris."

"I'm serious, Diamond. We've been winning and we can't take that for granted at all."

"Winning? Nigga, all I've got to show for this shit is a fake-ass construction company that hasn't made a dime, some bullshit-ass clothes and a car. That ain't winning."

"You've accomplished more than that, Diamond, come on, this is me you're talking to. You've cleared over four point six. How many motherfuckers can say some shit like that, huh?"

"That is before all the other expenses come into play. I—"

"You just need to start doing something else with the money you win for. Your brother didn't buy shit until he made his quota."

"I'm not stopping, Chris."

"I just want you to think about tomorrow. You have a business and you need to put it into play. You have an investment firm at your disposal, you have realtors on hand, use that shit, Diamond. This is what we get in this game for. To make something happen to where we don't have to take these penitentiary chances."

"Antonio set the bar and I'm going surpass that, nigga. I have to."

"Why?"

"Motherfucker, 'cause that's something I want to do."

223

Chris threw his hands up. "Hey, I'm supposed to be saying shit like this. This is what friends do."

"Naw, friends sell each other out, cut each other's throats and piss on their graves. That's what friends do. Me and you are more than that, nigga. We family."

"Yeah, we are that."

\*\*\*

KP was feeling pretty good about himself, thinking about the way things were turning around for him. He'd painted a pretty bad picture of the exact same people that went out of their way to help him. Here he'd accused both Chris and Diamond of trying to do something as crazy as killing him, only to be given a new Escalade truck and fifty thousands dollars. He was now more than sure it was done in an effort to see him do better and that was exactly what he was going to do. He thought about the first thing he wanted to do with the cash he had in his pocket, and giving some to the guy he'd taken on as an extra from the labor pool came to mind. It might not have been much, but it would definitely be a start and in his mind, since the guy wasn't working, he could make use of the twenty thousand dollars he planned on giving him. Since he was in the area, he decided to swing by the labor pool to see if he could catch him.

\*\*\*

Q got the call just as he was about to pull into the driveway. He'd made his rounds and wanted to be in pocket, just in case KP called, needing for him to pick him up. "Q speaking, what's up?"

"Q, hey, man. What's up?"

"Who's this?" he asked, not recognizing the voice.

"The nigga that almost died with you."

"Jeff?"

"Yeah. I um, I need to talk to you. I got something for you, man."

"Nigga, we haven't heard from you since the accident. You alright or what?"

"Um, yeah, yeah, that wasn't shit, but that's what I need to talk to you about.

"Man, I don't have shit to do with no lawsuit. Leave me out of that shit,"

"Ain't nobody talking about no damn lawsuit. Come by the house, nigga. I've got something you can use. You looked out for me when that shit happened and now I'm trying to look after you. Money, nigga."

Q thought about other things to do as well as other places to be, but since none came to mind, he told him, "Where are you now?"

"I'm still at the house. Swing through here right quick."

Instead of parking, Q drove, hoping what Jeff had for him wasn't about to waste his time. Hell, after all the money he just gave Somolia, any little bit could help.

***

KP made the block at the labor pool and pulled up on a couple of guys he turned on at one time. "What's up, fellas?" he yelled through the lowered window of the truck.

"KP, is that you, nigga?"

"Yeah, it's me. What it look like out here?"

"Motherfuckers trying to get some work. What you got going on?"

KP didn't want them to think that he'd lost or even sold his company and knowing they'd heard about the incident that happened in Houston, he had to save face. He told them, "I'm going to have a few projects coming up here shortly and I'm going to need a few guys."

"Well, you know where we at."

"Matter of fact, where's Jeff? Does he still come around or what?" KP looked past the guy, hoping to see the guy he'd come for.

"Hell, that nigga got some more shit going on now, KP. After what happened with y'all and the money he got from the insurance company, he's been hiring niggas the way you used to."

"What?"

"Hell yeah, that nigga came all the way up. Got new trucks and everything."

"Oh yeah?"

"You showed a nigga how this shit goes." The guy shrugged. "So, he owes it to you."

KP pulled off. He hadn't heard from anything from the insurance company and was hoping he hadn't been missing his notice to appear in court. He hadn't been thinking about the mail still being delivered to his home and since his wife hadn't been saying anything about it, it totally slipped his mind. Since he was in traffic already, he decided to stop by Jeff's house. He'd take the money there.

\*\*\*

Q couldn't believe what he was hearing and had to touch the money to make sure he was seeing what was being shown to him. "You did what?"

"I had to, man. You kept telling me about suing the insurance company, and then you started talking about three-hundred thousand dollars and all that shit, and I just thought you was trying to tip me off that KP had the money on hand."

"How in the hell you come up with some shit like that, nigga! I didn't say shit about shooting up my house and taking no money!" Q's anger was getting the best of him. He placed one hand on his hip and with the bandaged hand, he pointed at Jeff. "What the fuck's wrong with you, nigga!"

"Man, I didn't shoot up shit. I don't know where you get that shit from. I'm standing here telling you what I did, and you talking about a nigga shot up ya house. Nigga, I'm on parole. I don't fuck with no guns no more. Why you think I be at a fucking labor pool?"

Q looked down at the exact same duffle bag KP had in the rear cabin of the truck. It was the same bag that contained the six hundred thousand dollars he'd gotten for selling the company. He looked across the yard of Jeff's house. The brand-new Duallies, the heavy-duty toolboxes, the twelve-inch stepladders and the magnetized signs advertising Jeff's Renovations, explained more than he could ask, and seeing the hundred thousand dollars cash he was being offered, there was nothing to say.

"You want it or what, nigga?"

"This is some fucked-up shit, man. And, now you putting me in the middle of it." Q grabbed the handles of the duffle, walked it over to the rental KP entrusted him with and threw it in the trunk.

"That's what I thought, nigga. You'd better take that money and go on about your business."

"I still think you should have left that nigga's money alone." Q fumbled with the keys, climbed into the rental and added, "This some fucked-up shit, man."

\*\*\*

KP stopped the minute he saw Q and Jeff standing and talking in the front yard. He frowned, seeing the brand-new trucks out front, but seeing Q reach down and come up with the exact same duffle he'd got from Dell's, it all began to make sense. Chris and Diamond were right. It was his closest friend all along. The same guy that pointed at everyone else was only making sure he wasn't being pointed at. "Son of a bitch!" KP watched Q pull off and followed. He had to see who else was involved. He wanted to know who all he had to kill.

\*\*\*

Despite the money he had in the trunk, there were still questions he asked himself when it came to the fact that his house was shot to shit. The only other person that came to mind when thinking of that was Somolia and now that he'd paid her off, he

227

was hoping he was out of the water. All he had to do now was make sure KP never found out he'd taken money from the guy who'd stole it from him. The one hundred thousand dollars would not only cover the fifty grand he'd just given Somolia, but it would also tide him over until his insurance claim came through. The claim that would replace his car, as well as repairs needed for his house.

## CHAPTER TWENTY-TWO

As soon as King entered his apartment, he walked back to the third bedroom, counted out five thousand dollars from the stash he had there and walked it to the kitchen area. He was hoping Nava would drop by so they could talk. Camille's words continued to play in his mind and now that the choice was clear, he was praying both Diamond and Nava respected and accepted his decision. With so many things going on and not wanting to add to them, he went ahead and agreed with Camille on him not returning to the Ravinia mansion until things blew over.

He'd just concluded a call with one of his buyers and was about to check the window, when the doorbell rang. "Coming!" he yelled out so she wouldn't leave. He peeked out of the window and seeing the Town Car parked in the same spot as it was before, he made his way to the door. He opened it.

"Hey, babe!" Nava greeted him with as much excitement as she could muster.

"Hey, you. Come on in here."

Nava jumped into his arms and squeezed him. "I've missed you so very much, babe."

King held her with reserve. He tried so desperately to inhale the floral fragrance she was known to wear, but instead found himself recognizing alcohol and marijuana. He held her at arm's length and looked her over, her eyes were hardened but still beautiful to him. He pulled her to him and squeezed her, comforting her in the ways he used to. "Are you alright?"

"I am now. I've been so worried about you. I haven't been able to stop thinking about you, King. Everything reminds me of you and, and," Nava's eyes began tearing, her lips shaking.

"Shh, it's okay, Nava. I'm alright. I'm good." He pulled her to him again. He moved her disheveled hair aside and kissed her forehead.

Nava tried to meet his lips with hers. "I've been trying, babe," she cried. King walked her to the sofa, sat her down and went to grab her something to wipe her eyes with, as well as something to drink. "Where did you go, Nava, I mean, what happened, you were doing so good?"

"I, I went back home, King." Nava shook her head and sat upright. "I opened my own boutique, babe. I finally had my own, babe." She made herself smile, as if really remembering the event. "Then the hurricane hit and I lost everything, I lost it all, King. My boutique, my beachfront apartment, my car." Nava began sobbing quietly. She hid her face in her hands. "Now, I have nothing. I don't even have a place to stay, King."

"Shh, shh. I got you, Nava. It's alright, babe." King's heart broke when hearing all she'd been through. And, her father continually turning his back on her was something he wasn't trying to understand. Even then, he was all Nava had and it was the same way now. "Nava, look at me." King grabbed her chin and made her face him. "I got you, Nava, don't worry about it."

"I'm in debt, babe. I had a friend that's been looking out for me and—"

"I'm going to take care of that, don't sweat it." King thought about his most recent visit to Miami. He remembered the guys that hustled outside of the hotel he and Camille were staying in, remembered their descriptions of Nava, her partying, her drug use, her being abused sexually. It was the exact lifestyle he tried rescuing her from and it was the same thing she went back to. She'd been through enough and he wasn't about to add to it the fact that she lied about doing other things. He felt she was ashamed of her actions, her failures and no one understood that better than King. "You can tell your friend thanks for all he's done, but I got you now. I'm going to take care of you now." King went to the kitchen and came back with the five thousand dollars he'd taken from his stash in the back. "Will this cover those expenses?" He didn't even ask her about the money he'd given her just days ago.

"I gave him some of the money you gave me, but being that I lost everything, I had to buy me some new clothes so I can go look for me another job. I have to start all over, babe."

"Just give this to him and tell him—" King stood, took the money from her and headed out the door. That was about to be the conversation they had with each other.

***

Camille made the drive to Dell's estate as fast as she could. She wanted to be back in Las Colinas before it had gotten too late. She parked and climbed out. And, since Dell was walking his guest towards her, she waited at the bottom of the twelve stairs.

"We had an agreement," Dell told the guy.

"Yeah, that was before you started dragging this shit out. You promised my guys something and you need to make it happen, Dell. You've been making promises for the past eight months and now it's time to pay it."

"I gave you motherfuckers fifty thousand dollars already."

"They want more, Dell. I'm just the messenger. They're the ones with all the pull and resources."

"That's bullshit and you know it." Dell sighed, looked towards Camille and whispered, "Just give me a little more time."

"I'd hate for this little bubble to burst, Dell."

Camille was leaning against her Porsche when the guy walked up to her, wearing a mischievous smile. "Camille," he greeted her with a nod and kept walking.

"Officer Bell," she greeted him the same. She pushed herself from the car and walked to where Dell stood. They both watched the guy climb in the unmarked car and speed off. "Still feeding the snakes, I see."

Dell took a sip of the dark liquor he was holding and told her, "Fuck that bitch." He looked over at her and smiled. "How do you two know each other?"

"Aw, we've had a run-in or two. Nothing I'm stressed about."

"Well, enough of him." Dell led her up the stairs. "Let's talk business."

"After you." Camille looked back to where she'd saw the guy leave. It had been a while since she'd seen him, but she knew snakes didn't change colors, they only got bigger and greedier.

Dell poured himself another drink, walked down into the pitted den and handed Camille a glass of sparkling water. His phone chimed. He sighed, "Let me take this right quick, Camille. Hey, what's up?"

***

Chris had been telling Diamond about the things they needed to put in play and she was growing tired of his constant reminders. Now that she was the owner of a make-shift construction company, she was about to find some work for her employees. According to Chris, the last thing she needed was for them to wander off in search for other jobs. She phoned Dell.

"You take care of that or what?" she asked as soon as he came on the line.

"Most of it, but since the company wasn't registered by any professional means, I'm having to—"

"I need the shit done, Dell."

"I just need more time on it. I—"

Diamond took her frustrations out on him, instead of Chris. "I'm not paying you to put my shit on hold, Dell. How in the hell am I to get commercial contracts and I don't even have any insurance for my guys?"

"Just do what KP's been doing."

"Get on my shit, Dell, and find me some properties to renovate. I need to have my guys working by the end of this week. If not, we're going to have to pay them for doing nothing."

"And what does that have to do with me?" Dell asked.

"You're going to have to pay them. My brother wants this company up and running and that's what we're going to do," she lied. Diamond knew how to get results from the people she dealt with and it was now time she did.

232

"I'll take care of it at my earliest. No worries. Everything will—"

Diamond ended the call before he was able to finish his sentence. She'd been doing that a lot lately.

"What he say?"

"He's now understanding I don't have time to wait on his drunk ass. Every time I need the nigga to do something, he needs more time. I'm through with that shit."

"He's—"

"I don't give a damn about all that, Chris. I need my shit done now!"

***

Dell bit his lip in frustration, finished off the drink he had and returned to his bar.

"Seems as if someone's got up on edge," Camille smiled, seeing that the caller had apparently hung up on him. She felt whoever was on the other end of the line, had him by the balls.

"That's just someone that's getting beside themselves." Dell had been telling Raymond that Diamond was becoming more than they could handle and now that she was making a little money and allowed to call a few shots, he felt it was time to show her who really held the cards.

"Are you hearing anything I've been saying?"

He looked over at Camille and smiled. "Now, what were you saying?"

***

Chris knew when his friend was frustrated and watching Diamond, it was more than apparent. "Hey, let's go for a ride right quick."

"Nigga, I ain't got time for no rides. I've got shit to do."

"I got King's address and think it's about time we paid him a little visit."

He watched her watch him. Chris smiled, held up his phone and showed her the text from Datrina. He grabbed her hand and pulled her towards the car and when no resistance was met, he told her, "Let's surprise him."

\*\*\*

After having the conversation with the guy, King handed him the money and told him he could leave. He grabbed Nava's hand and pulled her back inside. "How in the hell you get caught up with some thug like that, Nava?" he asked, with both disappointment and contempt.

"Desperate times call for desperate measures, King."

King walked over and peeked out the window, making sure the guy took heed to his words. For tonight, he'd rent Nava a room at the Days Inn Hotel down the street and tomorrow, he'd take her to look for an apartment and some transportation to assist her in her job search. "Let me grab something right quick."

\*\*\*

Camille left Dell's home with more than a promise. He was going to look into several possibilities he had lined up. He whistled, hearing the price range she was willing to negotiate and she knew then she'd blinded him with the dollar amount.

And, since she knew personally what Officer Bell was about, she knew Dell was desperately trying to climb out of the hole he'd stepped in.

\*\*\*

Chris checked the address a second time. "Right there." He pointed.

"You and ya girl really going all out with this, huh?"

"Yep." He parked, killed the motor and asked her, "You ready?"

"Oh, I get to play too? Let's go with it." Diamond climbed out of the car and headed to where Chris had pointed. She looked around at the area. Nice, though she still wasn't about to believe King resided there. Once they were standing in front of the door, she looked back at Chris.

"Ring the bell, knock on the door, do something."

Diamond's heartbeat could be felt in her fingers. This sick joke Chris and Datrina played was one she was actually hoping ended better than any they'd played in the past. She knocked on the door twice.

Nava stood, hearing the knock. She looked towards the room King disappeared to and yelled, "I'll get it." She opened the door, saw the hazel-eyed woman standing before her and asked, "May I help you?"

"Um, does King live here?"

"And, who might you be?"

Diamond looked back at Chris and tsked. "Are you serious, Chris?" She backed away from the door and began walking.

Chris was speechless. The surprise he had, surprised even him. He saw in Diamond's eyes that her heart was broken. To finally have found King and for him to be with a woman. He shook his head. "Um, my apologies." Chris was just about to back away also, until King stopped him.

"Chris?" King asked, more surprised than either of them. He stepped past Nava and looked outside. "Is Diamond with you?"

"She's—" Chris looked back in the direction Diamond walked and before he could say anything, King pushed past him. Chris grabbed his arm. "Just let her go, King. Let her go, man."

King took a step towards Chris, looked him in his eyes and told him, "If you're not going to kill me, Chris, then let my arm go, man. I lost her once and I'm not about to lose her again."

Chris saw the sincerity in King's eyes, felt the love that drove him, then released his arm.

King ran after her. "Diamond! Diamond, wait, please!" He caught up with her, just before she was able to reach for the door handle.

She faced him. "What's up?"

"What the hell you mean, what's up?" King grabbed her, pulled her to him and wrapped his arms around her. "Where are you going?"

"Who's she, King?"

"Who's who?"

"The woman that answered your door, nigga! That's who."

"Nava, that's Nava, Diamond. She just popped up on me the other day. She's—"

Diamond stopped him. "Nava, the woman you talked about marrying?" She looked back towards the way King came and saw both Nava and Chris approaching.

"I'm not messing with her, Diamond. You are the woman I love now. I'm in love with you, Diamond, and you only," he pleaded. King looked deep into Diamond's eyes and lost himself as he'd always done. He asked, "Can I kiss you?"

"King!" Nava yelled from behind him.

Diamond wanted nothing more than that, but instead told him, "It looks as if you have some things to sort our first."

"There's nothing to think about, Diamond. I told Nava I was going to help her where I could, but that's it. I'm here for you, Diamond, remember?"

Diamond backed away from him, nodded for Chris to come on and told him, "Show me."

*** 

Chris drove them away from King's apartment. He watched King stand in the middle of the street until they'd turn the corner, but his mind was on the woman sitting next to him. "You alright?"

"Yeah, I'm good."

"You know he loves you, right?"

"Yep."

236

"That's what matters, Diamond."

Diamond nodded. Both Antonio's and Camille's words replayed themselves in her mind, reminding her of all she'd be willing to give up to keep love and the things she'd have to do for the people she loved. She'd thought about this very moment for a while and now that she was faced with it, she knew exactly what she was going to do.

"You hear me?" Chris nudged her, regaining her attention.

"What you say?"

"I said, are you willing to fight for him?"

Diamond faced him, looked him in his eyes and told him, "I'm even willing to kill for him."

NICOLE GOOSBY

## EPILOGUE

Camille followed Diamond down the arched hallways of the McClendon Estate, until they were standing at the doors of the eight-car garage. Today was the day they agreed to take the cars out so they could have a little fun and bet a small wager. The distance they were about to travel would take them at least three and a half hours and they were both looking forward to it. So much had happened since the last time they visited the Three Rivers Federal Facility and there were definitely stories to tell.

Not only was she able to remind Diamond of the things Nava was capable of, but with Buddy's help, she was also able to show the real Nava. The club-hopping, cocaine-snorting, gold digger bitch that was once engaged to her man. The video clips Buddy was able to produce would go no further than the three of them, and for the first time in a long while, Diamond didn't even let Chris know what her intentions were for the woman that plotted on her King. Despite King giving the guy who Nava claimed to have helped her five thousand dollars, he still hadn't left town and they were more than sure of his reason why. They'd watched Nava travel from the apartment King leased for her, to the various hangout spots she visited on a daily basis. Her claim to have been searching for a job was the lie she continually told King, and as bad as she wanted to expose the fact to King, she stayed out of his business. "You sure you're up for this?" Camille asked her, before climbing into her 911 Porsche.

"As sure as I'll ever be," Diamond smiled before closing the door to her Calloway Corvette.

Since the Dallas/Forth Worth area was where they laid their heads, Nava would surely be looked for there and that was also why they were headed to San Antonio, TX now. As planned, Diamond would become that understanding bitch King needed her to be. She'd also become that naïve, sympathetic bitch Nava thought she was and when all was said and done, King could look for her at the ends of the earth if he wanted, but she was bent on making sure Nava would never return.

\*\*\*

Nava laughed to herself, thinking of how well things had worked out. Although King had professed his undying love for the chick he called Diamond, she was still put up in her very own apartment, given a nice Pontiac convertible by the same woman and had cash in her pocket. It was only a matter of time before she'd push Diamond aside and reclaim what was rightfully hers. Her plan was simple. She'd move back in with King, find where he kept the bulk of his cash, and kill the woman that pushed her from the plans she had from the very beginning.

\*\*\*

She pulled the silver tray down from the bedroom closet, cut herself a couple of lines and filled her nose. "Y'all can keep whatever drugs we get, but I get to keep seventy-five percent of the money." Nava threw her head back, pinched her nose and added, "He can have that dumb-ass, square-ass bitch. By the time I'm finished breaking his ass, that bitch gonna be long gone. Watch."

## Submission Guideline.

Submit the first three chapters of your completed manuscript to ldpsubmissions@gmail.com, subject line: Your book's title. The manuscript must be in a .doc file and sent as an attachment. Document should be in Times New Roman, double spaced and in size 12 font. Also, provide your synopsis and full contact information. If sending multiple submissions, they must each be in a separate email.

Have a story but no way to send it electronically? You can still submit to LDP/Ca$h Presents. Send in the first three chapters, written or typed, of your completed manuscript to:

LDP: Submissions Dept
Po Box 870494
Mesquite, Tx 75187

*DO NOT send original manuscript. Must be a duplicate.*

Provide your synopsis and a cover letter containing your full contact information.

Thanks for considering LDP and Ca$h Presents.

**Coming Soon from Lock Down Publications/Ca$h Presents**

BOW DOWN TO MY GANGSTA

By **Ca$h**

TORN BETWEEN TWO

By **Coffee**

BLOOD STAINS OF A SHOTTA **III**

By **Jamaica**

WHEN THE STREETS CLAP BACK **III**

By **Jibril Williams**

STEADY MOBBIN

By **Marcellus Allen**

BLOOD OF A BOSS **V**

By **Askari**

LOYAL TO THE GAME **IV**

By **T.J. & Jelissa**

A DOPEBOY'S PRAYER **II**

By **Eddie "Wolf" Lee**

IF LOVING YOU IS WRONG… **III**

LOVE ME EVEN WHEN IT HURTS

By **Jelissa**

DAUGHTERS OF A SAVAGE **II**

By **Chris Green**

SKI MASK CARTEL **II**

By **T.J. Edwards**

TRAPHOUSE KING **II**

By **Hood Rich**

BLAST FOR ME **II**

RAISED AS A GOON **V**

By **Ghost**

ADDICTIED TO THE DRAMA **III**

By **Jamila Mathis**

LIPSTICK KILLAH **II**

By **Mimi**

WHAT BAD BITCHES DO **2**

By **Aryanna**

THE COST OF LOYALTY **II**

By **Kweli**

A DRUG KING AND HIS DIAMOND **II**

By **Nicole Goosby**

SHE FELL IN LOVE WITH A REAL ONE

By **Tamara Butler**

LOVE SHOULDN'T HURT

By **Meesha**

**Available Now**

RESTRAINING ORDER **I & II**

By **CA$H & Coffee**

LOVE KNOWS NO BOUNDARIES **I II & III**

By **Coffee**

RAISED AS A GOON I, II, III & IV

BRED BY THE SLUMS I, II, III

BLAST FOR ME

By **Ghost**

LAY IT DOWN **I & II**

LAST OF A DYING BREED

BLOOD STAINS OF A SHOTTA I & II

By **Jamaica**

LOYAL TO THE GAME

LOYAL TO THE GAME II

LOYAL TO THE GAME III

By **TJ & Jelissa**

BLOODY COMMAS I & II

SKI MASK CARTEL

By **T.J. Edwards**

IF LOVING HIM IS WRONG…I & II

By **Jelissa**

WHEN THE STREETS CLAP BACK I & II

By **Jibril Williams**

A DISTINGUISHED THUG STOLE MY HEART I II & III

By **Meesha**

PUSH IT TO THE LIMIT

By **Bre' Hayes**

BLOOD OF A BOSS **I, II, III & IV**

By **Askari**

THE STREETS BLEED MURDER **I, II & III**

THE HEART OF A GANGSTA I II& III

By **Jerry Jackson**

CUM FOR ME

CUM FOR ME 2

CUM FOR ME 3

An **LDP Erotica Collaboration**

BRIDE OF A HUSTLA **I & II**

THE FETTI GIRLS **I, II& III**

By **Destiny Skai**

WHEN A GOOD GIRL GOES BAD

By **Adrienne**

A GANGSTER'S REVENGE **I II III & IV**

THE BOSS MAN'S DAUGHTERS

THE BOSS MAN'S DAUGHTERS II

THE BOSSMAN'S DAUGHTERS III

THE BOSSMAN'S DAUGHTERS IV

A SAVAGE LOVE **I & II**

BAE BELONGS TO ME

A HUSTLER'S DECEIT I, II

By **Aryanna**

A KINGPIN'S AMBITON

A KINGPIN'S AMBITION **II**

I MURDER FOR THE DOUGH

By **Ambitious**

TRUE SAVAGE

TRUE SAVAGE II

TRUE SAVAGE **III**

DAUGHTERS OF A SAVAGE

By **Chris Green**

A DOPEBOY'S PRAYER

By **Eddie "Wolf" Lee**

THE KING CARTEL **I, II & III**

By **Frank Gresham**

THESE NIGGAS AIN'T LOYAL **I, II & III**

By **Nikki Tee**

GANGSTA SHYT **I II &III**

By **CATO**

THE ULTIMATE BETRAYAL

By **Phoenix**

BOSS'N UP **I , II & III**

By **Royal Nicole**

I LOVE YOU TO DEATH

**By Destiny J**

I RIDE FOR MY HITTA

I STILL RIDE FOR MY HITTA

By **Misty Holt**

LOVE & CHASIN' PAPER

By **Qay Crockett**

TO DIE IN VAIN

By **ASAD**

BROOKLYN HUSTLAZ

By **Boogsy Morina**

BROOKLYN ON LOCK I & II

By **Sonovia**

GANGSTA CITY

By **Teddy Duke**

A DRUG KING AND HIS DIAMOND

A DOPEMAN'S RICHES

**By Nicole Goosby**

TRAPHOUSE KING

By **Hood Rich**

## BOOKS BY LDP'S CEO, CA$H

TRUST IN NO MAN

TRUST IN NO MAN 2

TRUST IN NO MAN 3

BONDED BY BLOOD

SHORTY GOT A THUG

THUGS CRY

THUGS CRY 2

THUGS CRY 3

TRUST NO BITCH

TRUST NO BITCH 2

TRUST NO BITCH 3

TIL MY CASKET DROPS

RESTRAINING ORDER

RESTRAINING ORDER 2

IN LOVE WITH A CONVICT

**Coming Soon**

BONDED BY BLOOD 2

BOW DOWN TO MY GANGSTA

NICOLE GOOSBY

+

NICOLE GOOSBY